Mireya Book 1

Ty Spencer Vossler

This is a work of fiction. Names, characters, places, and incidents are products of the author's imagination or are used fictitiously and are not to be construed as real. Any resemblance to actual events, locations, organizations, or persons, living or dead, is entirely coincidental.

World Castle Publishing, LLC
Pensacola, Florida
Copyright © 2025 Ty Spencer Vossler
Hardback ISBN: 9798292144403
Paperback ISBN: 9798891264427
eBook ISBN: 9798891264434
First Edition World Castle Publishing, LLC, September 15, 2025
http://www.worldcastlepublishing.com
Licensing Notes
Cover: Cover Designs by Karen
Editor: Karen Fuller

AUTHOR'S NOTE

Two walls separate México from the United States. Most noticeable is a man-made barrier that runs six hundred and fifty miles from California into the southwestern United States. The second wall is constructed from stereotypes, ignorance, and fear. As a result, North Americans know virtually nothing about the *real* México or its people. Mireya carries readers back and forth across the Mexican border. Based on thirty years of experience living and traveling in México, this novel is a fictional composite of individuals I've known.

DEDICATION

To my BMW (beautiful Mexican wife).

PRELUDE
DISCOVERY (TLAXCALA, MÉXICO)

"Against all odds, a seed rises from darkness and beautifies the universe."
— Matshona Dhliwayo —

Unseasonable rains washed dust from the leaves of trees and plants in the garden. The fragrance of renewal permeated the air. Rita thought of her father, who loved tending it. She held back tears. He wouldn't have approved of anyone crying over him. At the base of the big pine, she stared at the spot where his ashes were strewn only weeks earlier. She raised her guitar and began to play Corazón Sin Vida.

"Rita?" Mireya's voice called from the upstairs balcony.

"In the garden, Mom!"

"Sweetheart, when you get a chance, would you look for an extension cord in the storage shed. I think there's one in a box marked 'Christmas stuff'."

"Okay!" Rita put her fingers to her lips and waved to the moist ground below the pine. "Duty calls, Pops."

Her father died three weeks earlier, and Rita took time off from school to be with her mother. She was finishing her bachelor's in music at the prestigious Bellas Artes in Coyoacan when her mother called with the news. It smelled earthy in the yard, and there were flowers blooming all around. *Dad, do you know I'm here*? She walked a dirt path to the courtyard, taking the guitar with her.

The early morning rain had stopped, and birds gathered to ambush worms as they surfaced. A hummingbird hovered over a bottlebrush tree and was chased off by another. Her father planted the garden with birds, butterflies, and bees in mind. *A garden isn't healthy without them*, he explained.

"The shed," Rita complained aloud. *Hate going in there. Dark, musty, black widows and mice.* She shivered. She didn't cotton to the idea of lifting boxes to find an extension cord. She considered fibbing that she couldn't find it, driving to a hardware store to buy one. Yet, she never lied to her mother.

She walked through the central patio and opened the steel door that led into the corrals. The cinder-block storage shed was there. The corrals were strangely quiet—no warbling turkeys, pecking chickens, laconic bawl of the family cow. They were years gone—*since grandma died*. Rita's mother had no interest in keeping animals, and the uncles were too lazy to try.

Mireya was fifty-eight, a PhD in Algebraic Topology. She taught at the University of Puebla. After years as a researcher, she had worked in Acapulco as a professor and even directed the Math Institute in Oaxaca for some years. She was glad to simply be in the classroom again. It was more satisfying, and teaching wasn't weighed down with politics.

The storage shed held prisoners of the past. Boxes and more boxes—some mummified with postal tape to deter mice, silverfish, and other scourges. A single dusty light bulb dangled from the ceiling to challenge the darkness. She leaned the guitar against a wall.

Creepy, thought Rita. *Wish I had a flashlight.*

Rita searched a particularly gloomy corner of the storeroom, where a dozen cardboard boxes were stacked. She brushed the dust off the top one. In bold permanent marker, two words: WYLER'S BOOKS. Rita didn't have a knife to split the sealing tape. Looking around, she found an old pair of hedge clippers with one blade hanging on a nail. She sliced down the middle of the carton and pulled open the flaps.

Copies of her father's books were there, spines staring up. *Seedlings, Meadowland, Deep Mud, LadySmith, Desperate Living,* and others. Her favorite was *Meadowland*, which reinforced her decision not to live in the dystopian US. *Something's missing there,* she considered. *An emptiness that can't be filled with better pay and opportunities.*

One title caught her eye that she didn't recognize — *Mireya*. "Hmm, what's this, Pops?" She lifted it from the box.

Rita stepped into the sunlight. Clouds were breaking up, and steam was rising from the tops of the adobe walls surrounding the corrals. The cover depicted a pretty Latina lying on her back naked on a bed, head resting on a pillow, one knee raised. Her eyes were focused on the bedroom doorway. The shadowy silhouette of a man stood at the entrance. Floating in the background were peculiar mathematical hieroglyphics, symbols, letters, and numbers that Rita recognized as Algebraic Topology. *It fits together to define space,* her mother tried to explain once.

Rita read the back cover:

"Even when I'm dead, I'll swim through the Earth like a mermaid of the soil, just to be next to your bones." — Jeffrey McDaniel.

Mireya pays homage to a remarkable Mexican woman who transcended poverty to earn a PhD in the male-dominated world of Algebraic Topology. The novel delves into social issues that plague México and the United States — double standards, inequality, misogyny, corruption, age discrimination — a society dominated by powerful, self-centered men.

That's changing in Mexico, thought Rita. *We have a female President and she's really smart.* She continued reading:

This epic novel follows thirty-five years of Mireya's life, highlighted by her pursuit of a higher education and experiences with dozens of lovers along the way. After marrying a North

American, she roams outside of the conjugal bed. Thirty-five years later, she confesses her infidelities to her husband, Wyler.

Note: This book has never been distributed. It's a self-indulgent labor of love.
— Wyler Costner

Rita closed the storage door. *The extension cord can wait. Got reading to do.* Grabbing her guitar, she returned to the garden with her father's novel. She sat beneath the big pine in a white plastic chair with Corona Extra stamped on the backrest. After leaning the guitar against the trunk, she read the dedication. Her throat grew tight:
To Mireya. No greater love can a man have for a woman than mine for you.
"What secrets do you have, Pops?" She gazed down at the ground where her father's ashes were.
"I'm going to the market, wanna come?" Mireya called down to her daughter.
"No thanks, Mom, gotta book. Pops likes me to read to him."
Mireya laughed. Her staccato giggle made her sound like a teenager. "Did you find the cord?"
"No, I'll look somewhere else."
"Ask your father."
"Okay."
Mireya disappeared inside the house for a few minutes and exited with several recyclable shopping bags. Thanks to Zumba classes and a healthy diet, she skipped down the stairs with ease. The garage was next to the garden. She threw the bags into the trunk of her red Hyundai Elantra, a recent purchase she'd made.
She looks younger, Rita mused. *Hope I got her genes.*
"Be back in a few, honey. Anything you need?"

"Chicharrones."

"Okay. I might pop in on Aunt Carmen."

"Say hi for me, and call if you're gonna be late."

"Okay, sweetie. I'll look for an extension cord at the market."

"Drive careful!"

"I will."

Rita turned to the opening chapter, and she placed a hand on her tummy. She was a week late. *Not great timing*, she knew. *See, Dad, you're not the only one with secrets.*

As the garage door closed, Rita began reading her father's mysterious, unpublished work:

Mireya
Wyler Costner

PROLOGUE

Giselle Lopez was twenty-two, renting a room in México City, cleaning homes for a living. She thought her newest employer, Epimenio, was handsome. She'd been working there for a few weeks. Her day began at 6:30 and ended when his excruciating wife said so. Rosa ordered her around like a general. Epi was kind, offering tender, surreptitious smiles when his wife was otherwise distracted. They were in their early forties and childless. He worked as the chief accountant for a food processing business. Rosa was a housewife, yet to hear her tell it, she was the glue that held Earth together. Then came the phone call. Rosa answered in a fawning voice.

"Of course I'm coming! Okay, I'll bring a change of clothes."

After hanging up, she started packing clothes into a carry-on suitcase. "Alma's having her baby baptized and wants me there," she explained to her husband. "Have to leave soon, it's two hours by bus. Be back sometime tomorrow after the service."

With only an answering nod from her husband, Rosa finished packing. Before leaving, she gave Epi a peck on the cheek and turned to Giselle.

"Finish the laundry, then you can go."

"Si, Señora."

"Hasta mañana, amor." There was no warmth in the farewell.

When she was gone, the house was quiet. Epimenio went into his office to catch up on paperwork.

———

Giselle was finishing laundry when Epimenio found her folding clothes on the dining room table.

"Let me help," he said.

"That's okay, I'll take care of it."

"Sorry for the way my wife treats you." He stared at her well-rounded ass.

"It's okay."

"Have a drink with me."

She thought, *If I say no, he may never be nice again.* "Okay."

In the kitchen cupboard, he took out a half-empty bottle of Herradura Reposado, poured two shot glasses.

"Salud," he raised his glass, draining it in one gulp. She took longer, and he poured again.

"How old are you, Giselle?" His eyes roved over her.

"Twenty-two."

"Boyfriend?"

She shook her head and blushed. When she was fifteen, she skipped school to meet an older man. He took her to a movie, bought her street tacos, and deflowered her in his dirty studio apartment. *The Mexican repayment plan,* she'd heard it called. Luckily, she didn't get pregnant.

"You're very pretty."

"Gracias, Señor."

"Epi. Please, just Epi." He refilled her glass.

When her head was spinning, his hands kneaded her shoulders as she folded laundry. Then his lips found the back of her neck.

In an even voice, "Ay Señor Epimenio, I have work to do." *Why don't you stop him?*

His hands roved beneath her shirt and dove down the front of her pants. "There's work here to be done, and we have all night."

———

Epimenio was insatiable, making good on his promise to keep her busy nearly the whole night through. *Resurrection is more than a religious reference*, she thought. Giselle enjoyed her first orgasm, and many others followed. By midmorning, she felt she loved him.

The sun streamed into the bedroom. She was laying on her side in a deep sleep when she felt a hand on her shoulder. Instinctively, she moved onto her back and lifted her knees, yet he was on his feet, looking down at her.

"Wash the sheets, then you can go." He quickly dressed and secluded himself in his office.

She did laundry and made him breakfast with a fresh pot of coffee. Then she tapped on the door.

"Breakfast is ready."

"I'll eat later. Did you clean the sheets?"

"Yes, Epi."

"You can go."

She stood at the door, not knowing what she'd expected. *A kind word, perhaps.* She heard the shuffling of papers, the squeak of the desk chair.

"Okay, see you tomorrow."

"Mmm."

———

As soon as she began showing, Epimenio privately asked if the baby was his. She told him it was. He fired her and told her never to return. Giselle thought of telling his wife, yet she knew how that would end. Rosa would call her a gold-digging puta (whore) and defend her husband. Then she'd make him pay dearly.

Giselle managed to find another job cleaning houses. *There are always jobs cleaning up after ricos*. Occasionally, she stole from an employer to make ends meet. She thought of returning to the small family ranch in Natividad, Tlaxcala, where her mother, doña Isabel, and the stepfather lived. Pride wouldn't allow it. Two years earlier, she'd left in a huff after a particularly abrasive argument regarding a man her mother wanted her to marry.

"Jorge's a good man, hard working, he'll provide everything you need, food, shelter, children," her mother said.

"He's an ugly old man! I'm not gonna end up like everybody else in this fucking place!"

Her defiance earned a hard slap across the face from her stepfather. Doña Isabel gave her a beat-up suitcase and told her to leave. Mireya was born in a community hospital in 1966. Giselle had an easy labor.

"What will you name her?" asked a nurse, handing her the baby.

Giselle looked at the nameplate pinned to her white uniform and read it.

"Mireya. I like your name. Good as any."

She was unaware that Mireya means miracle, admired, wonderful, and amazing.

———

A day later, Giselle carried Mireya back to the hovel she lived in. A kind neighbor lady brought over a pot of spaghetti and some tortillas. Giselle thanked her. She packed what she could manage to carry along with the baby and returned to the ranch.

She endured endless 'I told you so' lectures from her mother. Often repeated was, "Settle down. Jorge still wants you, don't ask me why."

"I'll consider it, Mama," she replied, not wanting another conflict.

Grandma Isabel doted on Mireya as if she were a separate entity, undefiled by her daughter's promiscuity. As soon as she was able, Giselle left with her daughter and returned to México City.

———

The next few years, two more children were added by married men, each promising the world in return for what was between Giselle's legs. One evening when Mireya was seven, her mother said they were moving back to the ranch. Mireya was happy. She'd been taking care of her little brothers while her mother went off to work, sometimes not returning until the following day. Once, they went hungry for two days until a neighbor lady brought over two dozen tortillas and a bit of milk.

"Where's your mother?" she asked.

Mireya shrugged, "I don't know."

The lady shook her head. Later, she brought over a bag of pastries from a corner bakery, a cigar box full of crayons for the young brothers.. Mireya never forgot her kindness.

When they arrived at the ranch, her grandmother greeted Mireya with a warm hug. Doña Isabel smelled like blue corn tortillas and spices. Most of her teeth were missing, yet her smile was the most welcoming sight she'd seen for a long time. Mireya's half-brothers, Hugo and Edgar, went into the corrals to chase chickens and cause other mischief. They were tumbleweeds blowing in a changing wind.

CHAPTER 1
MIREYA'S REFLECTION (1987)

Mireya lifted the hand mirror to her face. She was up before the rooster crowed. In the early mornings, she had time for herself — to think and dream. She undressed and stood in front of a mirror, plastered above the dripping sink. She gazed at her twenty-two-year-old face. Naturally wavy hair was cut short because it was unconquerable when it got too long. She never used anything on her face but red lipstick to highlight her full lips. She touched her eyebrows, wondering if she should pluck them. *No*, she thought, *a waste of time.*

It was a rare morning. Her mother had taken a bus with the younger half-brothers to visit the family of the latest man she shared a bed with. He was a truck driver, and they'd found each other a month earlier at the open-air market in Zacatelco. He purchased quesadillas for Giselle and Mireya's half-brothers, which entitled him to move in. *The Mexican repayment plan*, she thought. He would soon introduce Gisselle to his mother, who would judge harshly, and that would be the end of it. That's the way it always turned out.

Yet, this was Mireya's morning. No one bothered her on these special days. She had time to review goals and feel proud of her accomplishments. She turned on the shower to warm up before stepping beneath the water.. She closed her brown eyes and felt the water pouring down her body as she scrubbed with a washcloth. Fingers slipped over her shapely backside. She knew that men admired her body and saw hunger in their eyes.

Her jealous boyfriend, Enrique, grew angry when others ogled her. She soaped her moderately sized breasts, topped with tall brown nipples. Recently, she allowed Enrique's hand to reach beneath her shirt to fondle them. She stopped him short of slipping a hand down the front of her pants. She remembered the feeling — *Pleasure coursing through my body.*

Not yet, she counseled herself. Her cousin Chela came to mind. They were both twenty-two. Chela had four children, living a hardscrabble life. She thought of her mother — three children, three fathers. *Not until I'm ready.*

The water felt good, washing away bad memories, replacing them with aspirations. She shampooed her dark pubic hair, allowing fingers to slide over sensitive places. She closed her eyes, thought about Enrique, and shivered.

It'd been a long while since she'd had an opportunity to pleasure herself. Juggling classes at the university, having family responsibilities, left little time for self-indulgence. Her brothers were sixteen and nineteen, yet still depended on Mireya. *I practically raised them.*

When she started university, she put her foot down. They could feed themselves and do their own laundry. Giselle threatened, yet was unable to intimidate her daughter anymore. The brothers lived in a gypsy style addition on the bottom floor. Both dropped out of school and took factory jobs until they were either fired or laid off. Spare time was spent seeing how many community girls they could talk into a corn field.

The morning was young. Mireya pushed everything else out of her mind. She imagined Enrique kissing her, hardness pressing, tongue slipping over hers. She shuddered.

"Mmm, oyyy." Her sensitive clit emerged from its hood beneath her thumb. She slipped a finger past the lips, pushing inside. The bathroom walls amplified the sound of pleasure.

"Ay-ay, ayyy!" Her knees buckled as she imagined Enrique inside. She'd heard that the first time was painful. Beyond that, she couldn't imagine. She only knew the pleasure that was indescribably delicious. Her inner walls gripped and released her fingers. She couldn't help believing that Enrique could do even better.

After recovering, she rinsed and used the towel sitting on the toilet seat. Every time Enrique pressured her for sex, she thought of cousin Chela.

"I'm not ready," she repeated each time. She read his thoughts. *What does that have to do with it? Haven't I been nice?* Each time it was harder to say no, especially when her body demanded 'yes'.

After recovering, she toweled off, brushed her teeth, and reflected on life. She cleared the fogged mirror with the heel of her hand. *What is and what will be.*

———

Basic provisions were sold out of family home stores in Natividad. Her mother ran one from her bedroom. Bakery goods, tortillas, comida economica (cheap meals), and car repair, all were neighborhood businesses. No one there had finished high school. Natividad was typical in this respect. Girls got pregnant, were abused by the father, and despised by his mother. Men usually worked in nearby maquiladoras (foreign-owned factories) and drank up their salaries on payday. Many times, they simply ran away to avoid responsibility, and children were raised by grandparents.

Mireya had always been at the top of her class, regardless of additional responsibilities. Even as a child, she'd stayed up late to complete homework, not knowing at the time why her desire to learn was so strong. School was home, and she couldn't wait to get there, settle in, and discover something new. Teachers weren't the best, but they provided a framework, and she filled in the rest with hard work and extra effort.

Her academic ability was recognized without her mother's knowledge. She received medals and certificates for academic excellence, which she never shared with Giselle. *She'd never understand. It will remain a gift to myself.*

When she graduated, Mireya received a small academic scholarship and was accepted into the BUAP (Universidad Benemérita Autónoma de Puebla). It paid for books and incidentals. Unlike the United States, tuition was almost free. She took as many classes as she could find time for. Because of her other responsibilities, it would take her longer to finish, yet she was determined never to become fossilized in the community.

She recalled that Einstein said, 'Pure mathematics is, in its way, the poetry of logical ideas.' *Math isn't unfair or cruel, accepts all-comers with equal regard. Math challenges, never punishes.*

When she was ten, a movie called Rocky was popular. She'd never been to a movie theater, yet kids at school talked about the hero, who got knocked down and got up again over and over. *I'll be the Rocky of mathematics*, she determined.

Her mother resented Mireya for trying to rise above her station. Before she was allowed to devote time to academics, she had to help with cooking, cleaning, and feeding the farm animals. At least now her younger brothers fended for themselves. Every night, Mireya was up until the wee hours studying math. She used a plastic folding table beneath a single light bulb dangling from the cement ceiling of her bedroom.

Most Mexican ranches are *ejidos*, agricultural lands dominated by rich hacienda owners, returned to the people after the revolution. They've remained mostly unchanged for generations. In Natividad, campesinos (farm workers) still plow corn fields with stoic burros, or bony horses, using primitive farm implements to scratch out an existence. Homes are gypsy-style affairs, constructed of brick, adobe, or cement blocks.

When a girl gets pregnant, grandparents raise the children, and another cubicle is added onto the main house. Most additions look like gray tumors sprouting out of the main body.

In Natividad, aesthetics took a back seat to function.

The ranch house where Mireya lived was a two-story rectangle, the color of a cloudy day. Steel rebar was left uncut on the corners of the roofline, resembling insect antennae. A gravity tank provided water to the household and was only good for washing or to quench the thirst of farm animals. Parasites swam in the underground waters, making it unfit for human consumption.

She thought back to her first exposure to sex, a second-hand experience.

Like everyone around them, they grew corn. Mireya had grown up learning how to plant, harvest, and search for huitlacoche (an edible fungus) that could sometimes be found growing on the corn. It was considered a delicacy and brought a good price at the market. She remembered being twelve, walking inside the corn fields in search of huitlacoche. One late afternoon in a neighbor's cornfield, she heard a strange sound and quietly slipped through the stalks toward the source. There were voices.

"Ay papi si, qué rico!" a woman exhorted.

"Uh-uh-uh, ahhh!" was his impassioned response.

Then she drew near enough to see them — a man with his pants pulled to his ankles, a woman with her skirt raised. He moved rapidly between her legs, then called out, "Me vengo!" growling like an animal before collapsing on her.

Mireya backed away slowly, feeling a rush of dizzy pleasure.

———

Yes, Mireya pondered, *it's been an uphill battle*. She smiled in the mirror and hung a pair of earrings fashioned from kernels of red corn. Enrique bought them for her at the market in Zacatelco. As she laid out clothes to wear, she proudly surveyed her bedroom, built with her own money along with the tiny bathroom.

For eight years, Mireya worked summers, weekends, and

school vacations with her cousin Chela, making jackets to sell in the neighboring town of Xoxtla (Shoshtla). She gave half her earnings to Giselle and hid the rest taped beneath a drawer in her closet. After eight years, she hired a pair of local construction men to build two rooms on top of the main house.

"How did you pay? Who gave it to you?" Her mother demanded.

"I saved it." *She thinks I'm a puta (whore).*

"Hmph, you think you're a princess?" She didn't press the matter any further, knowing that the new upstairs addition added value to the property. When it was finished, Giselle wanted to move in with her latest boyfriend.

"You can take my room."

Mireya screamed, "It's mine! I worked for it! Do you hear me? Mine!"

"Pinche malcriado!" Giselle raised her hand, then lowered it. She saw that her daughter could no longer be threatened this way. She also realized how much harder life would be without Mireya to help with the endless chores. She balled up her fists and walked away, mumbling.

That was the first time I stood up to her. Taught me to continue advocating for myself.

————

Corrals were constructed with wooden pallets, strung together with bailing wire. Inside were two pigs, a dozen chickens, a rooster, and two filthy cows. Before and after school, Mireya cleaned the corrals and fed animals. A few times, she'd rushed to a university class smelling like animal dung.

Giselle ran a tiny commodity store from the front window of her bedroom. Her eighty-two-year-old grandmother, doña Isabel, sold handmade blue tortillas. That was their life, an unequal mixture of choice and no choice.

Mireya imagined life after university. *Everything will change.*

Since she was old enough to remember, she believed education would provide a better life. Some of the professors at the university earned PhDs in Russia, China, Canada, and England. Mireya's dreams took her far from Natividad. Her interest in Mathematics solidified when she studied Euler's famous equation for pi. Here was irrefutable proof of mathematical perfection, reminding her that humans will never fully grasp the meaning and reasoning behind math.

Beautiful, she thought. She processed much of what she studied with relative ease. Math made sense when nothing else around her did.

"Sweden," she whispered to herself as she combed through a tangle of wavy hair, *Greece, France, Japan. Mathematics will take me there.*

Logic was appealing. *Perhaps chaos can be explained.* Female mathematicians were rare in México. Math and science were dominated by men. "Pueden ir a follar a sus madres," she whispered to herself as she pulled on her jeans. *If it were up to men, I'd get pregnant and stay living like this. Mathematics doesn't make promises it can't keep.*

"I've got other plans," she murmured. *What is and what will be.* A mosquito buzzed near her ear, and she clapped it between her hands. "That's what'll happen to anyone who gets in the way." She noticed a spot of blood in the palm of her hand. The mosquito already had its fill.

Mireya applied simple red lipstick to her lips and remembered her mother's stinging words when she shared college plans.

"Who'll help with the work here? Hija, take my advice: find a husband, get a job close by, and get your head out of the clouds. This college nonsense is a waste of time. Sometimes we must accept who we are and learn to live with it."

"That's you, Mother, not me."

"We'll see about that."

CHAPTER 2
ENRIQUE

Enrique was a gentleman, and Mireya liked him. He was less macho than most young Mexican men. They'd met in high school, and he'd graduated a year earlier. He was a good student. He'd been shy around Mireya then, yet when they reconnected at the university, he set out to conquer her. Enrique studied engineering. He was as poor as Mireya, yet had a mother who doted on him—the prince of the house. They lived about seven miles further down the road in a small town called San Marcos. The father left when he was five. His three step-siblings were the creative efforts of three men, and they eagerly awaited his return each day.

Sometimes, if their schedules allowed, they took the bus together to the university. When they returned together, he walked with her a mile to the house before taking a combi (van) further on to his town. Lately, he was obsessed with getting her alone in a cornfield. He felt he'd spent a respectful amount of time waiting for her to fulfill her obligation. On weekends, he worked for a gardener and had nearly saved enough for a cheap motel.

After a kiss behind the big oak tree, he tried again. "Mireya, I want you so bad it hurts, it really does."

"Ay pobrecito." She stroked his face.

He dug into his pants and brought out a worn wallet. Where the peso bills should go, he pulled out a foil square. "I have this."

She nearly crumbled that time. Taking the packet from him, she examined it and saw that the expiration date had ended a year before.

Mireya's focus on mathematics helped her avoid traps. Since she was eleven, men had shown interest in her. At fiestas, church gatherings, quinceañeras, men tried their luck, plying her with promises, bribing with offers of small gifts.

"Come clean my house and I'll give you two hundred pesos," one offered. He was a bachelor in his forties. His teeth were stained yellow, and he had a pot belly.

"Thank you, Señor Guzman, but I don't have time."

"You have time right now. I'll give you the money for something else, and it won't take long at all."

She had an idea what that was based on gossip she heard at school. He had a crazed look on his face. She looked over his shoulder, pretending to see someone she knew, so that she was able to move past him.

Another time, one of her mother's boyfriends tried to kiss her while she was cleaning the corrals. She pushed him hard in the chest and he slipped in cow shit. She escaped before he made it to his feet and told her mother.

"What were you doing, eh?"

"Nothing! Just working!"

"Mmm. I'm sure he meant nothing by it."

Mireya walked away, knowing she'd have to look after herself as always.

It happened again in much the same way, yet this time Mireya was in a small alfalfa patch with a sickle, cutting fodder for the filthy cows.

"Here, let me help you. It's man's work."

She saw the look in his eyes and knew that he wasn't interested in cutting alfalfa. She held the blade in front of her.

"Cabrón, if you come near me, I swear to god I'll cut you!"

"Ay pajarita (little bird)…." He continued to walk toward her.

She didn't see when Hugo arrived carrying another sickle. Without a word, he stood by Mireya and began cutting. Every once in a while, he glared up at the man. Mireya did the same, and he turned and walked away.

"Gracias hermano," she said to Hugo.

"De nada."

After a week, the boyfriend left after an argument with Giselle regarding another woman he was seeing.

———

The dusty dirt road running in front of her house was a libro (toll-free road). Because it was free, a considerable amount of traffic whizzed by, slowed only by occasional handmade, unmarked speed bumps. They were capable of inflicting major damage if drivers failed to see them. When Enrique and Mireya returned from school together, they walked the final three kilometers along the libro until they arrived at Mireya's house. From there, Enrique hailed a minivan taxi seven miles further to San Marcos. Sometimes the minivan was so crowded that he had to squeeze in with fifteen to twenty others.

Early Sundays, Enrique and Mireya sometimes met at an outdoor market in Zacatelco, where they held hands and purchased fresh fruits and vegetables for their respective families. Mireya enjoyed strolling in the market. It was colorful and vibrant, alive with laughter and gossip. Giselle allowed the relationship because she hoped it would lead them to making a life together.

"When will you marry me?" Enrique would often ask as they walked.

"When we graduate, have good jobs, and if I still like you," Mireya giggled.

He loved to hear her giggle, a staccato jitter that made others laugh. He smiled. "That's a long time."

Mireya shrugged and smiled. "It'll go by fast."

"Like a caracol (snail) taking forever to find the flower.

"Patience."

Sometimes, as Enrique walked her home from the final bus stop, he pulled her behind a large oak tree that grew on the side of the road. They kissed, and he pressed against her. His hand would often wander, she'd capture it, and he'd make a frustrated sigh. Months earlier, Mireya had allowed their first real kiss there. As her tongue slipped over his, he shivered, and she felt his whole body quake.

"What's wrong?" she asked.

"Nothing." A sticky warmth crawled down his thighs.

Such moments reminded Mireya that natural instinct was stronger than logic. After such kisses, she immediately went upstairs to shower, letting fingers dissolve the ache between her thighs. She wanted Enrique, but not in a cornfield and not with expired protection.

Beneath the water, she squeezed a nipple. Messages were sent to her clitoris, which throbbed and twitched beneath her fingers. Sometimes she had to sit on the concrete floor to keep from fainting with pleasure. She wondered again what it would feel like to have Enrique inside.

Afterward, clothes needed washing, and animals needed tending. The oldest brother was Edgar, nearly twenty. Hugo was two years younger. Given her mother's propensity for finding men to share her bed, it was a miracle there weren't others. Her brothers were lazy and didn't share her enthusiasm for school. They worked off and on in local factories, dated local girls, and led more than a few into the corn fields.

———

Mireya's academic aspirations unsettled Enrique. She was determined to finish university and apply to graduate school. She even talked about earning a doctorate. *Her brain is intimidating.* Enrique knew he'd have to act soon, or lose her among the dreams she'd created.

Get her pregnant. Then we'll marry. Eventually, I'll finish my engineering degree. In the meantime, we'll live with my mother while I find work. He had it all planned. *Now I just need to find my way between her legs.*

Enrique heard friends brag about conquests, and he lied about his. His only experience was a college party he attended a few weeks earlier without Mireya. Three girls lived in a small Puebla apartment where the gathering was. After several slow dances and too much tequila, one of them led Enrique into a bedroom with a mattress on the floor. She didn't waste time, removing her pants and underwear, laying on the mattress and lifting her knees.

"Come on, cowboy," she said.

He nearly fell over pulling his pants down. He pushed easily into her dark, hairy pussy and shuddered.

"Uh! Ahhh!"

"Wow, that has to be some kind of a record," she joked.

She found a napkin next to the mattress. They returned to the party, and his buddies gave a thumbs-up. Throughout the night, she repeated the procedure with others she danced with. He asked for another dance, but she wasn't interested.

Nothing to brag about. Just something to go on until I get with Mireya.

————

The following semester, Enrique and Mireya took Calculus. One night, they studied late in an empty classroom at the university. Mireya charted problems on a chipped, portable blackboard in front of the lecture room. For Enrique, Calculus was a hoop to jump through for engineering. He was interested in applied math, didn't care how he got the answer, and always wanted shortcuts. Mireya enjoyed pure math, each step of the process. Her unhurried approach frustrated him.

She chalked: Find the volume of a region bounded above by the unit sphere $x^2+y^2+z^2=1$ and below by the cone $z=sqrt(x^2+y^2)$.

"Isn't this beautiful?" Mireya said as she worked on the solution.

"Yeah," Enrique said, staring at her ass. She scratched ideas, erased, and tried something else. Chalk turned her fingers white.

Mireya remembered a Cuban professor saying that Havana University often ran out of chalk. Mireya preferred the screech of chalk, announcing ideas to the darkness of the board. Dry markers sounded like squealing pigs and smelled bad.

Fronting the blackboard was a long, black laboratory table—a non-functioning relic left over from when the room was a science lab. Shiny chrome gas valves and aluminum sinks adorned its top. *Room for two there. Tile floor's too cold.* Enrique studied the location and walked slowly toward Mireya, who had her back to him.

Enrique's friends joked that Mireya was the reincarnation of Frida Kahlo. It was the eighties. Long filigree skirts were fashionable, paired with work boots, indigenous blouses, and jewelry made from seeds. Some called it a 'hippy dress'. She wore square, black-framed glasses for reading and homework.

Mireya carried an unconscious aura of sensuality. Even now her perfect ass swayed as she moved side-to-side, scratching formula on the board. Enrique felt his hardness demanding attention. He joined her at the board. Mireya turned, expecting an academic contribution, and saw his look. He took her into his arms, and his tongue skimmed over hers, causing a reflexive moan.

"Ay," she giggled, "what're you doing?"

"Mmm," he replied, sliding his hand up the back of her blouse to find the catch. As they kissed he lifted the bra and sucked a brown nipple into his mouth.

Mireya's head was spinning. Her legs quivered as his tongue flicked.

"Ay not here…ayyy." She was wet. "This isn't…" Mireya tried. Her legs were as weak as her resolve. *It's happening*, she thought. *Can't stop it. Don't want to.*

"No one's around." Enrique was trembling. He lifted Mireya's skirt to peel down her panties. She stepped out of them, and he led her to the lab table. They kissed for a while, and he left a blue mark on her breast. He helped her onto the table and pulled his pants down to the ankles before crawling between her knees. Mireya kept her glasses on.

"Ay, Enrique, what if someone — ?"

"We're alone," he assured.

"Do you have that thing in your wallet?"

He didn't answer. The beauty of her pussy was entrancing. The black down was soft, thin at the outer edges, with thicker tufts surrounding the pedals of her outer lips. When she opened her legs, they parted to reveal supple pink. Enrique had never seen anything so enchanting in all his life. He balanced above her on his elbows, legs straight out.

She felt him prodding. His thick uncircumcised cock oozed with precum. The outer lips surrounded his mushroom tip, and he pushed inside.

"Ow!" Mireya gasped and stiffened. "Slow, ay dios."

He pushed again. "Ohhh, baby." Slowly, he descended.

Mireya took a deep, discomforted breath. *Not too painful.*

Down, down, in, in, he pushed until his length was buried. Her head lolled to the side, and her mouth was ajar. A tear rolled down her cheek.

He squeezed his eyes shut. "Awww Jesus," he gritted his teeth. *So much better than that girl at the party*!

Mireya was panting, "Huh-huh-huh, ayyy." He was

tapping the beginnings of her womb. Despite a bit of pain, it was mostly pleasurable. Her body whispered, *Relax, we'll take it from here.*

Enrique stayed motionless, wanting so badly to explode inside her. Mireya lifted her head to kiss his chest and rubbed her hands over his shoulders. After regaining control, he pulled back slowly and returned.

"Ohhh, huh-huh-huh," Mireya gulped for air. "Ay si, ayyy," The feeling made her want to cry out. She felt the oncoming rush of a climax.

Enrique plunged and growled. "Oh baby, ohhh shit!" His balls compressed with the force of his spurt. "Rrrrawww! Aw-aw-awww!" His nut-sack pulsed and emptied. Mireya moved beneath him, needing to see where the glorious feeling would take her.

She felt him leaping inside, coating her with warm semen. Enrique stopped moving, yet she wasn't finished. Sperm, mixed with a spot of blood, seeped out and traveled to her anus. It gathered and clung before dripping to the black tabletop. Her clitoris ached. She'd been so close to something stronger than anything she had ever experienced in the shower. Enrique softened and slipped out. A rush of spunk accompanied his departure, followed by frothy queefs.

Enrique sat up to stare at the radiant leavings against the black top. He squeezed another glob from the tip of his cock and dabbed it at her glistening entrance. Pulling back on his foreskin, he tried to slip back inside. He wanted as much sperm as possible to swim toward an egg, making Mireya his forever. But his cock was too limp, and Mireya was too slippery. He kissed her and she returned it fervently, hips still moving as if a phantom cock were still there.

Enrique helped her off the table.

"Need a bathroom," she said.

"Okay," Enrique pulled up his pants and barely looked at her.

Mireya found an open bathroom down the frigid hallway. While sitting in a stall, she captured blood and semen with the tip of a finger. The outer labia lips were curled back slightly and tender to the touch. She looked at the thick substance on her finger, lifting it to her nose. It smelled briny.

Regaining control of her logic, Mireya began to worry. *Men enjoy bragging about conquests*, she thought. *In México it makes them heroes and turns women into whores.* Mireya didn't think Enrique was like that, but how could she be sure? Another glob dripped into the cold water. She didn't notice the lack of toilet paper until she was ready to wipe.

Should've known, there's hardly ever paper in these bathrooms. She used the hem of her skirt.

Enrique took her into his arms when she returned. Maidenhead vanquished, he covered her with conquering kisses and asked her to marry him—run away that very night. They'd be together, raise a family, live happily ever after.

It's what Mireya feared most—the trap, having dreams deferred, watching them dissolve slowly over time. Enrique would quit school and find a factory job. She'd stay home, have babies, cook, and clean. Weekends would be spent with his family, his friends, and any thoughts about earning a degree, traveling the world, living her life—terminated with extreme prejudice.

Mireya placed her hands on his chest. "We'll talk later. Let's go home. I have lots of homework."

"It's early," he replied, though well past midnight.

She felt his hardness pressing against her and warned, "My mother will have my suitcase packed and sitting by the road."

"Then we'll be together," he whispered, his hand lifting her skirt. "You can stay with me. My mother will—"

"No!" Mireya pushed him away, gathered her notes, and stuffed them into a faded backpack. A terrible thought came into her head. *What if I'm already pregnant?* A chill ran down her spine. She'd read once that *it takes fifteen to forty-five minutes for sperm to reach the egg.* Sperm could live for five days inside the reproductive tract. *Waiting for an egg.*

It took a minivan, a bus, and a long walk in the darkness to return home to the everyday lives they'd started the morning with. Along the dirt road toward Mireya's house, Enrique tried to pull her into a dry cornfield.

"Enrique, I have a lot of work."

"When?"

"I don't know."

His head was still swimming as they walked to the metal entrance of her house. Giselle's face appeared in a window, and Mireya knew she was in for it. Enrique gave her a small kiss and waved to the mother. Then he walked down the road, hoping for a ride to happen along. Even if he had to walk the seven miles, so be it. He reached down the front of his pants and felt stickiness, lifted the fingers to his nose, and smiled.

Mireya's mother tolerated Enrique. After all, he represented the possibility that her daughter would forget the college nonsense, settle down, and marry. They'd live together at the ranch, and Enrique could help with chores. Yet, getting in past midnight was unacceptable.

As Mireya closed the door behind her and turned, her mother slapped her hard across the face. "You think you're grown up enough to be out all night? Think again! This is my house, and you'll obey my rules!"

Mireya saw her mother's latest boyfriend eavesdropping from a side window. She was able to tame her response, keep the harsh words in her mind from spilling. "Si, Madre," she said.

Her mother continued to rant until she'd covered each

and every threat she could think to make. Then she stormed back into her bedroom. Mireya went upstairs. She let her backpack drop to the cement floor, turned on the bulb dangling from the ceiling, and heard a sizzle before it burned out. She stood in the dark doorway and sobbed.

Perhaps Mother's right — maybe I'm on my way to fulfilling her expectations. Still crying, Mireya shuffled out of her clothes in the darkness and stepped into the shower. The water did little to lighten her mood.

————

A few weeks later, Enrique paid for a cheap motel in Zacatelco. Motels in México have only one purpose. Depending on quality, the garage opening had electric aluminum doors or heavy canvas draw-curtains to protect customer privacy. Stairs in the garage led into the bedroom, and there was usually a cold shower to rinse off in. Payment was either made through a lazy Susan or handed through the privacy curtain.

After taking a bus and a minivan to get there, they strolled into the courtyard, and an employee rushed out to wave them into a garage. He closed the curtain, and Enrique handed two hundred pesos (about ten dollars) through the side of the enclosure.

The room was simple — a bed with a nightstand, an ancient television sitting on a stack of plastic soda crates, pre-set to a porno channel. There was a courtesy condom in an ashtray. The tiny bathroom had a dripping shower head. A couple in the next room was already in the throes.

"Ay papi, qué rico, ay si!" The lady screamed, followed by the rapid slap of balls against flesh, and the steady squeak of bedsprings.

Enrique kissed Mireya and slowly removed her clothing. When he took his clothes off, Mireya gazed at the thick brown uncircumcised cock protruding from his body like a living spear. The first time, she hadn't had an opportunity to see what was entering her body.

He was surprised when she reached out and lifted it, pulled the skin back, fascinated by how the mushroom tip emerged, glistening with pre-emergent—how it pulsed in her fingers. He lowered her to the bed, and she scooted to the middle.

"Shouldn't you have that?" she asked, pointing to the ashtray.

"Don't worry, I'll pull out."

"Please, wear it."

Reluctantly Enrique tore the foil, and rolled the condom over his cock. He crept between Mireya's open thighs and didn't waste time. Because the condom was lubricated, he slipped in easily, immediately battling the urge to cum. He focused on the blank walls of the bedroom, listening to the steady sigh of the broken toilet. The woman next door was exhorting her lover to fuck her harder.

Mireya felt less discomfort this time. She moved beneath him, hoping to pick up where she'd left off. The woman next door was cumming, her voice was deep and guttural.

"Oh-oh oyyy papi, ayyy!"

Enrique moved back and forth, and she instinctively swiveled her hips to match his thrusts.

"Ayyy si, ahnnn…" Quickly, Mireya was on the verge. "Si, ohhh oyyy…"

Without warning, Enrique buried his face in her neck. "Awww!"

The man next door was howling, "Me vengo!"

Enrique filled the reservoir tip of the condom. Mireya kept moving, hoping he'd stay long enough. Yet the condom was already loosening over his softening cock.

"Ay, dios mío." He slipped out.

Sighing heavily, she turned her head to the side away from him.

"Sorry," he said, stroking the smoothness of her belly. "Wait a bit," he said. Then he got up to turn on the television. A blonde was riding a black man. His long, thick cock plunged savagely into her waxed pussy, and she screamed, "Fuck me, yeah baby, fuck my tight pussy!"

"Is it normal to have one that big?" Mireya asked.

Enrique laughed, "Those guys get paid for being like that."

"Seems like it would be uncomfortable."

"Don't worry, baby, you'll never have to find out."

Mireya propped her head on a pillow and continued watching. Enrique still lay on his side, looking at her. *No more condoms*, Enrique thought. He stroked Mireya's smooth back, kissed her shoulder, licked a nipple, and explored between her thighs with his hand. She lifted her knees. The sight of Mireya's moist pussy lips surrounded by tufts of hair made him stiff. He slipped two fingers inside her snatch, and she thrusted, watching the screen. The man in the video announced, "I'm gonna nut!" The woman responded, "Yeah, baby, cum inside!"

Enrique's fingers moved back and forth, and Mireya liked it. "Mmm, huh," she gasped, "that feels good." Enrique was ready to fuck again, yet when he slipped his fingers out, Mireya gripped him by the wrist and guided them back. "Don't stop."

He probed until her movements made it almost impossible for him to keep his fingers inside. Then he rolled on top and balanced on his elbows. Enrique plunged to the hilt and began moving steadily. Mireya reached down to rub her clit.

What's she doing, Enrique wondered? This was strange indeed, but he kept stroking back and forth.

"Si, ayyy," she encouraged. The feeling was overwhelming. Something hidden deep inside was preparing to burst forth. "Oh, oh…ohhh…"

Enrique cried out and collapsed. He immediately softened and slipped out. A crawly flood of semen followed. She continued with her hand and erupted seconds later.

"Uh! Ohhh-ayyy! Ay-ay-ayyy!" She squirmed and bucked beneath him.

He tried to slip back in, but was finished for the afternoon. He moved off of her and watched her clitoris lifting, pussy lips opening and closing with each spasm, forcing frothy cum to issue forth.

After showering, Enrique admired the large wet spot on the bottom sheet. "I know a cheaper place we can go next week." Mireya didn't answer. He watched her dress and pictured them in their own place, fucking whenever they felt like it.

Mireya slipped into her pants and looked at herself in the bathroom mirror. She felt like slapping herself harder than her mother. A voice whispered — *What the hell are you doing? You want control of your life, now look at you*! Mireya realized at that moment her relationship with Enrique was finished. "Mmm," she nodded to herself.

"What?" Enrique said from the bed.

"Nothing."

The television was still on. A Latina was sucking a black man's cock at the same time a gabacho fucked her from behind. Mireya watched from the bathroom as the camera showed a close-up of the man's cock driving in and out of the woman's pussy. She felt a dull, unfulfilled ache, and it made her angry. She didn't know any black men. *Wonder what that would be like*?

"Let's go. I have exams to study for."

"What's the hurry, baby? We can watch TV, see what happens." He tried to kiss her.

"I have to go." She pushed him away.

"Ay, baby..." He reached for her as she walked past to find her shoes.

"No!" The word emerged with so much force that she hardly recognized herself.

"Hey, no need for that," Enrique said. "Okay, let's go."

———

They hardly spoke on the way back, stopping once for him to get off and continuing on to her house. When she arrived, she lit a candle, and although she wasn't a believer, she prayed to God just to be on the safe side. She prayed she wasn't pregnant, that her resolve would last until she finished her degree.

Four days later, Mireya started her period. A week after that, she broke up with Enrique. It was a pitiful scene. He poured out his heart and promised her the world on a silver platter. She held her ground, knowing the world wasn't his to give. She'd discover it on her own terms.

CHAPTER 3
DOMINGO

Domingo was strange and suspicious. He'd been bumping into Mireya lately at the university, repeatedly asking her for coffee or lunch. She politely refused each time, and now he was parked in front of her house in a faded blue Beetle as she arrived walking. She shivered and wondered how he knew where she lived.

Perhaps he knows Enrique. Enrique was incensed after the breakup. His only consolation was bragging rights. She was certain he'd left out the part about lasting four minutes total. *Yeah*, she thought, *this guy probably knows him. Explains why he's sniffing around.* She was marked territory — a target to be zeroed in on.

Since ending her relationship with Enrique, Mireya was focused on learning. *Men only get in the way.* Math studies kept her up most nights, and sometimes she got headaches trying to grasp more difficult concepts. Added to this, she was expected to do even more on the ranch because her mother was working for a rich family in Puebla with three young daughters. Mireya was certain they enjoyed more attention from her mother than she'd gotten as a child. Mireya's grandmother helped as much as she could. Mireya's own father was a ghostly memory. Her mother claimed Epimenio had wanted to divorce his wife to be with her.

"That man was crazy about me," she lied. "But his nutty wife threatened to take everything if he divorced her."

"What was he like?"

"A hurricane."

Mireya laughed. "Educated?"

"He worked with numbers at a factory. An accountant."

Giselle didn't understand Mireya's passion for academics. She quit elementary school when she was eleven to work in a fabric factory. Many in Natividad worked in the North American owned maquiladoras. Traditional expectations embedded the notion that women weren't cut out for math and science. Their rightful place was in a factory, waitressing, working as a secretary, or getting pregnant and staying home for the rest of their godforsaken lives. Natividad, where burros still pulled wooden plows in the fields, and gaunt horses towed carts filled with corn to the marketplace. *Higher expectations are unreasonable.*

Smart women threaten Mexican men. Because of Enrique's loose tongue, others expressed interest. Yet, they were intimidated by her stellar intellect and self-assuredness. Without fail, they fell short of bedding her and were happy to be rid of her by the end of the evening. *I won't play by their rules.*

Domingo wasn't intimidated. He liked that she was smart and invited her to a communist rally instead of a motel. Mireya politely refused. Now he was parked in an ancient blue Beetle in front of her house, pretending to read a newspaper as she passed by.

Domingo rolled down the window. "I wrote something for you."

"What're you doing here? How did you find me? What do you want?" *I know the answer to the last.*

"Please," he answered, holding up a sheet of paper for her. "Just read it."

She folded her arms and tapped a foot before accepting. "Okay, then I have to go."

"Fair enough."

As she read the poem, he recited it from memory in a soft baritone voice. Despite her reserve, it stimulated a pleasure zone in Mireya's brain:

Oceans, tempestuous churning water, cresting waves,
riptides pulling me deeper yet,
any risk is worth the cost
Your tempest triggers
tidal waves, tsunamis…
my pleasure

Mireya blushed. No one had ever written a poem for her. She smiled and reread it.

"Like it?"

She nodded.

"Good, that makes me happy. I'll go. You probably have a lot of studying to do."

"Yes," she smiled.

He took her hand in both of his, "Goodnight, Mireya." He kissed her fingertips.

She clutched the poem in her hand and went into the house. The blue Beetle popped in between shifts as he drove away in the direction of San Marcos.

———

Strange, this Domingo fellow, she thought as she finished washing dishes. His attention was different from Enrique's. With Enrique, she felt more in control. She was flattered by this man's pursuit, unsettled by his methods. *Perhaps I should give him a chance, out of curiosity.*

Domingo wasn't handsome. His face was pockmarked, and he wore a thin, black mustache. Still, he had a disarming smile, and looks alone were never a priority for Mireya.

Late that night, Giselle returned from her job in Puebla. She was in a foul mood because a recent boyfriend dumped her for a younger woman. Loneliness drove her to seek Mireya upstairs. It'd been a long time since she'd talked with her daughter.

Mireya met her mother at the door. *What does she want*? Her mother smiled wanly and asked her to come in. Mireya offered tea, and they sat on a threadbare sofa.

"How're you doing?" Giselle asked.

"Okay...tired," Mireya answered. *Why is she asking?*

"Me too."

She sipped tea and looked at her mother. Giselle did look tired. Her eyes were sad, and she avoided looking directly at her daughter.

"I want to say something to you, mi hija."

Mireya looked at her mother. *What's this about?*

"I'm sorry."

That put her off guard. "For what?"

"For..." Her lips quivered, "for not being a good mother to you." A tear streamed down her face and gathered at her chin.

Mireya put a hand on her mother's shoulder. "You did what you thought was right."

Giselle broke into gasping sobs, and Mireya held her. "I couldn't see...what you...what you needed."

"It's okay, mother, it's alright."

"No, I want to tell you how proud...how proud I am of you."

Mireya began to cry. "Gracias Madre."

"I feel...I'm so...lonely."

"I know the feeling."

"Forgive me."

"I do."

After a few more moments, Giselle pulled away and framed Mireya's face with her hands. "Mi hija...mi hija hermosa. Follow your dreams. Don't let them dry up and blow away like I did."

"I won't."

Giselle got up to leave. Mireya's legs felt weak, and she could hardly stand. They looked at each other. Her mother hugged Mireya, gave her a kiss on the cheek, and left. Mireya listened until she no longer heard her mother's footsteps. She smiled, then frowned, feeling a crazy mixture of happiness and sadness.

———

The next day, Domingo found Mireya in between classes and asked her out. She agreed.

He drove her to a posh restaurant in downtown Puebla. Mireya had never been in such a place. She didn't know why there were two forks on the white cloth napkin. She copied him closely so as not to appear ignorant. She placed the napkin on her lap, tried to eat slowly, deliberately sipped her wine, and didn't use bread to mop the plate when she finished.

She learned interesting facts about Domingo. He didn't attend classes at the university. He confessed to seeing her from his car at a bus stop close to the university. He double-parked nearby and rushed to follow until she disappeared into a classroom. When he returned to his car, a transit officer was removing his license plates. Domingo bribed him with two hundred pesos to get them back. Furthermore, he confessed that he worked as a security advisor for the Tlaxcala government.

"I followed to know where to find you again," he finished.

"How did you know where I lived?"

"Asked around."

"Stalking comes to mind."

"It's difficult to explain the whisperings of the heart. Sometimes you must follow blindly." Domingo changed the subject. "How are your studies going?"

"A long way to go, but I'll get there."

He asked about her dreams, interrupting at intervals to sigh and tell her how wonderful she looked. Mireya blushed each time. He didn't say much about himself, other than that his job was to protect politicians. Mireya wasn't thrilled that Domingo guarded the type of idiots who made México the fifth most corrupt nation in the world. She wondered if he carried a gun.

When they finished dinner, he lifted his hand, and a waiter presented the check. She excused herself to the bathroom, and then they left. He opened the car door for her, yet before she could squeeze in, he pulled her into his arms for a kiss. The combination of spontaneity, exotic food, and wine inspired her to return it. Another followed, lasting until they were breathless.

"Let's go somewhere," he whispered in her ear.

Silence made her complicit. In silence, they drove a short distance to the Motel Hacienda. Mireya's heart was racing, and she was wringing her hands as the Beetle was directed into a garage. The aluminum door made the sound of thunder as it closed behind them.

Haven't you learned anything? It was as if the logical part of her brain was anesthetized. Libido called the shots.

Domingo paid three hundred and fifty pesos through a trap in the garage door, and they took the stairs into the bedroom. More kisses led to a slow, measured removal of clothing until she was naked, and he stood in his underwear.

"You're a goddess," he whispered as he lowered her to the bed. When Domingo pulled down his underwear, Mireya saw that his cock was considerably smaller than Enrique's. Following her gaze, he said, "It's not the size of the spoon, it's how you stir the pot."

"Okay." She giggled nervously. He removed her glasses and set them on a nightstand. There was a mirror on the ceiling above the bed, and she saw herself lifting her knees. In the moments before he joined, her reflection showed a short, compact woman with pleasing curves, a dark triangle between ample thighs. Her toenails were painted red, as were her lips. The almond-shaped eyes stared down at her. *Is that really me?*

Domingo crawled between her uplifted knees. He sucked

her nipples and circled the areolas with his tongue. His kisses traveled slowly down, down until he arrived at her blossom. With thumbs, he spread the outer lips and flicked his tongue over the diminutive nub of her clit. Mireya had never experienced such a thing. Pleasure soon overwhelmed any reservations she had. A familiar ache grew, and she prayed a peak would be reached at last.

Mireya's first orgasm nearly doubled her over. She cried out and bucked uncontrollably beneath his tongue. "Huh-huh-huh, Guh...ayyy si, ayyy!" Her voice was unnatural to her ears—deep, guttural, desperate. As another arrived, Domingo sat up and plunged into her, angled his diminutive shaft so that it rubbed against her clit. Pleasure took Mireya's breath away. Her subsequent climax caused her to black out for a moment. "Uhhhnnn..."

"Oyyy Mireya!"

She caught her breath and saw them reflected in the mirror. It was the most erotic sight she'd ever seen, watching him pump, ass cheeks flexing with each thrust. She climaxed again as he worked back and forth, pausing to suckle her tits, leaving blue marks on the surrounding hills. Mireya grinded against him, her vaginal walls contracting. *This must be what Hindus mean by Nirvana*, she thought.

After considerable time, Domingo clenched his teeth and growled. "Me vengo! Aw-aw-aw-awww, ay dios, awww!"

What he lacked in size, he made up for in spunk. She felt it varnishing her insides, oozing, trickling slowly down into her ass crack. When he slipped out, another rush followed, gathering, making a cobweb before dripping to the top sheet. They faced each other on their sides, and she gazed appreciatively into his eyes.

"You really know how to stir the pot."

"Mmm, yours was boiling."

They rested like that for a time, kissing, rubbing fingers over the curves of their bodies.

"You really liked it?" he asked.

"What do you think?"

He answered with a long kiss and stiffened again. This time, he guided her over him.

"I'm not sure what to do," she said.

"I'll teach you." He put his hands on her hips to guide her forward and back. We'll bring you to a boil again."

Mireya found her rhythm quickly. He licked a finger, spread her ass, and began to insinuate it. She reached back to stop him. *What's he doing*? Yet, it felt good, and she moved her hand away. *Let him teach.*

They finished by Domingo taking her doggy-style. Mireya climaxed over and over, finally collapsing to her stomach, exhausted. Domingo grunted, pulled out, and spurted over her anus.

Mireya stayed on her tummy as he rested on his side. He kissed her back, shoulders, and face, and whispered into her ear. "I think I love you."

"I think you're nuts," she answered dreamily. The intensity of her orgasms lent wings to her fantasies. *There's a lot to be said for having a small spoon.* She giggled.

"What's funny?"

"Nothing."

———

For months, Domingo and Mireya experimented, and he taught everything he knew. She learned to give head, twisting, and jacking him as she moved over him. He especially liked it when she painted his frenulum with her tongue. She learned it isn't necessary to go all the way down, yet it wasn't difficult given his size. Sometimes he asked to leave her glasses on so he could spurt over them. When he didn't pull out, she let semen dribble from the corners of her mouth, coating his shaft before spitting into a tissue and rinsing. The taste and texture made her shiver.

"Smells like chlorine," she told him.

"You should try it in your coffee with sugar."

"No thanks."

————

He'd been living with his mother in the main city of Tlaxcala. A stern, ambiguous woman, she shrugged and wished them well when they moved into a small apartment in Puebla, close to the university. Some weekends, they went on small trips to towns she didn't know. Occasionally, they visited her mom. Giselle's attitude had changed a great deal. She welcomed Domingo and thought they looked happy together.

Giselle no longer let lovers stay at the house with her. Mireya's grandmother, doña Isabel, was sick and needed care. Her mother's nurturing side came to bear, and she lovingly attended her mother until the afternoon she died. She would no doubt have lived much longer had it not been for a car striking her down as she picked wild tomatillos alongside the libro. The driver didn't stop, and she died sprawled in the dust.

A tiny cement altar was erected at the site, and flowers were placed once a week by loved ones. No one had clearly seen the accident, and the authorities were useless. The color of the car was obscured by road dust, as were the license plates. To become a police officer in México required little training, and the results spoke for themselves. Crimes went unpunished, and most laws were unenforced or ignored. When officers needed money, they took mordidas (bribes).

"We'll do what we can," the police assured Giselle. Translation: We'll do as little as possible.

Mireya had always been close to her grandmother. She remembered turning eighteen and getting a warm bucket bath from her. As doña Isabel scrubbed, she told stories of the past, the revolution. Tlaxcala had been one of the few states that had escaped military conflict, yet her husband, Eugenio, had joined and fought.

Doña Isabel was buried in the local cemetery next to her husband. The half-brothers shed no tears and were quick to leave after the burial. Mireya returned to her life with Domingo.

A few weeks after her grandmother's passing, Mireya visited her mother.

"How are you, Mamita?"

"Well, you know, I keep busy, so I don't have time to think about it."

"Good strategy."

"Been thinking of writing a will so there's no confusion about the ranch when I die."

"We don't need to talk about this now."

"I want to."

"Okay."

"I'm giving the boys the farmland, corrals, and you'll keep the house, and everything inside the walls."

"Whatever you want."

"Someday you may raise a family here."

"Maybe." *When hell freezes.*

"I miss her blue corn tortillas," Giselle said.

"Me too. When we hugged, that's what she smelled like."

———

Domingo moved up in rank to become the chief security advisor to the Governor of Tlaxcala. The new position came with perks. He began staying out late or not returning at all. When questioned, he got angry, claiming his absences were work-related. It wasn't hard to find evidence of other women. Domingo was careless about leaving motel receipts in his pants and undeleted messages on his cell phone. When Mireya confronted him, Domingo didn't deny. Instead, he had the gall to ask if she wanted to try swinging.

She moved out of the apartment and back to the ranch while he was away on business. Domingo pursued, promising fidelity, proposing marriage, enticing her with promises of a house and family. *The trap*, thought Mireya. *Pendeja*, she scolded herself.

"You can continue studies," he added. "You know I love you, baby."

"Find another pot for your little spoon."

The words were wounding. His lips trembled with a mixture of anger and shame. He turned and left. A week later, he moved in with one of his other women.

From now on, nothing will come between me and my education — especially not a teensy dick.

Giselle was disappointed about the breakup even after she knew the truth. "That's the way all men are, hija. As long as they pay the bills, why should it matter?"

Mireya just stared at her mother. The cutting reply on her tongue stayed where it was. She put her house in order upstairs, didn't answer the phone, and called the police when she saw a blue Beetle parked in front of the house. They never arrived. *Domingo has them in his pocket.* He tried to get to her through Giselle. Her mother was sympathetic, yet reminded him that her daughter was old enough to make her own decisions.

CHAPTER 4
MARCOS (THE PHOTOGRAPHER)

Three months later, Mireya took a university art class for fun. She met Carmen Alvarez there, and they became best friends. Her December 7th birthday had come and gone. She turned twenty-four without anyone noticing. In the art class, she met a painter/photographer named Marcos Flores, who worked from his home studio. They became friends, and he seemed harmless enough.

"Eres tan hermosa (you are so beautiful)," he said to her over coffee one morning at the university. "Will you pose for me? I can pay a thousand pesos for a few hours of work."

"Pose?"

"For photographs that I'll use to paint you."

"What kind of photos?"

"Natural."

"Naked."

He nodded.

She narrowed her eyes. "Why me?"

"There's something about you. I can't explain."

"Posing, nothing else?"

"I'm a professional and a gentleman."

"Have you asked anyone else?"

"There is no one else to consider. My hope rests with you."

Mireya was confident in her body. She knew she wasn't built like air-brushed women in check-out stand magazines, yet she had something they didn't. Tiny luneta's (moles) dotted her arms. Her legs were short and stout, and her full backside turned heads. Firm, average-sized breasts were topped with brown nipples. She had a beautiful, full-lipped smile with straight white teeth. Her brown eyes were the shape of almond leaves. She didn't have to try to be noticed.

Cover models lacked reality. Mireya exuded a mysterious natural aura of sexuality. Men inevitably did double-takes when they saw her.

"What else will you use the photos for?" Mireya wanted to know.

"To practice lighting, experiment with development techniques. You can have the negatives afterward. I'll keep a set of prints for my portfolio if it's okay."

"Have you done this before?"

"A few times. I have examples at my apartment."

Mireya pursed her lips in thought. Then she nodded. "Okay, but it has to be professional."

Marcos clapped his hands together. "Ándale!"

———

Later that afternoon, she was having a torta with Carmen at a small comida economica close to the university, when the subject of Marcos the photographer surfaced.

"You're really going through with it?" Carmen's eyes were wide.

"Want to come with me? I'd feel much safer."

"In case he's a serial killer." She lifted an eyebrow..

"To keep his mind on business."

"When's this happening?"

"Thursday afternoon after my Calculus Two class."

"Can't make it, got a literature class until nine."

"Too bad."

Marcos will paint you with his tongue," Carmen grinned. "You're bad."

———

His apartment was tiny, neat, and well-organized. There were several paintings on the walls and photos he'd taken. Most of his art was steeped in metaphor. There was a canvas depicting at first glance to be a split peach, yet further scrutiny revealed a vagina covered in supple blond hair.

She particularly liked a photo that showed a young girl being bathed outside by a grandmother. It reminded Mireya of her own grandmother, who used to bathe her every once in a while, even when she was a teenager.

They didn't have a bathtub, so Doña Isabel heated water on a stove and poured it into a large galvanized steel pail. She told stories from long ago. Or eloping with Eugenio, getting pregnant, and starting their lives in a house he built with wooden palettes and particleboard wired together. She had been a little girl in 1910 when the revolution started, and it lasted ten years.

"Over a million died." Then she would make an all-encompassing hand gesture. "But now we have this land. Before the revolution, it all belonged to rich hacienda owners."

Marcos showed her a folder with examples of other nudes he'd done. She didn't recognize any of the models. One sat spread-eagled in a chair, another was face down, balancing a glass of wine resting on her lower back. She turned to a photo of a chubby woman lying in bed, knees raised. Poised at her entrance was a large cucumber. Mireya turned it toward Marcos.

"Vegetarian?"

He laughed. "She was pretty wild, actually."

"Well, I don't know what you have in mind for me, but this is out of the question."

"Don't worry."

Marcos explained that he used black and white film. "It showed details that color washes out."

He brought a tray of ice-cubes. Then, he arranged candles on raised pedestals all around a brass bed with a fitted white bottom sheet, creating a surreal atmosphere, darting shadows, and bursts of light. He set up his tripod, camera, and wore another around his neck.

"Please remove your clothes. You can set them on that chair." He pointed to the only one in the bedroom.

As she undressed, he tried not to gawk, but it was useless. *My god*! He grew painfully hard as he posed Mireya in the middle of the bed on her back with one leg raised. After smoothing out a few wrinkles on the plain white comforter, he gently turned her feet, adjusted her hands, and her head. His throat was dry. *Be a professional*, he reminded himself. *Goddamnit though!* He handed Mireya an ice cube and asked her to rub her nipples with it.

"An old trick," he explained.

She pursed her lips, yet did as he asked.

"Great." He took the ice from her and placed it in the bowl. "Let's get started."

His hardness throbbed painfully, yet he held up his camera, taking shots from all angles and distances. He zoomed on her tits—click click click—her snatch—click click click—her face—click click click. Pre-emergent oozed from his cock. He had an irresistible urge to join her in bed. *Maybe that's what she likes, spontaneity*. With great effort, he controlled himself. Then he decided on a new approach, switching to the tripod.

"Mireya," he said in a husky voice, "did you know that from the time we're born to the time we die, we're truly alive only three times?"

"When we're born, when we die. What's the third?"

"When we cum. It's like being reincarnated each time."

"Mmm." *Know where this is headed*. She began to feel betrayed.

"Almost done?" Mireya was ready to dress and leave.

"Un momento." He switched to video without her knowledge. He waved his hands apart. "Can you open just a little?"

Mireya sighed. *This isn't art anymore*. She spread her legs another few inches.

"Bit more."

"Marcos. I'm done." She sat up, and he quickly shut down the camera.

"Sorry, did I make you nervous? Okay, get dressed and I'll show you how I process film."

Mireya relaxed a bit. She dressed and followed him into his homemade darkroom (the bathroom). He had several pans filled with chemicals, and a string across the room to dry photos on. There was a special light he used when photos were immersed in the 'fixer'. He used a plastic paddle instrument to 'dodge and burn' with.

The end result showed Mireya as she never imagined herself — exuding sensuality. She was impressed.

"Is that me?"

"The lens can't lie."

She studied each photo. Black and white showed strengths and weaknesses in great detail, yet the results were pleasing.

"Mireya, these are beautiful. *You're* beautiful." *Take a chance. What've you got to lose?* "I've never...." He swallowed hard. "These will make men yearn, as I do."

"Remember what you said. Nobody sees those. I need to get home. Lots of homework."

He barely nodded. "Mmm. I'll make copies and give you the originals."

"Okay." *I don't trust you.*

He dug into his pocket and handed her a thousand pesos. She wanted to refuse, but anger and need overcame her pride. She thanked him and left.

————

Despite repeated requests, Mireya never returned to his studio. They met during class a few times, yet their conversations were stilted. He gave her a folder with negatives and kept printed copies.

"Please, work with me again. I have a wonderful idea for —"

"No, Marcos."

"No nudity. Two thousand pesos."

"Can't."

"Mmm."

There are other fish in the pond. Class ended, and he promised himself that if given half a chance, *I'll bring her around to my way of thinking.* In the meantime, a magazine paid for the entire series he'd created with her, fifteen thousand pesos (700 hundred dollars). He stopped short of giving them her information. They wanted her to act in a porn film. *Just the thought drives me nuts.*

"That's where the money is," said the promoter of the company. "I'll audition her myself."

"Don't think she'd be interested."

"Tell her we pay ten thousand pesos a day. That'll change her mind. She's a student. With that kind of money, she can buy a doctorate."

Five hundred American dollars a day to let strangers fuck her. A large lump formed in his throat.

Marcos lifted an eyebrow. "You know, I'm a pretty good actor."

"Just ask her, or tell me how to find her, and I'll do it myself."

————

Marcos caught up with Mireya in a hallway as she walked to a class.

"Hey!"

"Hi Marcos." *What the hell does he want now?*

"Listen, I submitted my portfolio to a media firm, and they want to hire me."

"Great, congratulations."

"Here's the thing, though, they wanna meet you."

"Why?"

"For a movie audition."

"I've no acting experience. What kind of film?"

"An art piece. The producer likes your look, and it pays ten thousand pesos a day, can you believe it?"

Art film, eh? She gathered all the information she needed from the sheepish look on his face. *Not much dialogue in this type of film.*

"No thanks, Marcos. Good luck with the new job."

"Ten thousand pesos!"

"Could be ten *billion* for all I care."

"If you change your mind," he said, handing her his new business card. "Would you just meet with them?"

She put it into her back pocket. "I'm busy these days."

"Okay. Well, think about it. You could try, and if you don't like it, quit."

"I'll think about it," she said to get rid of him.

As he walked away, she took out the card. Artes Exóticas, and emblazoned beneath, Marcos Flores, Photographer/Painter/Actor, followed by personal contact information. On the back of the card was a single image. The face was blurred, yet the rest was in sharp focus. Burning candles, legs open—*her* legs.

———

Mireya was depressed. Marco gave his card to everyone he knew. The campus was filled with predators wanting to pump her full of brine, as if she were a coffee cup needing refills.

In the solitude of her room, she painted a self-portrait of a woman sitting inside a wooden crate with unattended hair, sad almond-shaped eyes, and a defeated mien. Tears ran down her cheeks, dripping to the ground to become cockroaches. To her credit, Giselle tried to comfort her daughter. Yet her words were clichés that did nothing to assuage the pain and anguish Mireya felt.

"Time heals," her mother finished.

Mireya thought about that and shook her head. "Time heals nothing, Madre. It marinates pain and suffering until it's tender enough to swallow."

"You'll see, mi hija. You'll see."

Things only got worse when some university students (men) she didn't know began gesturing toward her as they shared a magazine. One of them approached with a pen for an autograph. A caption below a close-up said: Gateway to Paradise. She closed her hands into fists and went looking for Marcos. *Gonna make him regret the day he met me*!

Unfortunately, he'd dropped out of school to pursue his new career. *Pinche cabrón*! One after another, predators tried their luck. Many were professors. A few times, she was tempted out of loneliness and need. After a time, her cold demeanor managed to drive them away, and soon she was regarded as 'frigid', earning the name 'Ice Queen.'

—————

She skipped the next semester. The months that followed represented a temporary defeat in Mireya's life. She sought out a psychologist and attended a few group sessions. After the third meeting, Dr. Rudolfo Godinez asked to see her privately. His office was lush, and it included the stereotypical leather couch.

"Mireya, in order to overcome fear, we need to learn trust." A large desk separated him from the couch.

She lay on the couch, staring up at the ceiling. "It's difficult to trust men, but sometimes I need one," she said. "I'm weak."

"Men have lied to you."

"Yeah."

"If you trust me, you can learn to overcome your fear."

"How?"

"A step of faith, an act of spontaneity, can release chemicals in the brain to trigger positive receptors."

"An act of spontaneity?"

"Do you trust me?"

"Of course not. "

"Here's a hypothetical—I lock that door," he pointed, "and we make love on the couch."

Mireya gave a contagious giggle. "That's going to build trust?"

He smiled and lifted his hands. "Because I'm being completely honest."

"And when we're done, I'll feel better?"

"Headed in the right direction."

Mireya forced a smile. "Any luck with this therapy?"

"It's in the experimental stages."

"The couch. Why not the desk? It's certainly roomy enough," Mireya changed her tone. Now it dripped with sensuality.

Dr. Godinez licked his lips and stood. "Of course, if that's what you prefer." He began pushing books and papers aside.

"Need a bathroom first."

He nodded, placing a framed picture of his family face down.

"Be ready." She let her eyes rest on his crotch.

By the time she made it to the door, Godinez had already unbuttoned his pants. Once the door closed, he pulled them down to the ankles. His throbbing cock curved upward. A Woody Allen quote came to mind. *I don't know the question, but sex is definitely the answer.*

The bathroom was located in the reception area. His office secretary was typing. Mireya looked at a nameplate on her desk. "Ms. Fernandez, the doctor says he needs to see you right away. Said that it's urgent."

Ms. Fernandez stood as Mireya was leaving. As she made

it to the street, she began laughing. She stopped walking to lean her hands on her knees. She thought, *Laughter's the best therapy*, and immediately felt better.

CHAPTER 5
RENÉ

René Zepeda was the director of a long-distance learning program in Puebla. Mireya joined the faculty because it satisfied a desire to offer education to impoverished and underserved communities. It brought students living in remote villages together with teachers and materials. In two or three years, students qualified to take a high school equivalency exam. They could then apply to college.

Tetéla was a lush village snuggled high in the mountains, cut off from technology, shopping centers, anything that would thrust residents into the twenty-first century. Elders didn't believe Neil Armstrong walked on the moon. For them, la Luna represented the ancient goddess, Coyolxauhqui. The idea of men walking up there was ludicrous. The goddess would never allow it. On Fridays after university classes, Mireya rode a rickety bus four hours to Tetéla over winding roads filled with potholes. She taught all day Saturday and returned late Sunday afternoon. The trip was exhausting, yet deeply satisfying.

René was married, a father of two youngsters, yet such facts never discouraged men from trying their luck with Mireya. Now twenty-five, she was more exotic than ever, attracting bees in search of flowers to pollinate. Although her natural beauty was eye-catching, it was her aura that lured them.

Rene was a few inches taller than Mireya. He wore round rimless spectacles and sported a slight paunch. Mireya thought he was moderately handsome. She noticed that whenever he was around, he wasn't wearing his wedding ring, as if that legitimized his lust.

Mireya still kept her hair short, which was rare in México.

She had stronger lenses in her black-framed glasses and wore them full time. Her body was pleasing—strong thighs joined with, what Greeks called, a callipygian ass (beautifully formed). She wasn't skinny. Each curve was celebrated by admirers. Whatever clothes she wore showcased her attributes. Her full lips were promissory, brown oval eyes scrutinized her surroundings, catching details that others missed. Her smile was big and honest, and when her mouth was slightly open, her front teeth showed, giving an air of expectancy.

René was reminded of a poem he'd read by Roman Payne. He spoke it out loud one day in his office as he thought of Mireya: "She's free in her wildness, she's a wanderess, a drop of free water. She knows nothing of borders and cares nothing for rules or customs…." He couldn't remember the next line, but finished, "Her life flows clean with passion, like fresh water."

———

René occasionally accompanied Mireya into the mountains to observe teachers, and he was present for every graduation ceremony. She inspired Renés primitive need for conquest. She was exotic, intelligent, and passionate, and her teaching skills were unparalleled.

She attracted him the way hummingbirds are drawn to red flowers. When she wasn't looking, he admired her ass, prominent nipples sometimes noticeable through her top. Given half the chance, he'd feast on them.

René sat with Mireya on the long ride to Tetéla. She was excited about seeing hard-working students graduate.

"Imagine how their lives will change," she enthused. They've seen a glimpse of the world, and they're hungry for more."

Mireya's attitude was contagious. "You've done a wonderful job. Proves what we already knew—anyone can succeed if given an opportunity."

"They see education as a way out, like me," Mireya added.

"What will you do after you graduate?"

"Continue studies."

"Not many women choose math."

"True."

"But you're not like most women. Smart, kind, disciplined, and beautiful."

She smiled and looked out the window. Green hills rolled by. People were working in the fields, wooden carts pulled by skinny horses or burros were loaded with corn or alfalfa. There was a muddy field being used for soccer by a gaggle of young boys. Higher and higher the bus climbed, passing small villages.

"Is Carmen coming?" he asked.

"Yes, she had a late class. She'll be here tomorrow."

"Good."

———

The bus ground to a stop. Many students were there to welcome her. Others would journey four or five hours on foot the next morning for graduation. They handed her flowers as she stepped off the bus, smiling, wanting to touch her. René was enthralled. For them, Mireya represented the goddess of knowledge, a bridge to a better life. They knew she made personal sacrifices to be with them. She was one of them.

Sarasvati was the Hindu goddess of knowledge and learning, René recalled. *That fits perfectly.*

"Hola Maritza! Abel, how's your mother? Hi Xochitl." She knew their names, the names of their parents, brothers, and sisters. Students were respectful to René. He was no stranger there. Yet, they worshiped Mireya and carried her backpack to the tiny eight-room hotel called La Mariposa. She often stayed with student families, yet this time she opted for the only hotel, a simple affair with Spartan furnishings—a double bed, wooden dresser, cold-water shower, and a toilet that flushed by pouring a bucket of water.

She and René checked into rooms side-by-side and were invited to a family home for dinner. Visitors dropped by while they ate for a glimpse of la maestra. Many were young and dreamed of obtaining the document that gave them better odds in life. They believed the paper possessed magic, that Mireya was an academic curandera (a good witch). René's esteem for Mireya increased each moment in her company.

Mireya laughed, sang songs with them, and an ancient record player played standards they could dance to. At one point, the matriarch of the family took Mireya's hands in her own and tearfully thanked her.

"Mil gracias por todo, maestra."

"De nada. Es un placer."

———

They stayed late before excusing themselves to return to the hotel. The next day, Carmen and another teacher would arrive for the 11:00 ceremony, and a grand fiesta would follow. A new academic cycle would begin.

René brought out a bottle of Don Julio and invited Mireya to join him at a small plastic table in the outdoor patio. A few shots of tequila loosened her tongue, and she was comfortable sharing ideas that would strengthen the long-distance program. He listened patiently, waiting for an opportunity to move away from business. Yet, Mireya surprised him by bidding goodnight.

"Night's young," he argued.

"I'm very tired."

Disappointed, René drained his glass, sighed resolutely, and stood with her. "Goodnight, Mireya." He kissed her respectfully on the cheek.

Thoughts were haunted by Mireya's image when he took to his bed, and his erection kept him awake for a long time. He drank two more shots and finally nodded off, knowing *one thin wall separates me from a drop of free water.*

———

The following day, Mireya wore a traditional Poblana blouse with a white, filigree skirt and a pair of huaraches. Her earrings were made with red kernels of corn.

The day ushered in a whirlwind of emotions. They gathered in a small cinder-block building donated by the community for the school. There weren't any pupil desks. Students used a square of plywood sitting in their laps to write on. Folding chairs were arranged for spectators.

Graduates wore their finest clothes, pride beaming from their faces. Mireya was humbled by their kindness and generosity. Children brought more flowers, parents served homemade cheese and liters of pulque, a local drink made from fermented cactus. Students presented her with a handmade wooden plaque for her desk, Professor Mireya Lopez carved on it.

Every graduate was the first in their family to go beyond elementary school. The lives Mireya touched had been trapped in amber, and the only way out was for someone to go inside with them.

Her proudest moment came when she called names and handed them the official government graduation document. She gave each student a heartfelt abrazo, and many broke into sobs. The faces in the audience glowed, and youngsters looked on with hope for the future. Eleven students graduated.

Carmen and the other professor had arrived earlier in the morning. Carmen Alvarez was studying Spanish literature at Puebla University, and she was Mireya's best friend. They'd taken several undergraduate courses together. Carmen was pretty, yet suffered self-esteem issues because of the needy alcoholic boyfriend she lived with. Mireya met Carmen in the art class that the infamous Marcos was in.

After hanging out a few times, it was apparent that she

and Carmen shared much in common. They'd joined the distance program together, sharing a room when they traveled. The other girl was Victoria, an undergraduate in science at a private university. She was reserved, and Mireya didn't know her very well.

Late into the night, music played, and Mireya danced with everyone, including Carmen, René, and Victoria. Carmen leaned close to Mireya's ear as they danced.

"Professor René's flaming for you."

"Married."

"Think that makes any difference?"

"Does to me."

The song ended.

Mireya was an accomplished dancer, moving sinuously and suggestively without trying. More than once, she teased René during a cumbia by undulating, bending at the knees until her face was perpendicular to his beltline. He tried capturing her in his arms, yet she always slipped away.

By two in the morning, Carmen and Victoria bowed out to return to the hotel. Mireya and René followed soon after, leaving students to enjoy their triumph with each other and the families. René suggested sitting again at the small patio table to sip tequila.

"Quite a day."

"Amazing," Mireya answered. "They're filled with hope."

Me too, he thought. "Glad you're still awake."

"Sorry, I was exhausted last night."

"I imagine. Finishing your bachelor's, making time to be here. You're incredible."

"Thank you."

René raised his shot glass, "Here's to you."

Music began playing nearby. Franco De Vita was singing Te Amo.

They tipped glasses. After draining it, he stared at her.

"Do I have food stuck on my teeth?" she smiled.

"No." René stood up and reached for her hand. She took it expecting to dance, yet he drew her toward him. Mireya met his kiss tentatively, and it lasted a moment. The second was longer, and the tips of their tongues touched softly before sliding together. Sounds of moisture filled their heads with rows of cotton.

What will this cost? she warned herself. Even as the thought entered her mind, it was whisked away by chemicals flooding her body.

Renés hands caressed her back, and Mireya pulled back to look at him. His eyes confessed the need, and her heart whispered it's what she needed to.

Breathless, she raised an eyebrow and smiled. "My place or yours?" followed by giggling.

Renés heart thundered in his ears. "I'm two steps closer." They laughed and walked ten yards to his door.

As soon as the door was closed, they collided. Kisses were hungry and demanding. His hand slipped beneath her blouse to find the catch. He sucked a brown nipple into his mouth. Mireya drew a sharp breath and let out a satisfied groan.

"Ahhhmmm, what do you want?" she whispered into his ear.

"You know."

"Tell me."

"To make love with you." He lifted her skirt, squeezed her ass.

"Mmm." She shuddered. "That's what I want too." Her knees buckled as they kissed deeply.

"Ayyy Dios." Precum trickled from his cock as he slipped her underwear down. She toe'd off her huaraches and kicked them aside.

"Make me cum," she whispered.

"I promise."

Their tongues clashed again, and she was wet. His head swirled as they finished undressing. The rustle of cloth, clinking of his belt buckle, and zipper sounds, all performers in an erotic symphony. She reached for his cock—thick, broad-tipped, so hard that it lifted toward the ceiling. She started to remove her glasses.

"Leave them."

"Okay."

René lowered her to the bed. She scooted to the middle and lifted her knees. He crawled between, placed himself, and pushed down and in, not stopping until he was fully immersed.

"Ayyy Dios mío," he groaned.

"Huh!" Mireya gasped. "Mmmahhh." She crossed her ankles around his lower back. When he retreated, she pulled him back. Their rhythm was an erotic give and take, each getting what was needed.

"Ayyy si," she groaned, lifting to kiss his chest, taking a nipple into her mouth.

It was her first opportunity to put her experience with Domingo to the test with another man. She appreciated René's thickness. *Not a small spoon.*

"Ohhh, you beautiful thing," he said as her tongue flicked over his. *Thank god for the numbing effect of tequila*, he thought. Even so, he found himself pausing occasionally to gather his wits. *So tight, silky, so…*

"Huh! Ohhh, I'm gonna cum, ohhh…."

She froze solid for a moment, and then he held on for dear life as Mireya thrashed beneath him, astonished by the strength of her first orgasm.

"Ay-ay-ay, oyyy si!" Her pussy constricted over and over.

Carmen and Victoria shared a wall on the other side of them. Mireya knew they heard, yet as he drove into her, concerns evaporated with another climax.

With Mireya's hips lifted, honeyed pussy pulsing, René let go.

"Ahg, oh god, awrrr, ah-ah-ahhh!" His balls lifted and drew inward with the strength of his surge.

"Ay sí, tu semen se siente caliente!" (Your cum feels warm).

"Oyyy!" His cock throbbed, decanting so much semen that it flowed out, dripped in long thick cobwebs to the thin comforter. Subsequent thrusts were met with moist queefing. Mireya shivered with a smaller orgasm even as his hardness diminished. He pulled back his foreskin and pushed to stay inside, holding her tightly.

As they kissed, more oozed out. "You made me erupt like Popocatepetl," he breathed in her ear.

"Mmm, I feel your lava."

"Jesus." He kissed her again. "Cloudwalking. That's how you make me feel. Like my feet aren't even touching the ground."

"Mmm," she moaned with her tongue in his mouth.

They turned on their sides facing, and René slipped out. They stared at each other. Both had the ruddy complexion brought about by lovemaking. Cum flowed down the inside of her thigh, matting in her soft dark pubic hair.

Mireya heard giggling through the thin wall of the adjoining room. "Ay chismosas," she sighed. "I'll never hear the end of it."

"Don't worry."

She sat up. "I'd better go back to my room," she whispered.

"Please don't."

"It's better." She kissed him.

"How's that better?" He pulled her back down.

"What's the word I'm looking for? Incorrigible?"

"Insatiable, enamored, ruined for any other." He vacuumed a nipple into his mouth.

"Mmmm. Let's try to be quieter this time."

He pulled off her breast. "I'll fuck you quiet as a mouse."

————

On the bus homeward the next day, the four of them dozed periodically. For appearance's sake, René and Mireya sat separately. Victoria gave knowing smiles to Mireya along the journey, perhaps thinking she might want to sample him on a future visit. Carmen sat with Mireya, and they talked about students until René was fast asleep.

She narrowed her eyes conspiratorially. "So?" she whispered.

"What?" Mireya tried to be serious.

Carmen elbowed her in the ribs. "Don't play dumb."

"Mmm."

"Mmm?" Carmen raised an eyebrow.

"Mmm," she nodded. "He knows how to stir a pot."

They both laughed. René woke up with a snort, and they laughed harder. He went back to sleep.

"Were we that loud?"

"Ay sí, tu semen se siente caliente! Sound familiar?"

"Oh my. I guess we were."

Carmen nodded. "Does he have a big stick?"

Mireya closed her eyes. "Mm-hm." She rested her head in Carmen's lap and was soon asleep. Carmen stroked her hair affectionately.

————

It happened twice again. The first time, René drove them to a motel, and the idea of protection was never brought up until he'd already drenched her narrow confines with semen. The second time was also at a motel. Resting in each other's arms after the third lovemaking session, René intimated he was thinking of separating from his wife. Mireya grew queasy.

"Don't even *think* about it, René. You have children. I know what having a broken family is like, and I won't be the cause."

"I love you, Mireya."

"You love fucking me."

"Mmm."

"I have plans after I finish my degree."

"Okay, let's keep things the way they are."

"This has to be the end. You have a family to think about."

"In the meantime…" René's cock was in no hurry to leave the safety of the motel.

"Insatiable."

———

Thankfully, a week later, René was offered an elevated position in Morelia. He and his family were a seven-hour drive away. Mireya had worried that his wife would find out. *How humiliating it would be.* She promised herself, *No more married men.*

CHAPTER 6
CARMEN

Mireya's life took an interesting turn on a return trip to Tetéla with Carmen Alvarez. Carmen studied Spanish literature with the goal of teaching at a private high school, where something akin to a living wage was paid. In México, private schools usually pay better than public universities. Corruption is the culprit, undermining education to the extent that a full-time teaching position can't cover the bills. Most teachers worked two or three jobs to make ends meet.

Mireya and Carmen shared a philosophy that education wasn't a business, it was a human right. They had entered the long-distance program in order to show congruence. A tiny stipend covered travel expenses and a few meals. Mireya and Carmen felt needed and appreciated in communities such as Tetéla.

A month after the student graduation, new classes began. They splurged for a room in Tetéla's tiny hotel, La Monarcha. Ironically, they were assigned the same room Mireya and René shared.

"Surprised it doesn't still smell like sex in here."

Mireya giggled.

"Are you still…?"

"Not since he left for Morelia. It had to end. He was saying stupid things."

"The 'L' word?"

"He talked about leaving his family."

"No me chingas!"

"Yeah."

"Good while it lasted, eh?"

Mireya lifted her eyebrows. "Mm-hmm."

"Are you on the pill or what?"

"No," Mireya answered.

"Nothing?"

"No."

"Aren't you the brave one?"

"Or stupid."

"Why play Russian roulette with your vagina?"

Mireya shrugged.

"Jesus, you're the smartest person I've ever known, but that's just dumb!"

She nodded. "I finished my period last week. Four days late, so that was a relief. How about you?"

"I'm on the pill. Can't imagine having a baby with Jorge. He loves the bottle more than me."

"Does he still write poetry?"

"He sees himself as the Mexican Dylan Thomas, drunk half the time, crawling around, and barking like a dog."

"Why don't you end it?"

"I don't know. Guess being with a drunk is better than being lonely."

"You're pretty. You wouldn't be alone for long."

"Mmm."

"I'll find you a handsome black guy with a big chorizo."

Carmen laughed. "That's your fantasy, not mine."

"True. Okay, we'll share him."

"Deal."

———

Late that evening, they lounged on the tiny patio just outside the room, drinking a bottle of cheap red wine, laughing and talking about life. The conversation inevitably turned to men. Wine loosened their tongues, and they swapped experiences. Mireya talked about Enrique, Domingo, and René. She confessed to the strange events with Marcos, the back-stabbing photographer.

Carmen's eyes lit up. "He asked me where you lived. Creepy. He wanted me to pose too."

"There're lots of strange men out there."

"Last time Jorge fucked me, he fell asleep on top," she said. Mireya giggled.

"I love the way you laugh."

"Remember Enrique?"

"The guy who bragged to the whole university about fucking you."

"Four minutes total."

Carmen rolled her eyes. "Jorge has trouble getting hard. Do you think I'm codependent?"

"Both of us to some extent."

"You're right. What about Domingo? You said he had a tiny pito."

Mireya nearly spat a mouthful of tequila. She held up a thumb and forefinger to demonstrate.

"Shit! At least Jorge has that going for him, not that he can use it. Don't you agree, bigger's better?"

"Thicker definitely is."

"Think I'll take your offer to trade Jorge for a black man." She held her hands apart to show distance, then put her thumbs and forefingers together to show width.

"Let's go find one."

"In Puebla?"

"Cubanos," Mireya remarked.

"True. They have a place on Reforma that plays Cuban music. So, getting back to René, did he…?" Carmen wiggled her tongue lasciviously.

Mireya shook her head. "He cut to the chase."

"Culero. Men think tongues are only good for bragging."

"They just want inside."

"Could learn a thing or two watching how people eat soft-serve cones."

"Exactly." Mireya wagged her tongue, and they burst laughing.

Carmen caught her breath. "There should be a fuck academy."

A song drifted in from the hotel lobby. Mireya stood and gestured to Carmen for a dance. They took turns leading, making exaggerated moves that men were apt to try. In Tetéla, there was very little ambient light, and the moon was only a sliver. The next song was slow and steamy. Mireya put a hand to Carmen's face and kissed her. Carmen's soft tongue answered unhurriedly.

"Órale," Carmen said breathlessly.

"A psychologist told me I needed to be spontaneous."

————

It happened naturally. The song ended, and they walked wordlessly back to the room. Mireya took the male lead, undressing Carmen as they kissed. Her hands blindly found catches, snaps, and buttons. She pulled Carmen's T-shirt off and flicked her tongue over a rubbery nipple.

Carmen moaned softly, "*That's* what tongues are for." She ran her hands through Mireya's short hair, and her breathing quickened. Then she removed Mireya's glasses and tossed them onto the nightstand.

Mireya peeled Carmen's panties and pushed her onto the bed. Kneeling between her raised knees, she kissed the inner thighs, teased the soft fleshy lips of her cunt. She parted the lips with her thumbs and licked the musk-scented clitoris. Carmen arched as Mireya's tongue grazed lightly at first, then lapped hungrily.

Mireya enjoyed pleasuring her friend. It was the ultimate test of friendship. Carmen disengaged, moved into a sixty-nine.

Carmen had heard it called double-header, flip-flop, fork-and-spoon, head-over-heels, loop-de-loop.

"According to the Kama Sutra, this is the congress of the crow," she explained.

"Let's open a fuck academy."

Mireya's pearl was small and super-sensitive. Carmen's was sizable enough to suck on.

Mireya lapped and slowly pushed two fingers into Carmen's humid cunt, marveling how silky it felt. She curled the fingers to detect the upper ridges. Keeping a thumb on Carmen's clitoris, she rubbed circles as her tongue flicked. Carmen mimicked her movements, and soon they were writhing.

Satisfied sounds accompanied lovemaking. They twisted and cried out. Mireya's first climax was ushered in with a long seagull cry. She squirted a liquid the color of watered-down skim milk, and Carmen thought it tasted slightly sweet. She followed closely with a staccato groan and a bucking orgasm. Mireya moved her fingers deeper, as the inner walls twitched and squeezed.

———

Resting in each other's arms, Carmen broke the silence in typical fashion.

"We smell like pussy."

"Meow."

"You nearly drowned me," Carmen laughed.

"Doesn't happen all the time."

"I read about it. *A amrita*, nectar of the gods. That's what Hindus call it."

"How do you know so much?"

"I study literature, dear."

They kissed and fell into a deep, contented sleep. In the morning, Carmen was business as usual, although after brushing their teeth she allowed a good morning kiss.

They breakfasted in a house that served eggs and chorizo with fresh handmade tortillas. The woman making tortillas was silent as she worked. Even when they greeted her, she looked down at the hot grill and continued rolling masa into balls. Then she patted them, laid them on a wooden press covered with wax paper, and flattened them into perfectly round corn tortillas.

The woman who owned the eatery confided, "Her name's Esperanza. Her four-year-old daughter was struck by a car last year and killed. She hasn't spoken since."

Mireya and Carmen watched through tears, the woman making tortillas, pat, pat, pat—the rhythm of life in México.

———

Because of her high academic performance, Mireya's scholarship was increased so that she could afford a cheap studio apartment, twenty-five minutes walk from campus. Her mother was sad to see her leave again.

She enrolled in Zumba classes whenever time permitted. *Never wanna lose my shape.* So many women she'd known had let themselves go to seed. *Controlling what my body looks like gives me control over who I allow to enjoy it.*

Mireya recently met a poet at the university. She should have known enough about artists to be cautious. Yet, when her heart whispered, she listened. His name was Marcos, same as the obsessive photographer she'd posed naked for.

Mireya was taking an afternoon physics class. Sometimes she arrived hours early to sit on a green park bench and practice sketching people in the park. A colleague saw her there and joined. Miranda was short and stocky. She was funny, insecure, and gossipy. They took physics together, and when Miranda could stay quiet long enough, they studied.

Thus began a chain of events, leading to a wager and an unusual conclusion:

CHAPTER 7
MARCOS (THE POET), ONE WEEK AFTER THE WAGER

Marcos sat alone in an old tavern bordering the zócolo, a week after his first and only date with Mireya. Hungry artists came there to grip shot glasses and listen to their stomachs growl. He was reflecting on the experience that left him bereft. *As though I lost my soulmate. Mireya. Forgive. Please. Redemption.*

"What lies at the heart of you? Moonlight and ravens." Marcos murmured to himself. His poetry resonated with the pain. *Poetry's a condensation of thought, River Truth snaking toward oblivion. Poetry lurks within pain, salted memories rubbed into tiny fissures of the heart. I must forget, I must not forget.*

His head felt like a nest of Swallows—*conflicted voices, fighting for a corner to spit mud and build a home*. Beneath the moonlight, he couldn't see ravens, but he knew they were there, waiting as he did for the sun.

"Can I get you something else?" the waitress smiled.

"Another shot."

Poetry, he remembered, *that's what she was*. His memory of her took him down a lonely alley, reminding him why he now drank alone:

Spied her in the zócolo in downtown Puebla. She was sitting on a green bench, sketching.

"Feast your eyes," Marcos pointed Mireya out to his best friend, Eduardo. Another girl was reading next to her, and they both wore glasses.

"Which?"

"Are you blind?"

"Ah yeah, you've got an eye for chickens. Voy." Eduardo stood.

Marcos secured him by the arm. "A wager?"

Eduardo arched an arrogant eyebrow. "You still owe me from last time."

"Double or nothing," he challenged.

"You'll be eating rice and beans for months," Eduardo warned. Then he strode confidently toward the two women.

Marcos watched his friend's approach. Mireya smiled, laid the sketchpad in her lap, and gave Eduardo her undivided attention. After a time, she handed him the sketchpad. The other girl looked up occasionally from her book, yet said nothing.

Marcos knew Eduardo's routine and muttered a selfish prayer for his defeat. *Eduardo never penned a poem in his life.* Doesn't deserve recommence for the tired lines he's torturing her with.

Twenty minutes later, Marcos spied them exchanging phone numbers on scrap paper. The other girl looked up, rolled her eyes, and returned to the book.

Eduardo patted his heart when he rejoined Marcos, standing in the shadows. "She'll be writhing beneath me in a week."

"We'll see," said Marcos. He stood and stretched his arms.

"Be my guest," Eduardo gestured, "but rest assured, you're wasting time. I'm thinking of ways to spend your money. Condoms. Lots of condoms, or maybe she's on the pill."

Marcos waited a respectful amount of time before trying his luck, approaching from the other side of the green bench. It was a bad strategy to attack from the same direction.

"Buenas tardes," he began.

"Buenas tardes," Mireya replied. Miranda looked up, shook her head, and returned to her reading.

"May I?" he pointed beside Mireya.

Mireya's bookworm friend stood up. "I'm going to buy a

phone card."

After she left, Marcos sat and gazed at Mireya's hand, moving lightly over the pad, glancing up once in a while.

"Mind?"

Mireya shrugged and handed him the pad. She was drawing the beggar woman with three children who shuffled around the zócolo asking for alms.

"Ah, this is remarkable."

Mireya fixed her eyes on the beggar woman as Marcos turned pages back to the beginning.

"Landscapes without people feel empty," he said.

Mireya gave him a sidelong glance.

"Are you an artist?" she asked.

Marcos nodded, "A poet. Words are my colors."

"Do you attend university?"

"Literature."

"Do you know Carmen Alvarez?"

"Only by name."

"She's my best friend."

"I'll be certain to introduce myself. I'm Marcos."

"Mireya." She accepted his handshake. "Have a favorite poet?"

"Neruda, Lorca, Martí, immortalized by words."

"Do you dream of immortality?" Mireya resumed sketching.

He shook his head. "I've other reasons for writing."

"Mmm?" She looked up.

Eyes shaped like almond leaves. "There are two reasons to write — because you can, or because you must."

"You?"

"No choice. I must."

Mireya gestured to a legless beggar leaning against a tree with a collecting tin. "Do you write about them?"

Marcos nodded slowly. "Especially about them. Misery and chaos are strangely beautiful, don't you think?"

"I can't remember who said, 'Chaos was the law of nature, order was the dream of man'."

This woman's fascinating. Her words, carefully chosen, solicited from a golden realm where precious ideas thrive. Marcos knew Eduardo was watching, observing body language, counting smiles.

"That's beautiful, especially coming from such a lovely mouth."

Mireya blushed and turned away from him. Marcos focused on the sketchpad. Her name, Mireya Lopez, was penned on the cover. The first page was a drawing of an old woman scrubbing clothes over rocks at a river. He turned the page. Two young boys were happily wrestling among autumn leaves. One wore the mask of Santo, México's most famous wrestler.

"I have class," she said, glancing at her watch, and putting out a hand for her pad.

"These are wonderful. Do you make them into paintings?"

"Sometimes."

"What class do you have?"

"Physics."

"Physics," he repeated. "Are you a science major?"

"Math." She pulled the sketchbook from his grasp to place inside her backpack.

"Physics and math are poetry too."

"Mmm."

Marcos was losing her. As she stood to leave, Miranda returned.

"Can I walk you to class?"

"No, thanks," Mireya said.

"I didn't get a chance to see the rest of your sketches. I'd really like to." He dug into his pants to find the receipt for a coffee purchase and used it to scratch his number.

Mireya reluctantly fetched a scrap from her backpack and scribbled hers.

"By the way, I'm Miranda," said Mireya's friend scornfully.

"Forgive me," Marcos held out his hand, but Miranda turned and walked away.

"I feel bad," said Marcos.

"She'll live," Mireya smiled.

Marcos kissed her cheek. Then he watched until Mireya disappeared around a corner with her friend. He found Eduardo pretending to window shop at a variety store.

"Well?"

"She arouses both intellect and loins," Marcos proclaimed.

———

A few days later, as Mireya was walking to geometry class, Miranda stopped her in the hallway.

"I've news about your poet and the other one," she said.

"Eduardo," Mireya answered.

"Have you seen that new movie with Bernal—"

"Focus. What's your news?"

"Wait until you hear."

"How long will I have to?" She was growing impatient.

"I saw him and Eduardo this morning at the zócolo. They were at the little coffee shop. Fuckers didn't recognize me. I was sitting close to their table. Wanna know what they were talking about?"

"Eventually, you'll tell me."

"They were bragging about who would fuck you first. They have a bet."

"Cabrónes," Mireya clenched her teeth.

"Your poet—"

"Not *mine*."

"Anyway, he said, 'My poetry will spread her legs.' Swear to god, that's exactly what he said. Poetry will—"

"Heard you the first time." Mireya balled her fists beneath the table. Already, a plan fermented in her mind. *Men share a common weakness when it comes to women. They want control. I'll let them think they have it.*

"Sorry, maybe I shouldn't have said anything." Miranda looked away.

"Thanks. Glad you did."

"What're you gonna do?"

"Wouldn't want to disappoint."

"You're gonna fuck 'em both?"

Mireya smiled. "In a manner of speaking."

———

As they sipped tequila in a small bar at the zócolo, Marcos was pleased to hear Eduardo's date with Mireya flopped.

"At first, it was going well. There was chemistry, I could feel it."

"What now, Romeo?"

"We had lunch, went for a walk, chatted about this and that. Then I mentioned my apartment was close by and asked her over for a drink."

"So far, so good."

"After a few shots, I kissed her."

"Mmm?"

"Let me tell yuh, that woman can kiss. I almost nutted. But then she stood, thanked me for a wonderful time, and said she had things to do."

"Just like that?"

He nodded. "Nothing I tried worked. She doesn't answer my calls. We're both gonna lose this bet, my friend."

"Don't underestimate the power of poetry."

"Violets are blue, roses are red, you're never gettin' that bitch into bed."

"Not bad," smiled Marcos.

Marcos called Mireya that afternoon. She was enthusiastic over the phone and invited him to her apartment for dinner. After hanging up, he pumped a fist in the air and called Eduardo.

"Long way from the front door to the bed, cabrón," Eduardo reminded.

"Headin' to the pharmacy, wanna come?"

"Mark my words, you won't need them."

"Then I'll fill her flower with my nectar."

"They have chocolate and strawberry flavored ones now."

"She'll roll it on with her teeth," Marcos said.

"Or bite your cock off."

"I'll save the first one to prove how much she made me cum."

"Sick fuck."

Marcos prepared like a matador. He shaved the bottom of his shaft, trimmed his pubic hair, and wore his lucky shirt—an elegant black guayabera. He had flowers sent ahead to Mireya's apartment and was purposely ten minutes late to heighten her anticipation.

Mireya met him at the door in a short black dress, cut low in the front. Immediately, his body began preparations for a hedonistic fiesta. There were three condoms in the front pocket of his pants. *Won't use them unless she asks.* He handed her a red and white wine.

"Thanks for the flowers."

"Impossible to find any that match your beauty."

"Sweet."

The studio was tiny. The only separate room was the bathroom. Everything else, a worn sofa, the kitchen, and a double bed, were all within a few strides.

"Live alone?"

"Hardly room for myself."

"Smells wonderful. What are you cooking?"

"Pipian verde."

"Love it. My grandmother makes it. Can I help?"

"No, it's ready. Let's sit a while." They sat on a couch, making small talk and sipping wine.

"What will you do with your lit degree?" she asked.

"I want to write."

"Will you teach?"

"Have to. You're a mathematician and an artist. Interesting combination."

"Art's just a hobby," Mireya smiled.

"What are your plans after you finish?"

"A doctorate."

"Wow, ambitious."

"Let's eat."

The plastic kitchen table had a Victoria beer label stamped at the center. There were toilet paper napkins and paper cups. The wine glasses looked out of place amid the simple setting. The food she served more than made up for the accouterments. A candle burned at the center, held by a shot glass.

———

The food was delightful. As they ate, Mireya's voice spilled out as a fine mist, circling his ears before floating into his mind. He took out a pen and a small notepad. She looked on quietly as he made a quick sketch of her, candlelight illuminating her almond eyes. Then he wrote beneath, *Diamond eyes, multi-faceted, sparkling passion, suffused with promise.*

"You make it look easy. I've never been much of a writer." Seeing that they were finished with the meal, she reached for his hand. "Let's go to the sofa."

The dress rode up as she sat. Her upper thighs were smooth and brown. He wanted to knife a hand between them.

"I've something else," Marcos announced.

She leaned closer, fingers lightly touching his leg. He glanced at the swell of her breasts.

Taking a paper from his shirt pocket, he read, "Beauty holds lovers bold, consuming guilt with benediction. Leaping flames of passion lick, emptiness sleeps with moonlight and ravens."

She touched his face, and her eyes softened. "You're full of surprises."

Patience, Marcos advised himself. *Wait until she's flaming for you.* He gestured toward two canvases leaning against a living room wall covered with cloth.

"Yours?"

"Yes."

"May I?"

"Sure." She stood to remove the cover from the first one.

It was an oil of children falling from the heavens into a giant baseball mitt. Then she uncovered the other—an aged professor writing the formula for love on an ancient blackboard.

"Where do you get your ideas?"

"Same place as you, I imagine."

"How do you make time to study math *and* paint?"

"There's always time for things we're passionate about. Most of my colleagues paint or play a musical instrument."

"Still, it's impressive." His heart welled up. He was lightheaded with the notion that Mireya was more than the sum of parts. *This isn't only about the bet anymore.*

"Thanks." *Cabrón.*

She didn't explain what motivated her painting. Marcos didn't deserve intimacy with her story—raised in poverty, shackled by tradition, and low expectations, her fight to break free.

"When I first saw you smile, I tasted the sun." He moved

his hand to her face and stroked with a thumb.

"Did you burn your tongue?" She teased.

"Quite badly. There's only one way to make it better." Marcos kissed her.

At that precise moment, he knew that this poem in the shape of a woman was the other half of him. Mireya's answering kiss set him ablaze. When it ended, she stood and tugged him to her bed. Then she pushed him at arm's length to lift her skirt. Slowly, she peeled off her underwear and kicked them at him. He caught them and hastily pulled his pants down. Keeping her glasses on, she laid crossways on the bed and lifted her knees.

"Get inside," she said.

Marcos slid his hands beneath her shoulders and jackknifed awkwardly between her thighs, with his pants and shoes still on. He tried struggling them off, but she said the magic words again.

"Get inside."

Her brown eyes regarded him, and her lips were open slightly, showing her front teeth. He took a moment to gaze at the beauty of her pussy, dark thatch, outer petals parted slightly. He grasped his pulsing cock, pulled back the foreskin, rubbed the helmet over her lips until it was wet. Then he slowly sheathed himself until he could push no further.

"Oh my gawwwd, Mireya." His voice was raw with passion. *Nirvana!*

Mireya pushed him off so hard that her glasses fell off, and he tumbled onto the floor.

Role-playing. He jumped to his feet, fully erect. "Only struggle twists sentimentality and lust together into love!"

She stood on the opposite side of the bed. "Save your pretty words, pendejo," she hissed, pulling down her skirt.

What is this? "What's wrong?" He tugged up his pants and held his hands out in supplication.

Mireya threw her panties in his face. "Bring those to

Eduardo and collect your wager!" She moved past him to the front door and opened it.

Words deserted him. *How does she know about Eduardo?*

"How much was I worth?" Her lips trembled with rage.

"Please, let me explain? I don't know what Eduardo said, but—"

"Get out!"

"You set this up to *humiliate* me?"

"You gambled, you lost." She held the door open. "I never want to see you again."

Marcos left without another word. The front door closed without the emotional slam he deserved. Her panties were still gripped in his hand, and he quickly stuffed them into his pants to keep the condoms company.

"Please," he begged through the door. The porch light went off, and he was left in darkness. "For chrissake, Mireya! Lemme explain." *About what*, he thought.

A television was glowing in the next apartment over. A telenovela actress lamented, "Por favor! Por favor!"

Marcos could feel his cock, moist and sticky. *Moonlight and ravens*, he thought, making his way into the street to hail a taxi.

———

That night, Mireya showered and considered how it might have turned out differently. *What if he hadn't taken no for an answer?* The telephone rang. She lathered her pussy and set her jaw. *Nothing will get in my way.* She laughed, remembering the look on his face when she pushed him off. The bathroom's acoustics made her laughter echo rich and loud. *All bets are off.*

———

Marcos arrived at his apartment and immediately phoned Mireya. *Be honest, beg forgiveness, and work hard to make her forget the whole business.* Yet he knew that relationships engendered by lies are doomed.

CHAPTER 8
JAVIER

Javier Paredes was Mireya's favorite math professor. She never missed his office hours, even when she didn't need help. His face visibly brightened when she arrived, and they talked about a myriad of things unrelated to math.

Javier had large, luminescent eyes that hinted of deep mysteries and profound knowledge. He sported a full, graying beard, which he rarely trimmed. He was short and paunchy, not particularly handsome, yet the eyes conveyed intensity. What attracted Mireya was his profound intellect. He discoursed about laws of physics, world politics, social ills, and owned an impressive personal library of books on every subject. He once said he read three books a week.

When Dr. Paredes lectured, Mireya saw his love for math manifested through wild, arm-waving gestures, the timber of his voice, and the fervor with which he wrote ideas on the whiteboard.

Javier always made time for Mireya. He nicknamed her Curious George because she peppered him with countless queries and showed a desire to move beyond what he expected from average students.

Their friendship grew during the months following Mireya's misadventure with Marcos the poet, who was desperately trying to reconnect. She steadfastly refused his overtures. *Latinas have long memories. He wants redemption. Too damned bad.*

Javier and Mireya often shared coffee at an artisan brewery close to campus. He invited her to several plays, a symphony, and a Tania Libertad concert. As the friendship deepened, he felt comfortable telling her about his wife, Esmeralda. She was pretty, twelve years younger, and had recently left him for another man.

Javier was heartbroken. He loved his wife dearly and was willing to forgive if she returned. Yet he knew deep down she wouldn't. His depression deepened when she served him with divorce papers. They were childless, and he was to blame. Sterility was a sore point in their marriage. Being childless in México is culturally frowned upon. A specialist offered expensive alternatives—artificial insemination, in vitro fertilization—Esmeralda rejected them in favor of the live donor she was now with. Twenty-six years flushed down the toilet. A few weeks after he signed the papers, he found out that she was pregnant.

In the settlement, Esmeralda got the house without a protest from him. Javier didn't want to live surrounded by ghosts from the past. He moved into a small apartment close to the university. He had only to wake up every morning, dress, gobble a pastry or a piece of dry toast, and stroll to work. Every day at two o'clock, he bought lunch at the same corner kiosk. Then he returned to campus to grade papers or teach a class. He usually returned to his apartment by six or seven. The friendship with Mireya certainly made him feel better, yet he couldn't shake his despair. Mireya confronted him about it during office hours one morning.

"Are you eating enough?" She had noticed his recent weight loss.

"Ah, well, I think so…I don't know." He shrugged.

"Dinner this evening, my treat," she offered.

"I've a lot of work."

"An hour."

"Okay, but I'll pay. When you're a famous mathematician, you can treat me."

Mireya smiled. Javier carried sadness as if it were a botched tattoo. "When should we meet?"

"Six, if that's okay," he replied.

"Perfect, I'll stop by."

Javier watched Mireya exit his office. In happier times, he would have admired more than her intellect. *Happier times.* He thought of Esmeralda. *Maybe he'll leave her after the baby's born and come back to me.*

Mireya was prompt. They walked through dimly lit university hallways, taking the stairs down, until they exited into the waning sunlight. Colleagues and students smiled and nodded at them along the way. No doubt, telenovelas were created when they were seen together. In México, professors are discouraged from engaging in personal relationships with students, yet it often happens. There were seldom repercussions as long as the affair didn't disgrace the university. Mireya had friends and colleagues that fucked professors.

They walked to a pleasant little eatery specializing in quesadillas filled with mushrooms and flor de calabaza (squash flowers). When their orders arrived, Javier fell silent, looking distracted. He barely touched his food.

"Javier," Mireya said, "I'm worried about you. Is there anything I can do?"

He looked up from his plate, smiled, and reached for her hand. "Thank you, Mireya. I know you mean well, but I have to work this out alone."

"You don't have to do it alone."

He kissed her fingers. "I'll be okay."

Mireya searched the depths of her heart for a way to help her friend. "You've never invited me to your apartment, and every time I invite you to mine, you're busy."

"Mine's a disaster, I'm not kidding."

"You're a Chaotician, it's to be expected."

Javier laughed and threw up his hands. "Okay, but you've been warned."

He signaled for the bill, and Mireya insisted on leaving a tip. On the walk to his apartment, she captured his hand. She didn't care who saw them.

————

Javier's apartment was a catastrophe. Clothes littered the floor, unwashed dishes filled the sink, and dust balls skittered across the floor when the front door was opened. The only pieces of furniture were a ragged green sofa, a small desk littered with ungraded papers, and a mattress lying on the tile floor, covered with a bottom sheet.

Mireya looked at the papers. "You've got some catching up to do, my friend."

"To say the least."

"Okay, get started and I'll tidy up."

"No, please, you don't have to—"

"I want to." Mireya held up a hand to fend off additional protests. "Pretend I'm your maid," she giggled.

Javier knew better than to argue. Mireya's tenaciousness was well known. He'd heard a few colleagues refer to her as the Ice Queen. *They're the frozen ones*, he thought. *Frozen in time. Macho. Macho menos* (much less than macho), he amended. *Scared of a smart woman.*

He sat at his table and lifted a stack of papers. Mireya buzzed around the kitchen, interrupting only to ask where cleaning supplies were. She walked to a tiny family store across the street to purchase whatever was lacking—almost everything. Mireya busied herself until 11:30 PM. Javier cracked his spine on the wooden desk chair and stood. He looked at his watch and shook his head.

"My god, what happened to the time?" Then he looked around. "Am I in the wrong apartment?"

"Needed a woman's touch," Mireya said.

"I'll never be able to keep it like this."

Mireya shrugged, "Moping around in a filthy apartment, putting off work, wearing a long face, that's not you."

"You're only twenty-five? How did you become so wise?"

"Just turned twenty-six. Someday I'll tell you about my life, but for now, you need to get on with yours."

Javier opened his arms for a hug, and Mireya stepped into them. He held her loosely at first, and then tightened his grasp until he felt her whole body blend into his.

Mireya liked the way his whiskers tickled when they kissed. It was an awkward first kiss, short and friendly. When it ended, Mireya caught him by the beard to pull him back for another. This time, Javier remembered how. His tongue was soft. She tried to unbutton his shirt, yet he held her hands.

"Mireya, I don't know if I can."

"I read that the essence of math is not to make simple things complicated, but to make complicated things simple. Let's make this simple."

She kissed him again, and he let go of her hands. Mireya kissed his chest, teased a nipple. His hands tangled in her short hair as she unbuckled his belt. His brain slowly began reconnecting with his body. Mireya crouched as she slipped his pants down to the ankles. Javier's cock was semi-erect. She lifted it, pulled back to expose the broad mushroom tip, and licked there. His legs quivered, and he swelled rapidly.

Mireya jacked him slowly, taking him into her mouth, and down as far as possible, pulling off to paint him with her tongue.

"Ahhh." He couldn't remember the last time he'd been pleasured this way. His reservoir was at full capacity. Javier felt his climax triggered deep within his bowels. "Ahhh, oyyy Mireya, ahhh…." He tensed, shivered, and sent a massive burden into the back of her throat.

He gripped her hair. Mireya kept her lips sealed as spunk was pumped into her mouth. Her glasses fogged with the effort not to gag. Her cheeks bulged with the volume of semen he discharged. She held her breath, pulled off, tipped her head back, and swallowed with a strong shudder. Then she massaged out the remainder, licking it clean as it emerged. As he softened, she took him down one more time before letting him go. His cock slapped against his thigh and hung wet and limp. She stood on wobbly legs.

"Need your bathroom."

Javier gave her a satisfied smile. "Anything, you name it, it's yours."

Mireya rinsed her mouth in the sink and looked at her face in the mirror. She wasn't sure why she swallowed. She hated the texture, the briny flavor, and the chlorine smell. Yet, the satisfaction on Javier's face made her happy. *After a time, you get used to anything.*

Javier felt as though Mireya had swallowed his sadness. In the length of a day, she handed his life back. He thought he loved her, yet his conscience caught up with the sudden release of dopamine. *Twenty-six*, he reminded himself—*half my age.*

Mireya emerged from the bathroom, returned into his arms, and kissed him deeply.

"Better?" she asked.

"You can't imagine."

"Time for me to go."

"Do you have to?"

"I should."

"Don't go. Please."

"Okay."

———

They slept in underwear, facing each other on their sides. At dawn, Javier awakened with an erection. He kissed Mireya lightly, and she smiled and stretched. Feeling his hardness, she lifted to remove her panties. In the dimness of the early morning,

Javier rested on his elbows above her and pushed into her.

"Ohhh my god." He kissed her as he moved, and Mireya swiveled around him. A few minutes later, he spurted heavily, bawling out as if he'd stubbed his toe on a piece of furniture.

"Sorry," he apologized. "out of practice."

"Don't worry," she replied as cum gathered and spilled. "You'll have plenty of chances for redemption."

They slept again, and when they awakened, Javier lasted long enough for Mireya to climax with him. As they showered, Javier soaped her body and sucked her tits, glorying in the feel of their bodies, slippery together. She sucked his cock again, and the final remnants of sadness washed down the drain.

Mireya cooked a creative breakfast with what she could find in the kitchen. When they finished, she looked seriously at him from across his plastic dinner table.

"What?" He looked worried.

"It's your turn with the dishes."

They both laughed. His face beamed with a joy he'd never known with anyone else, even with Esmeralda.

"I love hearing your laughter."

"It's good to hear yours, too."

———

Javier realized that Mireya would soon finish undergraduate studies and was applying for graduate school. Most likely, studies would take her far away from him. He didn't care what colleagues would think. He loved Mireya. Yet, he knew she could never be his—not really.

Although the friendship endured, he reluctantly allowed the physical element to dry up in order to protect himself from another broken heart. For him, their lovemaking was an experiential pinnacle. Mireya took him on erotic journeys that left him contented, exhausted, and asking, *Esmeralda, who*?

Mireya didn't ask why he no longer seemed interested

in fucking her. Instinctively, she knew that he was aware of her ambitions and wanted nothing to stand in her way. They still enjoyed dining out and sharing ideas. One afternoon, as they were having coffee at the university's little cafe, he said something to her that made her eyes tear up.

"You gave me wings. I'll never forget how you made me feel."

She knew then that her time with him was nearly finished. Javier had chiseled his name into her heart, the first man to do so.

CHAPTER 9
SEBASTIÁN

Mireya remembered her grandmother's advice with regard to making a man happy—*Keep him well nourished in the kitchen and bedroom*. Doña Isabel had led a tough life, surviving her husband by twenty years. Mireya had barely known her grandfather, who died of pneumonia when she was small. Isabel worked the cornfields as hard as any man and was quick with her hand if you crossed her. She also provided warm hugs—something she rarely got from her mother.

The death of Doña Isabel reminded Mireya of how fragile life is, how important it is to live it to the fullest in a manner of your own choosing. As far as taking her grandmother's advice—Mireya was a fine cook, and her bedroom skills were becoming unparalleled.

———

Sebastián was a journalist for the popular Mexican liberal newspaper, La Jornada. A married man with children, he became completely infatuated with Mireya. He graduated from BUAP a few years earlier, yet Mireya didn't know him then. They met when he chose the distance-learning program to complete his community service requirement. In México, four hundred and eighty hours of community service are required by each student in order to graduate.

Sebastián was in the program for six months, yet when they travelled to the mountain communities together, Carmen was there too. She sometimes caught him gazing at her, yet the stars never aligned. He was attractive, and there were times when she thought it might be bold to see where it led. The day came when his requirement was completed, and she thought she'd never see him again.

———

As fate would have it, they bumped into each other at the El Dorado shopping plaza in Puebla, and he invited her for lunch.

Mireya looked exotic in her Mexican blouse, short black hair, piercing brown eyes, and full lips. The day was hot, and she wore a pair of blue denim shorts. He stole glimpses of her legs, the well-rounded ass, as they decided where to eat. They settled on a small comida corrida (fast food) and ordered quesadillas with horchata.

Sebastián stood at six feet, taller than most Latinos, and wore a fashionable six-day beard. Journalism had taken him all over Latin America—protests, celebrations, and political rallies. Over lunch, he shared a recent assignment in Guerrero, covering the drug cartel turf war. He'd seen charred remains of military vehicles, decapitated bodies dumped in trash bins, a man slumped at the wheel of a car riddled with bullets.

"Too much death," he told her. "Sick of it."

He lived in México City with his wife and two children, yet work kept him shoving around. La Jornada had small apartments in major cities for journalists on assignment. His best friend, Antonio, enjoyed a semi-permanent position in Puebla and was allowed to live rent-free.

Comparatively, Mireya's life was mild. Nearly finished with her bachelor's, she was deciding what should follow. She wanted to learn English, yet programs were expensive and usually taught by non-native speakers.

"I need to be proficient in English if I want to pursue a doctorate."

"Comes in handy for me once in a while," Sebastián agreed.

Sebastián's English was frightful, yet he switched over to

practice with Mireya. The results were humorous. Sheet became *shit*, focus changed into *fuckus*, and peace turned to *piss*.

They walked to a nearby hotel bar for a drink. She liked hearing his stories. Recently, he'd covered a protest over a gas price hike. An angry mob burned down a gas station.

"I can still feel the heat from the explosion. Knocked me off my feet."

After a few shots of tequila, Mireya hardly noticed when his hand covered hers, thumb making circles.

"How long are you in town?" She asked.

"Few weeks. I'm flying to Argentina to cover the economic crisis. What will you do if you don't get into a doctorate program?"

Mireya shrugged. The possibility of failure wasn't allowed. "I don't know. I haven't thought of that."

"Sometimes I teach a journalism seminar at the university." Abruptly, he leaned in close. "Goddamn, you're beautiful."

"You're off topic."

"Let's change the subject. This's a very nice hotel," he said.

Mireya looked around as though seeing it for the first time. "Expensive, I imagine."

He lifted her fingers to his lips. "I can afford it."

"Sebastián, I avoid married men. They bring nothing but conflict."

"You went into those mountains on weekends," he countered.

"What's that got to do with what I just said?"

"Risk. Without risk, we accomplish nothing."

The familiar tingling began, a delicious stirring between her thighs. She lifted her glass for a sip and stopped in mid-air.

"I'd end up like one of your news assignments — find out what you can, report on it, move on to the next job."

He shook his head. "You're an ongoing story that will require frequent updates."

She giggled. "Need time to think about that."

"Sex is like journalism. The more you think about it, the harder it is to do. Better to just let it happen."

"That's a rock'n'roll philosophy."

"Mmm, let's rock and roll."

————

Sebastián paid for a room and they took an elevator to the third floor. He was no stranger to having other women, yet Mireya was exotic even by international standards. He kissed her in the elevator, and the way she returned it caused pre-emergent to seep out.

He suffered sensory overload before her clothes were even off. Slowly, she unbuttoned her shorts and slipped them off. She carefully folded her clothes and set them on a chair, and he did the same. They faced each other in underwear.

Mireya smiled, "On three...one, two, three...." followed by a giggle.

They stood naked. His dark brown cock was thick, veiny, and rigid. They kissed skin-to-skin. Tongues touched at first, then slipped eagerly together. He pulsated against her belly, leaving a snail-trail of precum.

Removing her glasses, he tossed them on top of her clothes. Mireya lay on the comforter with her head on a pillow, lifted and spread her knees. He kneeled before her altar, and leaned forward to suck a brown nipple into his mouth. She ran hands through his hair as he scooted closer so that his cockhead butted against her chamoise-soft lips. She wiggled so that they surrounded him.

Teasingly, he licked her ear and whispered, "Ay Mireya, at this moment there's nothing else in the world but you."

She kissed him as he pushed, and was slowly enveloped within her velvety sanctuary.

"Ahhhayyy," she rewarded him with a low, throaty groan.

He trapped a nipple in his front teeth and surprised her by

thrusting to the hilt.

"Uh!" she gasped. "Huh! Ohhh." His cock touched the border to her womb.

He pulled back and shoved harder, so that his balls slapped against her. Slow back, hard return, over and over. Each time he plunged, she gasped and gripped his shoulders. Her body adjusted to his aggressive style, and she felt the stirrings of a powerful response.

His cock filled her nicely, and she floated in the ethereal world of deathless pleasure. Sebastián pulled back and returned forcefully, faster and faster.

Mireya took a sharp breath and let out a long, staccato moan. "Ayyy!" Her hips churned as he peppered her neck and shoulders with kisses, leaving blue marks on the firm mounds surrounding her nipples.

"Oh baby, you're gonna make me cum so hard."

Now he sat up, licked her feet, her calves, and continued pumping. The top of his cock brushed her clit back and forth. Her head snapped back. He felt her stiffen and watched her eyes roll up in her head.

"Huhhh," she inhaled deeply. "Nnn-nnn-nnn," grunting with savage thrust. Her voice changed, making sounds that shattering orgasms bring — unfettered, semi-conscious moans, banshee screams, ushered in with the vice-like contractions of her pussy. At times, she appeared passed out, only to tighten her legs around his back and twist her head side-to-side when another arrived.

She cried out a word she'd rarely uttered before. "Oy si, fuck me, oyyy fuck me!" She pulled him deep and trapped him there, thrashing, her pussy squeezing, releasing, gripping, over and over. Then she made a final demand. "Cum inside!"

Immediately, he complied. "Ohhh shit! I'm gonna…!" Sebastián's nutsack lifted and compressed over and over.

"Awww, aw-aw awww!" He grew dizzy with the force of his ejaculation. For a few moments, he was transported into a timeless dimension. Within that tiny fragment he realized that Mireya was the crown jewel in his fucking experiences. He sent jetstreams into her magical realm.

It took a while to recover his speech. Finally, he looked into her face. Her eyes were closed. Occasionally, her lower body shuddered as he moved slowly now.

"Now I understand what Shakespeare meant by 'a little death'."

"Mmm," she managed. She pulled him down for kisses. The aftermath of their lovemaking caused time to march forward again, yet it was slower than before. She looked into his eyes and smiled mischievously.

"Did you have fun?"

"It was okay," he joked.

She slapped him playfully. "Just *okay*?"

"You can never get the full story with a short interview."

Her clitoris was super-sensitive, and the slightest motion tickled. She felt him soften and crossed her ankles around his waist. "Where do you think you're going?"

"Need rest before the next interview."

"Mmm." She released him, and Sebastián pulled out. Semen rushed like a glowing waterfall beneath a moonless night. Trapped air sent another gush. Sebastián kept her knees lifted to enjoy the spectacle.

"Christ, that's sexy."

"Don't you mean messy?"

He lay against her. "You're the reincarnation of Rati Devi, Hindu goddess of sex."

"And you're a highly skilled journalist."

He laughed and sat up again. With the index, middle, and ring finger, he pushed it back inside all the way to his third knuckle.

"Mmm, you're a bad boy."

They faced side-by-side and silently caressed each other. He ran his hands over the soft skin of her shoulders and back.

Mireya knew this wasn't a one-and-done situation. That afternoon, after the fourth interview, they fell asleep in each other's arms. In the morning, they ordered breakfast in bed, and when the knock came, Sebastián called out, "Leave it at the door, please!"

The food was cold by the time they ate.

———

They connected three times the following week, meeting at motels, cutting to the chase. Before he left for Argentina, he invited her to the company apartment. His roommate, Antonio, was leaving for México City. He'd be gone for two days, and they'd have the place to themselves. Sebastián introduced them while Antonio waited for a taxi to the bus station.

He took her hand, "Mireya, it's nice to meet you. Now I see why Seb is always on top of the world." *Because he spends so much time on top of you*, he added.

Sebastián smiled and wiggled his eyebrows.

"Don't drink all my beer. If you're gone before I get back, be sure to lock up."

The taxi pulled up. Antonio stabbed a finger into Sebastián's chest and drew him to the side.

"Jesus Christ, you lucky bastard."

———

That first afternoon in the apartment, they didn't leave the bed until well after dark. He didn't hesitate to pour them shots of the forbidden tequila. Still naked, they sipped on the couch.

"Seb, you need to start wearing protection."

He pulled a sad face. "I'll pull out."

She shook her head, not letting on that her period was

already a few days late. Again, her conscience screamed, *Chela*! Her cousin was pregnant again, and now the face-slapping reality of her situation made Mireya offer up a hypocritical prayer. *Please, god, no.*

They returned to bed. In the nightstand, in addition to finding condoms, Antonio possessed an assortment of adult toys. A blindfold, soft cuffs, and a bullet vibrator. Reluctantly, Sebastián rolled a condom on. He fitted the blindfold on Mireya and cuffed her hands behind her back.

"What are you gonna do to me?" She groaned.

Without answering, he forced her legs apart and began lapping her pussy.

"Mmm."

He used the tip of the vibrator on her clitoris.

"Ahhh."

He slipped two fingers inside and curled them up.

"Ohhh!" She lifted her hips and bucked when her climax arrived.

He turned her over and tugged her to her knees, and opened her ass cheeks. He removed his condom and slathered lubricant over the vibrator. Then he slowly pushed it into her ass.

"Oof! Ahhhmmm." Her head was snuggled into the pillow.

He kept a steady pressure until the vibrator was buried, then he moved it back and forth.

"I want my hands free," she begged.

In answer, he pulled out the vibrator and replaced it with his cock.

"Ooommm, ahhhh!"

His journey was made easier by the toy, and he plunged forward.

"Guh! Ahhhmmm."

As he stroked back and forth, he pushed the vibrator up

her snatch.

"Ayyy si, ayyy," she trembled. "I'm gonna cum....oyyy!"

Sebastián felt her anal walls collapsing around him. He reached around to twist her nipples, driving deep.

"Uhnnn, uhnnn, uhnnn!"

His ejaculation began deep within the bowels, flowing up into his balls, where it was forced out like champagne when the cork pops.

"I'm gonna fill your ass with cum! Ahhh, ah-ah-ahhh!"

It felt warm as he spread it up and down her intestinal walls.

After showering and resting, she used her tongue to try to arouse him, but he was depleted.

"Got nothin' left, love."

"I'll wash Antonio's toy before we forget."

"Okay. I'll wait here. I don't think I can move."

———

Their final afternoon that week, she was on top, swiveling around him. He was watching.

"Oops," he said. There was blood on his shaft.

Mireya looked down. She smiled. "Should I stop?"

He thrusted upward in response. "You kidding?"

When they were exhausted, he put both hands around her face and looked deeply into her eyes.

"What would you do if I said I loved you?"

"It's better if you don't."

———

Sebastián left for Argentina. Mireya knew the score—married, with children. She resolved to focus on math, finish her degree, and to move on from the relationship. Jealousy, possessiveness, and other commitments prevented a long-term relationship.

They want the whole enchilada, even if they're married. All but Javier, who thought he was too old, or I was too young.

CHAPTER 10
ANTONIO

Antonio was Sebastián's best friend. Mireya met him briefly before he left for Mexico City. He was a computer tech for La Jornada and was semi-permanent in Puebla.

While Sebastián was away, Antonio returned, and once again had the apartment to himself. Before landing a tech job with La Jornada, he lived with his mother. Though he was thirty-one, it isn't unusual for Mexican children to stay with their parents after they become adults.

Weeks earlier, over drinks, Seb made him privy to his relationship with Mireya. "She's really something, Tonio."

"Put her hooks into you?"

"She's all I think about. Smart, funny and whew…!"

"That good, eh?"

"She makes me cum so hard I see stars."

"What're your plans with her?"

"No plans."

"What line of work is she in?"

"Finishing a bachelor's in math."

"Careful, my friend, you of all people know how news gets out."

"Yeah."

"Gotta admit though, she's hot."

"You've no idea."

I think I do, Anyonio thought.

———

When Antonio returned from México, Sebastián was winging his way to Argentina. Seb's wife hated that he was a ghost in their lives. Yet, his chosen profession would never allow him to settle without a few more years under his belt.

Antonio found Mireya's telephone number on the floor of the bedroom. *Probably fell out of his pants, he was in such a hurry to get them off.* He pictured her in his mind. *Short, curvy, fuckable.* The way Seb rambled on about her piqued his curiosity. *What do you have to lose?* He called her.

The voice on the other end numbed his brain.

"Hello?"

"Hi Mireya, this is Antonio. We met briefly the other day."

"Sebastián's friend."

"Yeah. I was wondering if you like dancing?"

"I do."

"Would you like to go with me? I know a salsa club."

"Can I invite some friends?"

"Of course."

"Heard anything from Sebastián?"

"Nope. You?"

He must know about us. "Nope."

"Par for the course."

"Where should we meet?"

"I'll pick you up. What's your address?"

————

Miranda called a few friends, yet Carmen and Jorge were the only ones available. Antonio picked her up in an old Nissan Sentra, and they stopped for Carmen and Jorge on the way.

Mireya had reason to celebrate. She finished her bachelor's thesis and turned it in for her advisor. Her mother was proud and boastful, which was annoying. She graduated as a result of iron will and perseverance that kept her focused through tough times. Her cumulative grade report was 9.5 out of 10. *My passport to the world.*

At the club, Mireya was the show. Agave nectar lowered

inhibitions, letting the genie out of the bottle. She was coquettish, uninhibited, and exotic. She'd chosen to wear a pair of form-fitting Pepe jeans, which accentuated her generous upper thighs and well-rounded behind. Her top was East Indian with beads making flower patterns on the front. Red lipstick made her teeth shine when she smiled..

———

Most of the night, she danced with any man who asked, including Antonio. Occasionally, she pulled Carmen onto the floor. Jorge deferred his interest in favor of tequila and beer. He and Antonio discussed the North American Trade Agreement, how gringos treated Mexico like a lapdog.

"Pinches gringos, someday *they'll* be the ones sneaking across the border into México," said Jorge.

"Powerful and ignorant." Antonio shook his head. "Bad combination."

As the night progressed, Antonio watched Mireya's dancing transform, becoming even more suggestive. Her hips swiveled and teased, and men hovered over her like red-tail hawks.

Dancing with Antonio, she curtsied until her mouth was level with the front of his pants. Antonio's head swam with desire, bolstered by agave.

After 2:00 AM, the party moved to Antonio's apartment. They danced, had more drinks, and Jorge passed a joint around. Mireya had never tried. She enjoyed the floating feeling it gave her.

Just before dawn, Jorge crashed on the living room couch, and Carmen took space on the floor next to it with a blanket. Antonio invited Mireya to his bed, too tired and drunk to enjoy his good fortune when she agreed. They lay down fully clothed. He kissed her a few times, and soon they were fast asleep.

Half past eleven, Antonio woke up, turned on his side,

and gazed at Mireya. His erection pushed roughly against his pants. He lightly kissed her awake. Mireya opened her eyes a slit and smiled.

"Good morning, or is it afternoon?"

"Noon."

"Mmm," she replied. "I better get going."

He kissed her again. "You don't have to."

"I need a shower, a toothbrush, and more sleep."

"I have everything you need." He touched her face.

"Carmen and Jorge….?"

"We'll be very quiet."

"Ay pobrecito."

"Have any idea how much I want you right now?" His hand crept beneath her blouse.

Mireya captured it. "Tonio…" she warned him off.

He gave his best pout-face.

She gave him a short kiss. "Gotta go."

"Mmm," he replied. "Rain check."

"I had fun. Thanks."

"Wait, I have an idea." He really didn't, yet he made one up at the moment.

———

Antonio suggested they walk in Puebla's main zocalo that evening. Most large cities have a large park with surrounding restaurants, museums, art galleries, and businesses. Jorge and Carmen were still sleeping when Mireya left in a taxi for her apartment.

They met at 7:00 PM. It was a lovely evening. Vendors were selling homemade sherbet, ears of corn slathered with mayonnaise, sprinkled with cheese, and arbol pepper. There were beggars, musicians, and smooching lovers sitting on green steel benches. Mireya accepted Antonio's hand as they walked. After a while, they found an empty green bench.

"I feel peer pressure," he said, pointing to another couple kissing passionately.

"Wouldn't want that."

Antonio leaned over to kiss her. The softness of her tongue, the way she glided it over his, made him lightheaded.

"My mother lives close by," he mentioned. *Why the hell did I say that?*

"See her often?"

He shook his head. "Not as much as I should."

"Let's go."

"Now?" he protested. *Shit!*

"Why not?"

Because I want you in my apartment! he thought. "Guess we can stop by. She's always home. My father died five years ago."

"Never knew my father. Let's go."

It was a twenty-five-minute walk. They saw her in the kitchen window as they approached. She greeted them with a huge smile and pulled them inside.

"I was just thinking about you, hijo."

Antonio introduced Mireya, and his mother took both hands in hers. "Mireya, you're lovely."

"Thank you."

"And what a beautiful smile," she added. "Relax in the living room, and I'll bring some snacks."

"Let me help," Mireya said.

"No, you go with Tonio."

"I wanna show her my jazz collection."

"Okay."

Mireya followed him upstairs to his room.

He locked the door and faced her.

Mireya giggled. "What's on your mind?"

"Mamá takes forever in the kitchen, and she's hard of hearing."

"Are you insane?"

"Swear to god, Mireya, I'm dying for you."

"Antonio....?" She put her hands on her hips.

He put on a record and started the turntable spinning. Billie Holiday's voice filled the room with 'All of Me'.

Mireya's mind whirled. "Let's go to your apartment," she advised.

"I'm on my deathbed." He took her into his arms..

His quirky humor and spontaneity overwhelmed Mireya's logic. She pushed him back and looked sternly into his eyes.

"Un rapidíto (a quickie)," she said.

"I can manage that." He unbuttoned his pants, slipped them down, hooking the underwear along the way, and stumbled out of them. His throbbing cock was broad and uncircumcised.

Mireya toed off her shoes and peeled off her jeans before removing her panties.

"Jumpin' Jehoshaphat!" Antonio was wide-eyed.

She put a finger to his mouth. "Shhh."

They kissed briefly, and he almost spurted. She sat on his double bed wearing her glasses. The mattress creaked loudly, and she stood back up.

"Too loud." She spread the comforter on the floor, laid down, and raised her knees. "This is crazy," she giggled.

"You're the sexiest creature I've ever known."

Antonio kneeled between her thighs, splayed his legs, placed his cockhead within the parentheses of her lips, and slowly pushed in.

"Ohhh my god!" His eyes rolled up in his head.

"Pull out when you cum."

"Ohhh baby...."

"Shhh." Her eyes veiled. "Mmm."

When he was completely immersed, he paused to gather his wits. "Nnnn," he gritted his teeth.

She knew that he was fighting his urge. "You should cum." Mireya gasped.

Antonio pulled back, returned, and grunted loudly. "Ughnnn! Oh my god, oh my god, ohhh my god I'm gonna!" As he pulled out, she lifted the front of her blouse. Enormous spurts were directed onto her belly and over her pubic hair. It crawled down her sides. Still hard, he entered again and pumped furiously.

Pleasure muted her surprise. She sucked in a lungful of air as her cunt walls collapsed around his cock.

"Huh-huh-huh, ayyy!" She muted her pleasure with a pillow.

Antonio pushed to the hilt and clenched his teeth. "Sssyyy," he hissed, nutting inside of her. Collapsing on top of her, he found her lips as Billie sang, 'All of me, why not take off of me...'

There was shuffling on the cement stairs. Antonio stuffed his legs back into his pants, Mireya giggled, and finished buttoning just as his mother knocked.

"Taquitos are ready!" his mother announced over the loud music.

"Gracias, Madre, be right down," he responded.

"My god, what a mess."

He laughed and held Mireya. "You're adorable."

There were no tissues to wipe with, so Mireya pulled her pants back down and used the comforter.

"You didn't pull out," she scolded.

"The first time I did."

"I need a bathroom."

"Downstairs."

"Jesus." Semen was creeping down her inner thighs. She wiped again. They went downstairs, and she excused herself to the bathroom before they sat at the table. Flan was served afterward. It was as rich and sticky as she was.

They stayed long enough for mother and son to catch up on gossip, and he promised to visit more often. As they took to the street, he suddenly stopped to face Mireya.

"That's the best Mom visit I've ever had."

"Ha-ha."

"Seriously, though, thanks for reminding me of what's important."

"You're a good son, I can tell."

He kissed her. "We have unfinished business."

"I have unfinished homework."

"You're done with your thesis."

"I still have to defend in front of a committee."

"I'll help you study."

"Another time, okay?"

His hangdog face was etched in disappointment. "Mmm."

"Call me."

"Mmm. Okay."

———

That night, she thought of how fortunate she was. *A miracle I finished a bachelor's without getting pregnant. What would I have done?* A baby would ensure a life of mediocrity. Slowly, her desire to rise up would drown in a flood of responsibility. *The child would come first, and my dreams would finish last.*

Mireya lifted her underwear off the floor before she showered. The front was starched with spunk. Her belly and sides were glazed with dried semen. The phone rang, and she knew it would be him. She ignored it, stepped into the shower, and scrubbed away the evidence of her weakness.

The following day, she went to a pharmacy. She didn't want to be on the pill. She'd read about side effects—likewise, shots and implants. She chose an IUD and paid a doctor to place it—a T-shaped device covered with coiled copper. The doctor used a speculum to dilate the cervix. Then she inserted the device into the uterus using a long, pencil-thin tool. The procedure was painful, yet afterwards, she couldn't feel it.

As she left the doctor's office, she felt more in control. As a further precaution, she took a morning-after pill.

CHAPTER 11
RICHARD

Once in a while, Sebastián returned to Puebla to conduct business. Mireya would meet him for a bite to eat, then they rushed to a motel. Antonio always knew about it and grew jealous. When Seb left, he grilled her.

"Have fun with Seb?"

"Antonio, this won't work if you're going to be like this."

"He's married. I'm less complicated."

"Tonio."

The thought of losing her was too much. He clamped his mouth shut.

———

Sebastián knew nothing about them, yet regaled Antonio with sordid details regarding his time with Mireya.

"Mireya's pussy is magic. Never felt anything like it. When she cums it's like being trapped inside a tight silk cocoon. My god, she loves to fuck. She has these whole-body orgasms."

Antonio finished the story in his head based on his own experiences. *I don't cum, I explode!*

When Seb was in town, Mireya was a hypersexual juggler. On numerous occasions she fucked both on the same day, and a few times she had them on the same morning.

Others release stress with art, exercise, cooking, and music. For Mireya it was fucking. She read a medical study that explained, 'When we orgasm, our brain is flooded with dopamine in the reward pathways of the limbic system. This feels so intensely pleasurable that it's like a heroin rush to the brain. *I'm hooked on dopamine.*

She took Rhumba classes at least twice a week, yet there was nothing like the rush she felt with an orgasm. There were times when she climaxed a dozen times before her lover growled, flooding her narrow confines.

——

On December 7th, Mireya turned twenty-seven. On the cusp of Christmas, she traveled alone into the Sierra Norte Mountains of Puebla. Her family didn't celebrate holidays or birthdays. Her brothers were leeching off their latest girlfriends, spending holidays with them. As for Giselle, she had a new man in the house, and Mireya didn't much care for him. When he was around, she felt his eyes crawling over her. *Perhaps*, she hoped, *he'll be kinder than others*. But she doubted it.

Mireya enjoyed her independence, although she barely scraped by, teaching as an adjunct at various colleges. At that time in México, you could teach with a bachelor's degree. There were a few teacher certification programs. She enjoyed taking short trips alone.

On one such bus ride into the mountains, she thought of life. Her sights were set on a Master's, and she'd applied for scholarships.

After arriving at Ixtlan de Juarez, a hamlet snuggled deep in the Sierra Norte, she checked into a small posada and went for a walk. The air was crisp and refreshing, fragrant with pines and the scent of street food. She gave alms to a beggar with three children, who would never enjoy the luxury of a normal childhood. Mireya was fortunate. The poverty she endured as a child was nothing compared to this.

She found a tiny comida corrida and ordered a torta. Two men were sitting at a nearby table. One was Latino, and the other was white. During a lull in their conversation, they stole glances at Mireya. "Do you live here?" the Latino asked.

"Visiting," Mireya nodded.

"Where're you from?" The white man used broken Spanish.

"Puebla."

"Me too," said the Mexican. He gestured. "I'm Juan Mendoza, and this is Richard. He's Canadian."

"Richard Lamplier," the gringo added. "You have family here?"

"No." Mireya thought, *No matter where I go,* she reflected, men find me. Antonio called her a vixen.

"Where're you staying?"

"Posada Pino."

Juan nodded and gestured to Richard and himself. "Pretty sure it's the only place in town."

"Please join us?" Richard nodded to a chair beside him.

"Sure."

Juan ordered a round of Victoria's. Tortas arrived, and the men told her how they met in Ixtlan. Juan was an energy specialist, and Richard was a semi-retired architect living in Montreal. Juan wanted to practice English with Richard, and they became friends.

Mireya didn't reveal much. It was enough to say she was a math professor, wayfaring for pleasure, and that she wanted to learn English too.

After lunch, they invited her for a hike to a local waterfall. The Canadian was quickly enamored with Mireya and didn't hide it.

"I'm gonna frame this," he said as he snapped a shot of her. "Pretty as a picture."

Juan was more discreet. *Bide your time*, he thought. *She'll tire of the gabacho.*

Each time Mireya got ahead of them on the trail, they gave each other knowing glances and lifted eyebrows.

"How long are you here?" Richard asked.

"I'm leaving tomorrow," she answered.

"Perhaps we'll travel back together."

Mireya laughed. "You've no choice, there's only one bus, and it's leaving at 1:30."

"Should we buy tickets now?" Juan asked.

"It's always a good idea," she advised.

"Yeah," Richard said, "we might end up taking a burro."

They walked to the bus station and bought tickets. That afternoon, they visited the marketplace and found a cozy restaurant with a vista of the valley below.

"Beautiful," remarked Juan as he gazed at the valley.

"Yeah." Richard had his eyes fixed on Mireya. "Absolutely."

At sunset, they sipped tequila and talked. While Richard was in the bathroom, Juan gossiped about Richard and confessed about himself.

"He's sixty, divorced, a weekend father with two teens. I was married to a Poblana and lived in México City. Divorced when the boys were five and six."

When Richard returned, Juan excused himself to the bathroom. Richard gave her a rapid briefing.

"Juan's fifty, twice divorced, lives in Puebla with a jealous girlfriend. He's here to escape his girlfriend for a few days."

It was fun hearing them lay the groundwork for conquest. She didn't feel chemistry with either of them, and even if she did, *I'm not taking that road again.*

Late that night, Mireya excused herself after dinner and thanked them for footing the bill. They made no overtures regarding the Mexican repayment plan.

"Before I forget," Richard handed her a personal business card. Mireya wrote her contact information on a napkin. Juan fished in his pants for a receipt to write on, and settled for another napkin.

"You should visit Montreal," Richard said.

"I'd like to," she said politely.

After spending the following morning together, it was Richard who sat with Mireya for the bus ride back to Puebla.

I'll still be here when the güero leaves, thought Juan. He eavesdropped as Richard regaled Mireya with the wonders of Montreal.

"Seriously, you should come," he said.

"I'll save up," she answered. She did the calculations in her head. *On a Mexican academic scholarship?*

————

When they arrived in Puebla, Mireya guided them around a few spots in the city. She invited Carmen, and they visited the pyramids in Cholula, ate chapulines (roasted grasshoppers), and visited local artisan markets. The day ended with drinks at the Alleyway of Artists near downtown.

Juan showed interest in Camen, yet switched his focus when he saw that Richard was getting the lion's share of Mireya's attention.

Both men were thankful to Mireya for spending time with them. Juan had already seen the sights, yet never with someone like Mireya. Her enthusiasm for life and her exotic appeal made the tour refreshingly new. Carmen felt like a third wheel, but Juan still managed to exchange information with her.

Plan 'B', he thought.

"Which one's winning?" Carmen asked when Richard and Juan visited a men's room..

"What?"

"Don't play dumb. They're flaming for you. Why not kill two birds with one stone? The French call it a ménage à trois.

"Mmm, go for it."

"You never found me that black man you promised."

"We can go to that club where the Cubanos play."

Carmen changed the subject. "Are you using protection

yet?"

"An IUD."

"About time."

———

Richard was taking the airport express bus to the Mexican airport the next morning, and he yearned for a stronger alliance with Mireya.

"I'll pay for your ticket. You can leave with me tomorrow. I checked, and there are still seats."

Warning buzzers went off in Mireya's head. In México, such offers always contained a hidden payment clause. "Very kind, but I'm starting a Master's soon."

Juan was relieved. *Tomorrow's my chance.*

"Standing offer, no expiration date," Richard said.

"Thank you."

Juan couldn't wait for Richard to disappear. He had three condoms in his pocket and an alibi ready for his girlfriend, who owned a beauty salon.

———

Juan bought Richard a bottle of tequila to take, and Mireya gave him a box of camotes (rolled fruit candies). When he said goodbye to Mireya, his lips strayed from her cheek to her mouth. Mireya concealed her embarrassment and waved as he stepped onto the bus.

Juan invited her to a nearby bookstore/coffee house and purchased a biography of Frida Kahlo for her. "You remind me of her."

"Thanks, I've always admired her."

They walked in the zócalo, and she politely fended off his advances.

"Mireya, can I be honest?"

"Sure."

"You're all I've thought about since the first moment I saw

you."

"You have a girlfriend, Juan."

"That's why I was escaping in the mountains. Need a breath of fresh air."

"She's still your girlfriend."

"We're history."

"I don't have time for a relationship."

"Doesn't have to be that serious."

Mireya smiled. "Friends for now."

———

Juan didn't press. *Other opportunities.* There was something special about Mireya. Sensuality oozed from her pores. *Je ne sais quoi. That's what the French call it.* She bewitched him.

Another week passed. They attended a concert and picnicked in the mountains above Atlixco. She allowed a few kisses, but when his hand strayed, she captured it.

"Mireya," he gasped after a long kiss one evening, "I'm ready to burst."

"Your girlfriend can take care of that."

"No strings attached," he argued. "One and done if you like."

She shook her head. "No." It was getting easier to say that word.

"Once?"

"Once is never enough for men."

"Mmm." His cock was pounding. *She has me there.*

———

That night, picturing Mireya as he showered, Juan jacked himself and spurted down the drain. When his girlfriend arrived from work, he took her from behind while imagining Mireya. Afterward, she shared her day as if nothing had happened. Juan watched semen march down her thighs as she droned on about a weird haircut one of her clients had requested.

"Get me something to wipe with," she demanded.

Richard called Mireya at least twice a week. They exchanged Emails, and once he had flowers delivered to her apartment. She was nice to him, yet did nothing to reciprocate his romantic interest.

When the first teaching semester ended, he asked her to come. She still hadn't heard from the graduate schools she applied to, which wasn't unusual. Bureaucracy in México moves like molasses through the veins of progress. Eventually, she'd need to contact them directly over and over. *Squeaky wheel gets the grease.*

Mireya didn't like the idea of traveling alone to Canada, her first time outside México. She barely knew Richard, yet she itched for an adventure, and came up with a plan. The next day, he called.

"Could I bring a friend?" she asked with uncertainty.

There was a pause. "Yeah, why not?"

"Okay, great."

"I'll pay *your* ticket and book a hotel."

"I'll ask my best friend, Carmen."

"If she can't make it, will you still come?"

"Let me ask her first."

"Sure. Looking forward to seeing you."

"Is it cold?"

"Freezing. Bring warm clothes."

When the conversation ended, Richard sipped coffee and picked up a newspaper. Staring past the headlines, he thought of Mireya. He pictured taking her home, getting the preliminaries out of the way, and bedding her. *Got a feeling she'll be phenomenal!*

When he first met his ex, Claudina, the sex was good. She got pregnant right away. Following the birth of her second son, early menopause struck. She didn't want to be touched. First came separation, then he served her with divorce papers.

Yeah, Richard thought, *been a long time.*

————

Carmen was starting a Master's in literature and was unavailable for the Canada trip. Mireya went down a short list of other possibilities, yet no one had time or resources for the adventure. She thought of a new friend, Lourdes, finishing a bachelor's in psychology. They met during Mireya's last semester.

Lourdes was pretty, with long black hair flowing halfway down her back. Her eyes were large and luminous because she originally hailed from Guadalajara, where there was an Italian influence. She was four inches taller than Mireya, and her ample breasts worked as stoplights for men. She attracted various types — professors, students, married men, and virtual strangers.

On several occasions, they went out dancing or took time for coffee together before class. Lourdes invited her to a party given by the psych department, yet Mireya couldn't make it. Later, she was glad she had.

Mireya called Lourdes on a whim.

"Of course I'll go! Let's see, I have seven thousand pesos saved and I'm sure I can scrape up more even if I have to do table-dancing."

"Let's hope it doesn't come to that."

That afternoon, she called Richard to accept his offer to pay her ticket as long as he understood that she'd repay him as soon as she could.

"No worries. Don't have to think about that right now. Find your ticket and I'll wire the money."

"I'm bringing a friend. Her name's Lourdes.

"I'll arrange the hotel. Just get here."

————

They visited a travel agency downtown. Each round-trip ticket was five thousand pesos. They could make it work if they traveled on the cheap. She was hoping Lourdes would provide insulation from any notions Richard might have. *I'll pay him back without my body.*

Mireya found a gallery willing to display some of her paintings. As fortune would have it, she sold two of them a week before their departure—the children falling from the sky into a giant baseball mitt, the other paying homage to Marcos (the poet), depicting a man inside a volcano, his brains erupting.

"Who bought them?" she asked the gallery manager.

"Another painter. His name is Marcos Flores. Said he knew your work."

Flabbergasted, she was paid seven thousand pesos ($400) for the two. *Breathing room*, she sighed. *Marcos. That cabrón must be doing pretty well for himself.*

Lourdes sold a beat-up Renault for twelve thousand pesos ($700). Together, they'd stay at hostels and eat wisely.

The trip to Canada would be the first trip outside México for either of them, and they planned carefully. A week before the flight, they sat in Mireya's apartment and sipped wine. They mapped out places to visit, and Lourdes began laughing.

"What's so funny?"

"I'll visit these places alone because you'll be on your back most of the time."

Mireya shook a finger at Lourdes."That's not gonna happen, I told you."

"Are you protected just in case?"

"An IUD."

"I'm on the pill. Got pregnant when I was fifteen, and had an abortion. I don't take chances."

"Fifteen?"

"He was thirty-six.

"Did he force you?"

She shook her head. "Daddy issues, which is why I study psychology. You've got to understand yourself before you can climb into other people's heads."

"Do you understand yourself?"

"Fuck no."

Mireya thought of her time with Javier. Perhaps she had similar issues.

"That party you asked me to, how was it?"

Lourdes made googly eyes. "The wildest shit I've ever seen. You've no idea how crazy psych students are! Wanna hear?"

"Sure."

"Okay. The house belongs to a nutty professor, Dr. Hernandez. It's huge. Three other professors were there, and about thirty students. After drinks and dancing, they cleared a large space in the living room. We divided into groups of ten to play, spin the bottle."

Mireya giggled. "The teenager game?"

"Not quite. As I was saying, there were three groups of ten, each team had five women and five men. We sat in a circle, boy-girl-boy-girl, and in the middle was an empty tequila bottle and a stack of index cards. Professor Ortiz and Dr. Hernandez were in my group. We all took turns spinning."

"What did the cards say?"

"I'm getting to that. Hernandez spun first, and it pointed to a girl named Abby. She picked up a card. Each card had a side for men and one for women. Her's said, 'Show your tits.'"

Mireya put a hand to her mouth. "Did she?"

"Of course. Then she spun, and it pointed to a guy. His card said, 'Kiss the girl on your left. '"

"Glad I wasn't there."

"Dr. Ortiz passed around a pipe full of hash, and we all took a hit. The guy who kissed the girl spun, and it landed on me. You won't believe what I had to do."

"What did your card say?"

"Good thing I had a buzz going. It said, 'Give head to the man on your left for two minutes. If you make him cum before time is up, you'll receive five hundred pesos. If you swallow, you'll receive five hundred more.'"

"And?"

"He lasted about a minute, and I snagged a thousand pesos."

Mireya shook her head. "Mathematicians are hedonistic, but nothing like that."

"Anyway, they passed the pipe again. I was floating, and as luck would have it, I soon had to pick another card. Couldn't even read it. Handed it to the guy I'd given head to. 'Golden Ticket!' he read the bold letters. 'Fuck the men in your group within a half hour, receive five thousand pesos for each. If you let them cum inside, you'll receive another thousand pesos.'"

"Let me guess. You earned thirty-five thousand pesos?"

"Should've been more. When those five were finished, others took turns. Like a baseball game, after the seventh inning, you get in free."

"That's sexual assault."

"I barely knew they were there. After that, I passed out. It was noon the next day when I woke up in bed alone, naked, covered with dried cum. Next to me was an envelope full of cash. A note said, 'You were spectacular! You're welcome to stay. I'll be back this afternoon. We can have a late lunch.' signed by Hernandez."

"What did you do?"

"Rinsed off in a shower and left."

"You should say something. Those professors need to be fired. Think of how many other women—"

"They didn't force us. Let's change the subject."

"You were coerced."

"You're about to find out what that's like."

"No, I won't."

"Hmm, anyway, I've got plenty of cash for the trip."

———

The day before they left, Juan called and asked to meet in the zocalo.

"I've exciting news," he said.

"Me too."

It was a blustery day, and they were dressed warmly. They sat on a green bench in the park.

"You first," he insisted.

"I'm going to Canada."

"Fuck."

"What's the matter?"

"You know what Richard wants."

"He'll be disappointed."

"Sure about that?"

"I'm going with a friend."

"Christ."

"I can take care of myself. What's your news?"

He took a deep breath. "Split with my girlfriend. Wanted to celebrate with you."

"When I get back," Mireya said.

"Christ," he repeated.

"I'll be fine."

"Mmm."

"I've got packing to do. I'll call when we get back." She gave him a short kiss.

He watched as a black and yellow taxi whisked her away. *Richard's the one who'll be sightseeing in Canada—between your thighs.*

———

The weather was cold and clear when they arrived in Montreal.

It was late January. Another year had come and gone. She only remembered celebrating her December birthday once with Domingo five or six years earlier. He took her to the Frida Kahlo museum in Mexico City.

It was their first experience with snow. Mireya scooped some while they waited for the hotel shuttle. Richard had business on the day of their arrival, and promised to join them for breakfast the next morning. She'd argued about him footing the bill for the hotel as well.

"My pleasure, the price was reasonable. I'll make sure you have a great time here."

He's making an investment, she thought.

Breath fogged from their mouths. The jackets they brought were woefully inadequate. Lourdes began running in place. A few men standing around watched with interest as her breasts flounced up and down.

"Hot shower, warm bed—preferably with a man in it," Lourdes said.

Mireya shook her head and pointed, "There's the shuttle."

———

Hotel Nelligan was in downtown Montreal. A uniformed bellboy showed them to their room. They had exchanged pesos for Canadian dollars at the airport, yet neither was sure how much to tip. Mireya took an educated guess and handed him five Canadian dollars. The bellboy smiled.

The spacious room had two queen-size beds, a small living room, and a refrigerator stocked with liquor and snacks. On a bedstead was an envelope addressed to Mireya. She opened to find a note folded around a debit card with a PIN number:

Dear Mireya,

Welcome to Montreal! Please use the card for anything you need. I'll meet you downstairs in the morning at around

10:30. Call you tonight. Rest up!
    Yours,
    Richard

Lourdes opened the mini-fridge and took out a tiny bottle of whiskey. "*Yours*," she teased, reading over Mireya's shoulder. She unscrewed the cap and downed it. "A credit card, too. Ooee-ooee-ooee, you've got your work cut out."

"It's a *debit* card, and no, that's not gonna happen," Mireya shook her head emphatically.

"C'mon, you said yourself, he's not bad looking for an older dude."

Mireya narrowed her eyes. Since their arrival, Lourdes had flirted with men in the airport, a man on the elevator, and gave the bellboy a once-over.

"You're the one with daddy issues." Mireya parried. "You have my blessing."

———

Mireya didn't use the card and kept it away from Lourdes. After an evening walking downtown, they returned to the room. Richard called shortly after.

"How's everything?"

"We just got back from a walk. It's beautiful here."

"Sorry, I couldn't be there when you arrived — pressing matters." He would never say that those matters dealt with a property dispute with his ex.

"Warm enough?"

"It's very cold."

"Use the card to buy jackets."

"We'll wear more layers."

"How's Juan?"

"Saw him a few days ago. He's fine."

"Did you tell him you were coming?"

There it is, she thought. *The competition*. "I did."

Bet he turned white, Richard reflected. "Mmm. Are you dating him?"

"Just friends, like you and me." *There, I made it clear.*

As they talked, Lourdes lifted a condom from her purse to wave in Mireya's face. Mireya pushed it away.

When the call ended, Mireya wagged her finger at Lourdes. "You're terrible! Why do you carry condoms if you're on the pill?"

"I'm not crazy about STDs."

———

Ten-thirty on the button, Richard greeted them in the lobby. Looking fit and younger than his sixty-plus years, he was dressed in a light green linen suit with a black trench coat, sporting a short, graying beard. His blue eyes sparkled when he saw Mireya. He greeted Lourdes courteously, eyes roving over her as well.

"You look wonderful," he said, "So glad you're here."

"Thanks for the invitation."

"My car's parked outside. I'll tour you around a bit, and then we'll grab a bite.

"Okay."

Richard drove an Audi SUV. He held the door for Mireya to sit in the front. They visited the Notre-Dame Cathedral and the Old Port, then stopped for lunch in Old Town. By late afternoon, they were touring the botanical gardens, enjoying the warmth of the hot houses, filled with lush tropical plants. Richard suggested dinner and drinks at the Hotel.

Lourdes was no help at all. She gave them plenty of space to themselves, taking pleasure in Mireya's discomfort. *If I were in her shoes*, she thought, *this gabacho would be taking the ride of his life by now.*

After dinner, Richard excused himself to the men's room. Reaching into his front pocket, he took out an oval yellow pill and swallowed it with water scooped from the wash basin. The effect would last up to thirty-six hours. *That should do it*, he thought.

While he was away, Mireya reprimanded Lourdes for trying to push her into Richard's bed. "You're no help at all."

"C'mon, what do you have to lose? Not your virginity."

"There's no chemistry," Mireya argued.

"Pretend you're a Vegas whore and he's putting money in your slot machine."

"Lourdes, be serious. I really don't want—"

"Shhh, here he comes."

Richard returned to his seat, and the bill arrived. Mireya opened her purse, and he held up a hand. "You're my guests."

"Let us pay the tip."

Lourdes took some cash from her pocket. "Yes, it's only fair."

"As you wish." He glanced at the bill. "Thirty dollars?"

That would pay for a family of five in Mexico, Mireya thought. She split responsibility with Lourdes.

Suddenly, Lourdes announced, "I'm taking the tourist tram around the city. That'll give you time to get reacquainted."

Mireya's eyes grew wide, and then narrowed.

Lourdes stood."Richard, thank you so much for your kindness and generosity. Mireya was right. You're truly a wonderful man." Then she smiled at Mireya. "Don't wait up."

I never said that, Mireya fumed. *The trap is set.*

"Splendid," Richard enthused. "The tram will take you just about anywhere you wish to go."

She smiled. "Have fun catching up."

Mireya was seething as Lourdes sauntered away. Richard's hand covered hers.

The waiter collected the card, asking if there was anything else he could get for them.

"I think we're fine," Richard answered.

He smiled, took her hand, and rubbed the other over it. Mireya's eyes softened, and she smiled.

"You're more beautiful than I remember." Richard fished into his pocket and brought out a rectangular box. "Thought this would go well with your lovely brown eyes."

"Richard, I—"

"Open it."

Resting on a velvet lining was a silver necklace with a pendant inlaid with green jade and red coral. Richard stood behind her to help fasten it and kissed the back of her neck.

Mireya shivered. "It's beautiful."

Richard sat and recaptured her hand. "My pleasure."

"Please, don't spend any more on me."

Richard shrugged, "You must know how I feel about you, Mireya."

She slowly nodded, "Yes, I can see, but—"

"Tomorrow," he cut in, lifting three tickets from his jacket, "the Canadian opera."

He's narrowing my choices. She fingered the necklace and sighed.

He glanced at his watch. "It's only seven." He lifted an eyebrow. "I took a room for the night, and it just so happens, there's champagne on ice there."

"Mmm," Mireya pursed her lips. "What a coincidence." The setup was complete.

Both of his eyebrows were lifted expectantly. *The moment of truth.* After a lengthy pause, she cleared her throat and looked directly into his eyes.

"Richard, let's be clear. A serious relationship is out of the question. I have years of study ahead."

He nodded slowly. "I understand." He kept his eyes locked on hers.

She folded and unfolded the cloth napkin in her hand. *The*

repayment plan is about to go into effect.

"Okay," she said. "Let's go have some champagne."

Richard swallowed hard, kissed her hand, and nearly knocked his chair over standing up.

In the elevator, he drew her into his arms. Mireya placed her hands on his chest and looked up at him.

"This is just for fun."

He gave a thumbs up and kissed her.

Diffidently, she kissed him back, and the elevator door opened.

"Same floor we're on."

"Imagine that," Richard said slyly.

He was also next door to theirs.

"Home sweet home."

"You're confident."

"Hopeful," he amended.

Safely inside the room, Richard hung the Do Not Disturb card on the outside door handle. Mireya removed her jacket and laid it on the sofa. Richard did the same and led her to the side of the bed for a kiss. The feel of her tongue caused his cock to swell in moments. Still kissing, his hand crept beneath her blouse to find the catch.

Mireya stepped out of his grasp. Keeping her eyes on him, she methodically removed her clothing down to her underwear. As she had with Sebastián, she carefully folded them, set them on a chair, and left her glasses on. Richard popped a button on his shirt and nearly fell over his pants. Then he held her. Slipping the bra off, he bent to a nipple, slipped his thumbs into the elastic of her panties, and eased them down over her sumptuous ass. She kicked them free. He removed his underwear and stepped back.

"My Lord," he enthused, his thick, pale cock jutting fiercely, noticeably throbbing. "You're celestial."

Mireya laid on the bed and lifted her knees. She spread

as Richard kneeled before her, marveling at the beauty of her Venus — dark hair, downy at the edges, thicker around the borders of the mocha-colored lips.

His cock oozed with pre-cum and lifted with each beat of his heart. Mireya's inscrutable brown eyes gazed up as he scooted forward. She lifted her glasses off and tossed them onto a chair.

"Queen of beauty." His hips shifted forward, and he pressed into the constricting throat of her pussy. *Mon Dieu, elle est délicieuse*, (My god, she feels delicious), he thought.

"Mmm," Mireya moaned. Her mouth opened, showing her front teeth. *Feels good.*

"Ohhh Jesus," Richard whispered, peppering her face, neck, and breasts with kisses. "So tight." Richard drew back and plunged, feeling a snug welcome into the depths of her velvety throat. *Hold on*, he warned himself. He paused to lick an earlobe.

"Huh-huh-huh," Mireya was panting, pleasure mounting. "Ayyy si, mmm."

Richard moved slowly back and forth. She lifted her hips to meet him. *Yes*, she thought, *I'm a Vegas whore.*

The exquisite ache in his bowels warned Richard of an impending release. Squeezing his eyes shut, he paused to let a steady stream of semen flow out. Pressure relieved, he began moving again. *Christ*, he thought, *this is incredible.*

Mireya felt warmth glazing her insides. Her clitoris was sensitive, and the top of Richard's shaft was in contact.

"Oh!" she cried desperately. "I'm cumming!"

"Together!"

"Huh-huh-huh…Oyyy!" Her anus contracted, her cunt closed and opened over and over. Ay-ay-ayyy si, ayyy!" She stirred around him.

Richard's nutsack drew inward. "Ahhh! Ah-ah-ahhh! Jesus Christ, ahhh!" He poured spurt after spurt into her.

She thrashed so wildly that he slipped out, sending a spray

over her lower tummy before he got back inside. Streams of cum crept slowly down the inside of her thighs.

Mireya climaxed again, and Richard sat up to watch her contractions flexing around him rhythmically.

"Uhnnn," she repeated with each spasm. "Uhnnn!"

Richard's cock tingled and tickled as he lost hardness, yet he pushed in and held on until her final quiver. Then he rested on top and whispered in her ear, "You're enchanted."

Mireya squeezed him out, followed by a rush of semen. "Excuse me." She tucked her panties between her legs and hurried to the bathroom.

While she was away, Richard lifted his wet cock and jacked himself, willing it to fill with blood again. *Patience.* He opened the champagne as Mireya returned to bed.

"Watch something on TV?" She asked, trying to keep it as casual as possible.

"If you like."

"BBC News."

"You're an angel, you know that?"

"Mmm."

"Mmm," he nodded and handed her the remote and a glass of champagne. "My turn." He got up for the bathroom.

His exit hole was glued shut with cum, so he pulled the lips apart before peeing. Even so, he shot a stream of piss against the toilet seat.

After the champagne, Richard recovered. Mireya lifted and impaled herself. He clutched her hips as she swayed forward and back. She was soon jittering around him. When he sploshed, his eyes rolled up in his head, and he blacked out for a moment.

———

"Let's go for a walk," she suggested as they showered.

"If I *can* still walk."

He soaped her tits, lathered her pussy, ran a sudsy knife-hand down her ass crack, all the while kissing her. He loved how it felt to have her body slipping against his.

"Lourdes can't know about this," she warned as she rinsed.

"Okay."

———

Mireya made certain their stroll lasted a long while. Richard spilled his whole life along the way. Semi-retired referred to a need to pay continued child support.

"She maintains her standard of living, what about mine? She got the house, a car, the kids, spending money...ah, well."

When they returned, Mireya checked her room. Lourdes was still gone. Richard asked Mireya to spend the night, but she politely declined.

"Lourdes isn't dumb, she'll know."

"Mmm," he pouted. "Goodnight quickie?"

"You're a teenager," Mireya remarked. It wasn't the first time she inspired feats of stamina.

"You're to blame."

"Rápido."

"No problem."

They entered his room. She narrowed her eyes and bit her lower lip.

"This's for you." She removed her jeans and underwear, laid on the bed, and presented herself.

He quickly placed himself. "Oh my god, Mireya," he moaned as he slipped inside. "Ohhh...." his voice rose an octave.

"Cum," she invited. "I wanna warm inside."

Richard shuddered and she felt his cock twitching, warm semen coating her inner walls.

"Mmm, that feels nice."

She's the fountain of youth. I want this forever. He began brainstorming ideas to inspire the cancellation of her return flight.

———

Lourdes showed up soon after Mireya returned to their room.

"Let's go dancing."

"I wanna sleep," Mireya replied. *I smell funky.*

"Bet I know why."

There was a knock at the door. Richard stood there, looking past Lourdes to Mireya.

"Just came by to say goodnight."

Lourdes turned toward her. "Mmm-hm."

"Goodnight, Richard." Mireya tried to fight an incoming blush to no avail.

"Goodnight, see you in—"

"Richard," Lourdes chimed, "would you take me dancing? There's a place open until five just down the avenue."

Richard looked at Mireya for signs of jealousy. Nothing. She only pulled the covers higher.

Mireya nodded and smiled at Richard. "Lourdes is a great dancer."

"I'm afraid I—"

"C'mon Richard, Mireya had you all evening. My turn."

"Well, okay," said Richard, smiling lamely. "Be warned, I'm a terrible dancer."

"I'll teach you," gushed Lourdes.

"Okay."

"Meet you at the lobby in fifteen."

When they were alone, Mireya didn't have the energy to castigate Lourdes.

"So, how was it?" Lourdes said as she wiggled into a short skirt.

"You'll freeze in that thing."

"Richard will keep me warm. You didn't answer my question."

"Use your imagination." Mireya turned away from her. *Shower later.*

"Come on. I need to know what to expect."

"You'll find out soon enough."

"Are you okay with that?"

Mireya lifted a hand. "Be my guest. By the way, he's right next door."

"You'll hear us."

"Tomorrow, let's leave for Quebec."

"What about Richard?"

Mireya coldly replied, "What about him? Got what he wanted."

"Quebec, eh? Alright, let's do it."

Lourdes was all in favor of another adventure. They examined their budget and decided it would work if they were thrifty. Richard's generosity had saved them a lot of expense.

"Use the card," Lourdes suggested, "Let's have some fun before he cancels."

"No," Mireya said emphatically, glaring at Lourdes.

Lourdes foraged around in her purse and lifted a three-pack of condoms. "Won't be needing these." She gave herself a once-over in the mirror and hung a pair of earrings. Then she ran her hands down the front of her dress and smiled.

"Ciao," she waved and left.

Mireya fell into a deep sleep. At 4:30, she was awakened by a headboard butting rhythmically against the wall, corresponding to her travelmate's response. Tap, "Ooo!" Tap, "Ooo!" Tap, "Ayyy sí!"

Just after dawn, Lourdes dragged in.

"How was the dancing?" Mireya asked sleepily.

"Club was closed for refurbishing. You must've heard us."

How does a man that age have so much endurance?

"He asked about having a threesome. Kinky old fart. I told him you're exhausted."

"Is he still there?"

"Out like a light. He won't be up till this afternoon."

"Got a bus to catch."

She waved a hand in front of her crotch. "Huele a pescado (I smell like fish). Let me shower first."

When Lourdes was out, Mireya showered. She dressed warmly and advised Lourdes to do the same. They left the debit card and a thank-you note at the front desk.

When I get back to Puebla, I'll have my phone number changed. She thought of leaving the necklace with the card. *I earned it.* They had a small breakfast at the bus station and were soon on their way.

Mireya tried to sleep. Lourdes wouldn't let her.

"How could he keep going like that? We'd finish, and ten minutes later," she lifted a finger, "boing."

Despite herself, Mireya laughed and lifted a finger, "Boing."

CHAPTER 12
BYRON

Lourdes finally slept. When she awakened, she conversed in broken French with a man sitting across the aisle. As they spoke, Mireya watched Lourdes' legs wagging back and forth. *Jesus*, Mireya thought. They planned for two nights in Quebec City, and Mireya figured Lourdes would spend them hopping from bed to bed.

They arrived in Quebec in a little over three hours and decided to eat before checking into a hostel. At a small French cafe, they ordered poutine, French fries smothered in gravy and cheese curds. Within minutes of placing their order, Lourdes attracted the attention of a gentleman at another table. He looked to be around fifty, and his flaming red hair was paired with a fiery goatee. Ruggedly handsome, he showed dimples as he smiled confidently and joined them at their table.

"Byron Smythe," he said in perfect English.

Mireya shook his proffered hand, and Lourdes clung to it, allowing her fingers to slide away when she released. Mireya answered his questions generically in broken English, while Lourdes used French to fill in words she didn't know. Byron was more divested in the livelier Lourdes, yet stole curious sidelong glances at Mireya.

"Rarely see women traveling alone. When I was a teenager, I hitched to Montreal every so often—got a ride to Detroit once. Not safe now." He shook his head, "World's crazy."

"Especially the gringos," Mireya blurted. "They use Mexican sweat to build their empire."

"Ay yi-yi," Lourdes interrupted, "your poutine's getting

cold."

Mireya hated being interrupted, especially by someone like Lourdes. Byron saw dark clouds form on her face. She shoved her plate aside.

"Listen, if you're here only a few days, you're welcome to stay at my castle."

"Castle?" Lourdes said.

"Yeah, I own a castle in the mountains. I'd be honored to have you as guests."

"Castle?" Lourdes repeated.

Here we go again, thought Mireya.

Lourdes didn't hesitate to accept—yet Mireya rested a hand on her arm and squeezed. "Lourdes, let's think it over. No offense, Byron, but we barely met."

Lourdes turned to Byron. "You're not an axe murderer, are you?"

He extended two fingers and crossed his heart. " I promise to keep my axe locked in the woodshed."

"Lourdes?"

"I'd love to see your castle. Is it guarded by brave knights?"

Byron smiled and shook his head. "By spirits of the past."

"Ghosts?"

"Friendly ones."

"Lourdes, there are lots of things to see here, the river cruise, museums, the Old City, castles—"

"None of which compares to actually staying in one."

Goddamnit! She was about to tear into Lourdes. Mireya hated losing control.

Byron lifted a finger. "I have a solution. If you're not comfortable staying, I'll return you here."

Lourdes lifted a challenging eyebrow to Mireya.

She knew how stubborn her companion was. Yet, her conscience wouldn't let Lourdes leave with this man alone. A small knot formed in her throat.

Mireya pursed her lips and nodded, "Okay."

"Excellent." He held up a hand to the waiter and paid cash for their lunch from a wad of bills he kept in his pocket. Before they left, the owner of the cafe beckoned to him. They spoke in rapid French, shook hands, and shared a laugh.

He helped them with their bags and guided them to a beat-up Jeep Cherokee, the back filled with groceries.

"She's not much to look at," he referred to the Jeep, "but on mountain roads, it comes in handy, especially if it's muddy." He opened the front passenger door, and Lourdes took the initiative to ride shotgun.

As they wound their way up the mountain, Mireya understood what he meant. The road was long, narrow, and full of bumps and potholes. It reminded her of some Mexican roads leading into the small towns.

As he drove, Byron explained the history of his one hundred and twenty-five-year-old Scottish baronial castle.

"My parents made it into a resort. Twenty years ago, they died in an accident driving down this mountain. Brakes. At the tender age of thirty, I was left with the castle and a trust fund. When I was a child, the castle was a wonderful place to play hide and seek."

"Married?" Mireya asked.

"There has never been a Mrs. Smythe. Look there!"

In a grassy area off the road was a family of deer. Mireya smiled. It was the first time she'd seen them outside of a zoo.

"Do you have bears, the ones that eat people?" Lourdes asked.

Byron laughed. "There are no Grizzlies in Quebec. Black bears, but they only eat Canadians. Mexicans are too spicy."

Mireya laughed. Lourdes pursed her lips.

"You're making fun, but I'm really afraid of wild animals."

Mireya thought, *Except human ones.*

————

It took an hour to reach the massive iron gates, and on the other side loomed the castle.

"Oh my!" Lourdes exclaimed when she saw the massive residence. Towers rose from the corners, turrets and steeples graced the roofline. She thought it looked like something out of King Arthur.

Byron flipped down his window visor to access a remote clipped there. As the gates slowly swung open, he explained, "Gave thought to reopening, yet the cost of renovations and upkeep, phew! Besides, I'd be tied down for the rest of my life. My folks never went anywhere."

"You live here alone?" Mireya wanted to know.

"Friends come and go—stay a week, a month, a year. The groundskeeper and his wife live in a small cottage close to the main keep, and house cleaners come up three times a week, all Mexican by the way. This week they're taking a holiday, so we have the place to ourselves."

Byron parked the Jeep in a circular drive in front of the castle. After unloading their meager belongings, he faced the castle and spread his arms. "Welcome to Château Dans le Ciel, Castle in the Sky."

"Can't imagine living alone here," said Mireya.

Byron lifted an eyebrow. "Never alone. There are deer, moose, elk, mountain lions, black bears, and ghosts, of course."

"Wait a second….lions?" Lourdes wrinkled her forehead.

"Don't worry, they're very shy." Then he looked at Mireya. "And very formal. You have to send a written invitation before they eat you."

Mireya giggled. "Good to know."

Byron used a large skeleton key to open the ornately carved front door.

"After you, ladies."

The floor in the foyer was green marble, and immediately to the left was a dining hall, with an oak table long enough to seat thirty guests. Straight ahead was a spiraling green marble staircase.

"That leads to guestrooms." He gestured to a pair of swinging doors, "Kitchen's through there."

"How many rooms?" Mireya asked.

"Sixty-eight," he said. "The Fairmont Le Château Frontenac in Quebec City has about a hundred and twenty."

"You *really* grew up here?" Lourdes asked.

"Yep. I'll tell you all about it. Would you like a small tour to get an idea of where things are? There used to be a pool house, but it cost too much to maintain. I have a steam sauna, though. On cold winter nights, there's nothing better."

Byron led them up the staircase, and Mireya got goosebumps. *We're alone in a castle at the mercy of a complete stranger. Did I leave my brain in México?*

Lourdes smiled fawningly and commented on the Renaissance artwork adorning the walls leading up. Some depicted naked women frolicking in autumn leaves, men spying from bushes.

The tour took two hours. History saturated each room. There were portraits of famous actors, politicians, and history-makers dotting the hallways.

"This is where Humphrey Bogart stayed when he visited, with a different woman each time." They entered another room. "Spencer Tracy always reserved this room. He was such a nice man." Then he led them into a room at the end of the grand hallway. "Cantinflas stayed two weeks after he won the Academy Award for—"

"Around the World in Eighty Days," finished Mireya.

Byron smiled and nodded. "Funniest man I ever knew.

Never stopped entertaining. Marilyn Monroe was an occasional guest, very sweet as I recall." He led them into his personal bedroom. "This bed is a French Juliette Shabby Chic," he informed them.

"Not too shabby."

Byron raised his eyebrows, "Like sleeping on a cloud."

A huge armoire and various pieces of Baroque furniture filled out the room. Lourdes sat on a sofa and crossed her legs coquettishly.

"Baroque is elegant, yet uncomfortable as hell," Byron said. "I prefer the Biedermeier — elegant, modern, and a lot more cozy."

Neither Mireya nor Lourdes knew anything about antiques, yet they nodded. He showed the claw-footed metal tub and pedestal sink in the bathroom.

"Let's go downstairs to the library."

Lourdes made google-eyes, and Mireya tried to ignore her as they followed. Double doors opened into a library filled wall to wall with books.

"My goodness!" Mireya put her hands to her mouth. She loved books. When she wasn't studying math, she read for pleasure — Saramago, Allende, Marquez, Poniatowska, and Llosa — anything that struck her fancy.

"Bogart smoked cigars and drank brandy here. Einstein stayed whenever he guest-lectured at the university."

"Growing up around so many famous people must have been like living out a fantasy," Lourdes remarked.

"Actually, I wasn't old enough to be of worshiping age. For me, they were only guests. I was told to leave them alone most of the time. Yet, Joe DiMaggio showed me how to swing a bat and signed it for me. I still have it."

"Any particular ghosts we should keep an eye out for?" Lourdes asked.

"Honestly, I haven't seen any, but I wouldn't mind terribly if Marilyn paid me a visit." A phone rang, echoing in the library. "Excuse me."

Byron answered, said a few terse words, and hung up. For a moment, his countenance darkened, then he beamed a smile.

"Sorry," he said, "business — shouldn't take long. Make yourselves at home, feel free to roam. I'll find you, then we'll have dinner."

"Can we help with the cooking?" Mireya volunteered.

"You're guests, just relax and enjoy." He pointed to a full-sized bar in the living room. "Help yourself to anything."

As he took his leave, Lourdes' eyes were ready to pop out. "Can you believe this?"

Mireya shook her head. *What's the catch?*

"Don't know about you, but I could use a drink," Lourdes made a beeline for the bar. She went behind the counter and slapped the top. "What'll it be, stranger?"

Mireya laughed, "Whisky, make it a double."

"Two bits."

Mireya joined her behind the counter. "Look," raising a bottle of absinthe. "Ever tried?" She uncorked the bottle and sniffed. "Whew! Never mind, I'll stick to whisky." She found a whiskey bottle labeled Famous Grouse and poured a quarter inch into a tumbler. Lourdes preferred a VSP brandy, filling the glass halfway.

"Wo cowboy, take it easy," Mireya advised.

"Not to worry, I have a high tolerance. So, we're staying, right?"

"Mmm."

———

They wandered the castle, drinks in hand. Lourdes snooped into everything, and Mireya kept nudging her to stop. She revisited Richard's bedroom.

"Shouldn't be in there," she warned.

Lourdes ran her hands over the soft, thick comforter. "Not shabby at all," she said.

"Least he makes his bed," Mireya observed.

Lourdes laid on it and made her arms into a cross, "Take me, Lord Byron."

"Get off!" Mireya hissed. "You're such a kid."

"According to Carl Jung, sex is the natural discharge of tensions. I'm feeling tense."

"Leave me out of it."

"Where's your sense of adventure? The French have a word — ménage à trois." She reached to tickle Mireya in the ribs.

Mireya slapped her away. "You're loony."

Byron was at the door. They had no idea how long he'd been there.

"Dinner is served." He bowed ceremoniously and offered a crooked elbow for each.

"You cooked for us?" Lourdes asked.

"I enjoy it. Most everything was ready except the fresh salmon.

Mireya was still blushing with embarrassment. Lourdes hopped off the bed and snuggled into him. Mireya grasped him by the elbow, and they went down into the dining room. The long trestle table was bare but for one extremity, where dinner awaited.

Byron paired a French white cabernet with poached salmon, fresh baked bread, tossed salad, and finished with crème Brûlée.

"Delicious, Byron. Thank you."

"Most welcome, Mireya. Have to be a jack of all trades up here."

"You said you have a trust fund, but do you also have a regular job?" Lourdes queried.

"I have investments and a side business that keeps me busy. Sometimes I rent out space here for catered events, weddings. What about you?"

"I study psychology."

Byron smiled broadly. "A psychologist. You've certainly come to the right place. And you, Mireya?"

"Mathematician. When we get back to México, I'll start a Master's program."

"I love math. There are several interesting books in the library regarding its history."

"That sounds interesting."

Mireya impressed him with her sterling intellect and wit. He treated her with deference.

"And after that?"

"A doctorate, so I can see the world doing research."

Lourdes jumped in. "I wanna start a private practice. That's where the money is."

"Hmm," Byron said. "Let's retire to the smoking room for brandy, shall we?"

The room was ten times the size of Mireya's apartment in Puebla. Byron lavished them with tales of growing up in a palace. "Grandfather taught me to hunt in the forest, Christmas brimmed with interesting guests, and I once played chess with Boris Spassky. He pretended to lose."

"So many beds to choose from with lady-friends," Lourdes commented offhandedly..

"My god, Lourdes, you really don't have a filter." Mireya shook her head.

Byron laughed. "Yes, a great place to bring girls, but my first experience was with a Mexican housekeeper when I was fifteen."

"You're kidding." Lourdes leaned over to touch his thigh.

"Her name was Fernanda. She made it clear that discretion

was of the utmost importance. We made love in nearly every room of the castle."

Mireya smiled, "Must have taken some time."

"I was young and virile. Sometimes we'd meet in three or four rooms on cleaning day. Fernanda was responsible for the most important part of my formal education."

"Every room?" Lourdes repeated.

"Until Mother caught us."

"My god, what did she do?"

Mother sometimes wandered the castle, inspecting rooms. She heard some noises, found us on a balcony, sniffed loudly and said, 'Bit chilly for that sort of thing'. Then she left.

Lourdes laughed so hard that tears formed in her eyes.

Mireya covered her giggles with a hand. "Did she fire Fernanda?"

"She got pregnant and quit."

"Was the baby…?"

Byron shrugged, "Probably."

"My first time was in a cornfield when I was thirteen," said Lourdes.

Mireya nearly choked on her brandy. She recalled the classroom science table with Enrique. Last she heard, he'd gotten a girl pregnant and worked on a construction crew.

"What about you, Mireya?" Lourdes was scissoring her legs.

"It is getting late," said Mireya. "I'll help with dishes."

"Leave them," said Byron. "The groundskeeper's wife will collect them later. She does a few things like that when the others are away." His focus was diverted to Mireya's neck. "That's a lovely necklace you're wearing."

Mireya looked down at the reminder of the price she paid. "Thanks."

"A gift from a verdant admirer," Lourdez blurted.

"I imagine you've received many," said Byron.

———

Mireya could barely keep her eyes open. She peered into her brandy snifter and suppressed a yawn. Lourdes was still animated, energetic, hanging on Byron's every word. Mireya thanked him for dinner and asked to be excused.

"Of course, you must be exhausted. We'll have a late breakfast, and I'll show you the grounds. There's much to see."

"Thank you. Where should I sleep?"

"Any room you choose, Mireya. Room fifteen's where Marilyn slept. It has a private bath, fresh towels, shampoo, everything you need. I'll help with your things." He got up to retrieve her suitcase.

"Thanks, I can manage."

He gave her a cheeky kiss. "The castle has five boilers, so it stays cozy in Winter, but there are working fireplaces in every bedroom."

"Okay."

"Buenas noches." Lourdes winked at Mireya. "Fifteen?"

She nodded. "Maybe I'll see Marilyn."

"Join you there later."

"Goodnight," Mireya said.

"Sleep well," Byron's words followed her toward the stairs.

Mireya showered before going to bed. The soap and shampoo were French, and smelled of fresh lavender. She slipped beneath a thick quilt and crisp covers, and it was so warm that she wore a fresh pair of panties and an oversized white T-shirt.

The room was spacious, filled with Victorian furniture and oil paintings. One depicted a nude lying in bed with a knee raised, pretending not to notice a young man standing in the bedroom doorway.

Mireya's eyes were heavy. She closed her eyes to listen to

the steady hooting of an owl and the distant yip of a coyote.

———

Byron beckoned to Lourdes. She came, and he took her into his arms.

"Mexican women are exotic for Canadians," he said.

"How much did you learn from Fernanda?"

"More than you can imagine."

"I have a very good imagination."

The first kiss was an exploratory dancing of tongues. Then he gently nipped her neck and licked her ear. Lourdes relaxed into his body.

"You're gorgeous," Byron whispered. He led her by the hand up the stairs.

Lourdes was wet. This would add to other experiences she'd had. *Fucking on horseback in Morelia, in a canoe in Xochimilco, on top of the Pyramid of the Sun in Teotihuacan, caught by Japanese tourists. And now, in a castle!*

Once inside his room, they kissed and stripped each other. Lourdes gawked at Byron's broad ivory shaft, glistening at the tip with pre-emergent. He admired her denuded triangle, the scalloped edging of her pussy lips. He pulled her onto the bed to lick them up and down before applying his tongue to her clitoris. Within minutes, Lourdes was writhing, gripping his hair, grinding against his face.

"Mmm, delicious," he said.

She lifted and climaxed, her raptor call echoing in the bedchamber..

"Your turn." She shifted onto her knees.

Byron lay on his back, Lourdes clutched his heavy cock and cleaned precum from the tip. Then she dragged her tongue down and up again and again, only hesitating at the sensitive frenulum.

"My god, you've got a wicked tongue," he moaned.

Controlling her breathing, she moved him down her throat as far as possible. He lifted his head to watch, and to listen to the moist slurping sounds.

———

After a time, Lourdes laid back and he poised at her glistening entrance, teasing his broad tip over her smooth cunt lips.

"Get inside, ohhh, I want you inside!"

Byron obliged, pushing down and in, her lips opening, stretching to accommodate.

"Oof! That's a big, ooommm."

Lovemaking soon developed into a frenzy of thrusts, parries, groans, and sharp cries of pleasure. His thrusts were accentuated by his steady mantra.

"Mmm-mmm-mmm!"

Each of her orgasms was accompanied by falconish shrieks.

"Oh! Ohhh, I love your cock, ohhh my god, fuck me!" Her demand echoed in the bedchamber.

Byron changed rhythm, guided her into new positions, some she'd never tried. In the Lotus, she rocked him in and out. At one point, Byron lifted her and they fucked with her back against a wall. They finished with him thrusting from behind, taking her by surprise when he pulled out and pushed into her ass.

"Slow…oof! Oof!" She reached between her legs to massage her clit.

Air escaped from the tight seal as Byron buried himself deep within her bowels. Her orgasms were long, rippling convulsions.

"I'm gonna cum!" He warned. "Aw-aw-awww fuck! Awww fuck!"

She rested her face on the pillow. He stayed inside for a while, kissing her shoulders and neck. When he pulled out, she launched a mixture of sperm, feces, and trapped air from her anus.

——

After she cleaned up in the bathroom, they rested with legs akimbo for an hour, touching, kissing, and making small talk. Byron fetched a tin box from the nightstand containing a dozen neatly rolled joints. He lit one, took a hit, and handed it to Lourdes.

"How do you and Mireya know each other?"

"We met at the university." And then she went on to explain how they came to Canada, sparing no details except for the fact that she'd also fucked Richard.

"So, playing hard-to-get." He felt his cock stirring again.

"She's cautious."

"Maybe we should invite her to play."

"She won't." Lourdes shook her head vigorously. "I know her well enough."

"Alright, lass. Can't wait to see what tomorrow brings."

"I should join Mireya."

"You don't have to."

"She'll be afraid to stay alone."

"Okay. But before you go…" He was hard again.

——

Lourdes used a warm washcloth to clean herself, and slipped into bed next to Mireya without waking her up.

Mireya was up at dawn to pee. She showered and dressed, and bundled up in her coat, scarf, and gloves for a morning stroll. Her best investment in Montreal was the down jacket she'd found in a second-hand store. *Lourdes must have had her work cut out for her last night*, she thought, gazing at her sleeping form. *Can't wait to leave this place. It's starting to give me the creeps.*

She walked a trail that led to a stream and watched five deer lapping. There were woodpeckers hammering on fragrant pines, and she took amusement from a pair of squirrels chasing each other. Wind sifted through the trees, swaying the tops. Dark clouds threatened in the sky. She knew a snowstorm would trap them here, and shivered at the thought. *I'll go back alone if I have to.* Occasionally, the sun peeked out before being swallowed again.

A few hours later, Lourdes and Byron discovered her sitting on a boulder by the water.

Glad we found you," said Byron, "Have to be careful out here alone."

"I saw deer," she said.

"Yeah, lots of those," he replied. "And poachers."

"Hungry?" Byron asked.

"Starving."

"Mireya and I will make breakfast," Lourdes volunteered.

"You'll spoil me," said Byron.

He slung an arm over Lourdes' shoulder as they returned to the castle, yet he couldn't keep his eyes off of Mireya. *Something's different about you. Lourdes follows orders. You're gonna make me work for it. Well, I've never been accused of being lazy.*

———

After breakfast, Byron lit a bong-pipe and passed it to Mireya. She politely declined and gave it to Lourdes.

"Tonight we'll barbecue, and I was thinking of having some friends over." Byron's eyes were red, and he smiled dully.

"We've got a flight to catch," Mireya informed him. "We can't stay."

"Move it up a few days. No big deal. I've got a landline in my office."

"We have discount tickets with restrictions. They'll charge extra."

"I'll pay the difference, no worries."

"I'm starting a Master's program in a few days. I can't." Mireya was emphatic, though it was a lie.

"What about you, love?" He looked at Lourdes.

"I'm afraid we both have to go."

Byron sighed, "One more night? You'd like my friends."

"Can't," Mireya said, "but we've had such a wonderful time." *Keep calm. Don't panic.*

"You can visit us in México," added Lourdes. That seemed to satisfy him.

"Count on it," said Byron.

"Mireya and I love to cook," Lourdes interrupted his thoughts.

"Right this way." He led them through the large swinging doors into the massive hotel kitchen — pots hanging from hooks, stainless steel basins, and marble islands. He showed them where the ingredients were.

"Relax, we'll do the rest." Lourdes and Mireya busied themselves.

"Need to make some calls. Back in a jiffy," Byron said.

When they were alone in the kitchen, they whispered.

"We have to get out of here," Mireya said.

"Yeah," Lourdes replied. "Sorry, I got us into this."

"Save it."

"Yeah." Lourdes was unusually docile.

"An omelet." Mireya found cheese and eggs.

"Here's some rolls," said Lourdes.

"What I wouldn't give for some of my grandmother's blue corn tortillas," Mireya added.

————

Byron was on the phone in his study. One of his associates had a new client ready to airdrop two 100 pound bales of his Canadian *Grade A White Widow* into Florida. Camouflaged greenhouses in the backwoods of the castle overflowed with cannabis. Byron had bales ready for shipment at a moment's notice. He was preparing to expand into growing opium poppies, a dangerous but lucrative business.

For surrounding folk, he was the odd fellow with a castle on the mountain—the one that used to be a grand hotel. He was an eccentric. Unbeknownst to them, Byron had developed the biggest pot-growing industry in Canada.

My folks would roll over in their graves. He made a hundred times the yearly profit of the hotel in its heyday. A dozen workers, mostly illegal immigrants, helped him maintain the plants. He paid them fairly, and they had everything to lose, nothing to gain by ratting him out.

"Too bad you're not here, Carlos. Two gorgeous señorita's are staying here. Tourists from Mexico."

"For how long?"

"Not sure."

"Hittin' it?"

"What do *you* think?"

"Órale güey."

"I'll be down to see you next month. Need to pick your brain."

"Ándale."

————

Byron rejoined the girls as they finished cooking.

"Mmm, smells delicious. Sure you won't stay on as cooks? I'll reopen the hotel, and you can run the kitchen."

"I'm a mathematician," Mireya said. "I can't be in the kitchen all day."

"Cook my books then," he joked. "What about you, Lourdes? What's your analysis?"

"Never mix business with pleasure."

"Speaking of pleasure, there's something I haven't shown you."

————

They finished breakfast, and Byron invited them to see 'something special'.

"You two go ahead, I'll do dishes," Mireya was quick to say.

"You don't have to," Byron protested. "I have help coming in today."

"It's okay, I want to."

"Alright. You're a headstrong woman. I admire that. Shall we?" He crooked an arm for Lourdes and winked at Mireya. "Perhaps later."

"When will you drive us down the mountain? It looks like a storm's coming."

"Snow's likely. We'll have a look this afternoon."

Lourdes took his arm, and they walked away. Lourdes glanced back to give Mireya a look that would have curdled milk.

Her penance, Mireya thought, *for all the trouble she's caused.* Then she felt guilty for thinking that way. *I'll get her things ready for her and bring the bags down.* Briefly, she considered going into his office to use the phone — *call a taxi. Would they come all the way here? I don't even know where* here *is.*

———

Byron led Lourdes through a long hallway until they arrived at a knick-knack shelf built into a wall. He found a secreted latch beneath a shelf, and it swung inward when he pushed. He took her hand at the top landing of a small stairway, and closed the shelf behind them with a click. They were left in total darkness.

"Byron?" Lourdes was petrified.

Another click, and a light illuminated the stairwell.

"Come."

At the bottom of the steps, he found another switch. A chandelier blazed to life above a king-sized bed centered in a large room.

"You're gonna love this." Byron gripped her elbow and led her down into the room. There were straps built into the head and footboard of the bed. A high table stood next to it.

Furnishings were spare—a sink, a toilet, and an open shower off to one side. Another pair of straps dangled from chains anchored to the ceiling.

"Father had the playroom built for clients with special needs. Presidents, Chancellors, various luminaries required discretion, a safe place to play."

Lourdes swallowed hard. His psychological profile was now clear in her mind. *Byron is a maniac.*

Byron went to a large closet and opened double sliders. Shelves were filled with various sex aids—vibrators, dildos, butt-plugs. On hooks were whips and harnesses. Strange leather clothing filled wooden hangers.

"What do you think?"

"Ever thought about making the castle into a tourist destination? So much history." *Focus him on reality.*

"Not really."

There were dildos of every conceivable size, including one that might have been replicated from an elephant. There were handcuffs, strap-ons, lubricants, and devices she hadn't a clue about.

"It's like something out of the Spanish Inquisition," she breathed.

"Sometimes I rent to filmmakers. This room's been on quite a few adult websites."

"Mmm." Her mind stabbed in every direction for a way out. "Will you show me the grounds now? We haven't been outside yet."

Byron reached for Lourdes and rubbed his hands gently over her shoulders. "It's cold out there. Trust me."

"The cold is invigorating."

"So are you." He pulled her into his arms.

———

Mireya finished the dishes and went into the library. She found a large section of erotica and picked up an ancient copy of The Perfumed Garden, by Muhammad al-Nafzawi. She fanned through, stopping at the full colored illustrations depicting couples doing things she never imagined. She replaced the book and found a shelf filled with horticulture books. Most were specifically written about the care and cultivation of marijuana and opium poppies.

Finally, she discovered a biography of the famous Indian mathematician, Srinivasa Ramanujan, a college dropout who became one of the greatest math-minds of the twentieth century. She sat in a leather armchair and immersed herself. The book reminded her of the promises she'd made to herself—keep control, work hard, never give in. Ramanujan had been very poor, yet in his short life, he'd come up with over three thousand important results, most of which he worked out independently.

Hours crept by. Mireya cracked her back on the back of the chair and stood to stretch. She was worried. They needed to get down the mountain, catch a bus to Montreal to make their flight the following afternoon. She looked out a window. It was snowing lightly.

She returned the book to the shelf and wandered the house, listening for signs of life. A young Mexican woman arrived to tidy up the castle. *The groundskeeper's wife.* Mireya spoke with her.

Emelina was from Oaxaca—tiny, swarthy-skinned, and young. She wore indigenous clothing. Mireya began by asking how long it took to clean the castle.

"Two weeks to do the rooms, when all of us are here. I don't know where the other girls are. He sent them away."

He lied. They're not on vacation.

"Do you work here?" the girl asked.

"I'm with a friend. We're guests."

"Mmm." She had a funny look on her face. Her eyes were wide, as if she were listening with them.

"Emelina, how do the others get here?"

"There's a bus that goes to a lodge further up. It stops at the front gate."

"When will it come again?"

"Twelve, and then six depending on the weather."

"I think my friend and I will take that bus today."

"Mmm." She sounded skeptical.

"Byron said that your husband works here."

Emelina narrowed her eyes. "Yes. He takes care of the plants and does gardening. Well, I have work. It was nice to meet you."

"Igualmente."

Emelina turned her head side-to-side, as if a monster might be lurking in a darkened corner. Then she walked toward the kitchen.

——

Mireya went outside to stand in the sun, which had broken through the clouds. It looked as though the storm was moving away from the castle. A half hour later, a man approached her from an outbuilding a hundred yards from where she stood. As he neared, she saw that his neck, face, and hands were covered in tattoos. He smiled.

"Buenas días."

"Buenas días," she returned.

"Did you see my wife by any chance?"

"She's inside."

"Gracias." He nodded and went through the main entrance.

From inside, she heard yelling. She moved closer to the door. They were speaking an indigenous language she couldn't understand, but it was clear he was upset. When the exchange ended, she moved away from the door. He barged out and marched past, giving her elevator eyes on the way by.

"Hasta luego," he said.

Certainly hope not, Mireya shivered. She hugged herself in the cold and waited. Breath fogged from her mouth, but it was better than returning inside.

Lourdez found her standing there an hour later. She looked disheveled.

"Where were you?" Mireya demanded.

"Sorry," Lourdes said in a defeated voice.

"I talked with a housekeeper. There's a bus that comes by. We missed the first one. It comes back at six."

"Byron's going to drive us down the mountain."

"Sooner the better," Mireya whispered. "I packed your suitcase for you."

"Thanks."

"Let's wait in the library. It's freezing out here."

"Okay." After a pause, she added, "Mireya?"

"Yeah?"

"I'm really, *really* sorry."

"Let's just get out of here."

————

When Byron found them in the library, he was bright and cheerful. "Ready, ladies?"

He loaded their things into the Jeep, and they began the bumpy descent down the mountain. Nothing much was said on the way. Lourdes hugged herself as she sat in the passenger seat next to Byron.

At the bus station, he asked for their contact information. Mireya found a piece of paper in her purse and wrote out an address, phone number, and an email, entirely false. She handed it to Lourdes, who flipped it over and followed suit.

When the bus arrived, Byron hugged Mireya goodbye and said he'd visit México as soon as possible.

"México will be waiting," she said. *With a baseball bat.*

He took Lourdes into his arms and kissed her. "I'll call. Maybe you can visit during a school break. I'll pay round-trip for both of you," he added. "Maybe you have other friends that would like to stay."

"Sure," she said lamely.

He kissed her again, and the bus to Montreal boarded. As they pulled away, Lourdes began crying softly. Mireya put an arm around her, and pulled her close. Whatever her feelings for Lourdes, the Mexican culture allowed for compassion under most circumstances.

"He wanted you…he…he told me…I said you…you had a…a yeast infection."

"That was smart."

"He was…"

"A monster," Mireya finished.

"I think he's into some bad business. Drugs, porn, I don't know. He said he had to fly out of town for a few days and wanted both of us to stay as guests. I said our families knew where we were and would be expecting us home."

"Good."

They stayed in a cheap hotel the evening before their departure. Mireya felt sorry for Lourdes, yet resolved to end the relationship when they returned — after she called the authorities in Canada. *There's something fishy going on.*

————

It was good to be back safely. Her phone was ringing as soon as she arrived at her tiny studio apartment. She ignored it, put her backpack and suitcase down, laid on her bed, and resolved to call the Canadian authorities the next day.

A Spanish-speaking translator was found. She told her tale. They listened carefully, yet after over an hour, she heard the officer speaking in French. The translator said, "No hay pruebas suficientes para continuar." (There isn't sufficient evidence to go on). But they will look into it.

After the conversation, Captain D'Aboville rubbed a hand over his face. He picked up the phone.

"Detective Laurent, could I speak with you for a moment?"

"Of course, Captain. On my way.

D'Aboville had a gut feeling about this Byron character. *Put some feelers out, see what comes of it.*

————

She changed her phone number. *Richard, Juan, Antonio, Sebastián — better to cut ties with them and get a fresh start. Wake up! You don't need a man, Mireya!*

Antonio came over a few times when she wasn't there. He left notes saying that her number didn't work, that he wanted to see her. He wrote that Seb had a desk job in Mexico City. *Good for him*, she thought.

To simplify her life further, Mireya moved into another studio apartment relatively close to the university. She wanted to be invisible. Lourdes was out of the picture now. *Self-destructive. Me too, actually.*

Four weeks after returning, a mutual friend told her that Lourdes had an abortion. Mireya visited a doctor to have the IUD removed. *Never liked the idea of having a foreign body inside me.* She kept busy with tutoring, teaching an Algebra class, painting, and taking Zumba.

CHAPTER 13
ALFONSO

Four months after returning from Canada, Mireya met Alfonso Soriano, a physics instructor. She was *still* awaiting word regarding her Master's status. The wheels of bureaucracy turned slowly in México, or not at all. In the meantime, she taught two lower-division algebra classes and took a physics class for fun.

Mireya was attracted to smart, older men. She suspected it had something to do with the absence of a father. One afternoon, as she sipped coffee at the university cafeteria, the physics professor, Alfonso, spotted her.

He was above average height, slender but not skinny. He wore his dark hair short and combed back. His smile revealed dimples, and his eyes were large, brown, and sparkly. A full mustache reminded her of a popular television series about a private eye in Hawaii.

"Mind?" he gestured to the seat across from her.

"Of course not, professor."

"How's the coffee here? I've never tried."

"My treat."

"Thanks."

"What would you like?"

"Americano, black."

Mireya ordered, thinking wryly, *A black Americano. Always been curious.*

"Seeing you here alone reminds me of Einstein's Grand Unification Theory." She smiled, "How so?"

"It states that a beautiful woman should never be left alone for too long."

"Did he really say that?"

"I don't think so."

"Well, if it's true, then I'm lucky you came along," she giggled.

"Nick of time." Alfonso gestured toward several men staring furtively at them.

Coffee arrived. Mireya judged Alfonso to be mid-forties. She remembered seeing him in a grocery store, holding hands with his three-year-old son. *Doesn't wear a ring. Doesn't mean anything.*

He asked about her future plans, and she explained her frustration with finding a Master's program.

"If I don't get in soon, I'll have to teach full-time."

Alfonso shook his head. "Where have you applied?"

"Puebla, Guadalajara, Cuernavaca, Morelia, Mexico City."

"Why not skip the Master's and apply directly to a PhD?"

"Is that possible?"

"Not in Mexico. I studied in France and Germany, but there are opportunities in Russia, China, and England.

"My dream," Mireya said, "to travel and see the world."

"Anyone keeping you here?"

"No." She blushed.

"México has academic partners all over the world. Once or twice a year, I attend a conference in Europe or Asia. I just returned from Sweden. Let me place a few calls on your behalf, see if we can get the ball rolling."

"Thanks, professor."

Alfonso shrugged. "Write the names of universities you've applied to, and your contact information as well."

Mireya fished out a piece of paper from her briefcase to make a list. "It's not an imposition?"

"Of course. You will owe me another coffee."

Mireya laughed, "Gladly."

"What's your focus in Math?"

"Algebra."

"Physics and math produce offspring together. Where are you living?"

"A small apartment."

He nodded, "You have classes this afternoon?"

"An evening class in basic Algebra."

Alfonso shivered. "Undergraduates."

"Be nice," she chided, "I was one of them only a few months ago."

"No, my dear, you were never one of them." He lifted an eyebrow.

Mireya smiled and glanced at her watch.

"Heading home?"

She nodded. "Papers to grade."

"I'll give you a lift."

"That's very nice, but I'm close by."

"Then it will be a short drive."

"Okay, thanks, professor."

"Friends call me Fonso."

————

Rather than butt heads with her mother's boyfriend, Mireya struggled to keep her own apartment. Yet, she barely made enough to cover her rent and eat. Zumba classes were free at the university. *Time's running out.*

As Alfonso drove, he wisecracked at the obstacle course that was every day Mexican traffic. Her apartment was on a dirty side street. The neighborhood was dilapidated, with outer walls covered in graffiti. She thought of warning him that it wasn't safe to leave his car parked, yet decided against it. It would be rude not to invite him in.

Ragged furniture came with the apartment—a worn sofa, a small round plastic patio table with two chairs, and on the floor of the studio was a sleeping mattress. Alfonso gazed around, and Mireya saw a sad look in his eyes. She didn't want anyone feeling sorry for her. This was her reality for now, yet she was determined that circumstances would change.

She only had water with a squeeze of lime to offer, and gave him a glass. They shared the sofa, and she sat cross-legged facing him. They discussed Mexican politics, the looming election, and a bevy of clowns vying for Los Pinos (The Mexican White House). Mireya's eyes sparkled when she talked of her plans to use education as a way to earn a more comfortable life. Alfonso was enraptured. He told her of places he'd been, of opportunities that awaited.

"I've no doubt you'll fulfill your dreams," he said. "I'll call the universities tomorrow."

"Thank you, professor—

"Fonso," he reminded her. "Don't thank me yet."

"Okay, Fonso."

They talked about his physics class. It was a pleasure to delve deeper into a subject Alfonso was so passionate about.

"We're close to understanding how to reach the stars. Physics will make it possible. Ever heard of Miguel Alcubierre?"

"No."

"He's known for his Alcubierre Drive, a theoretical means of traveling faster than light."

"Star Trek."

"Precisely. Miguel teaches physics at the UNAM (National Autonomous University of Mexico). I met him in Sweden. He has an amazing mind."

————

Alfonso talked about a starship that could shatter speed barriers, allow exploration, and find habitable zones. He explained how important math was to the mission, and of the many disciplines found within Algebra.

As they talked, hours flew by. Mireya looked at a clock on her kitchen wall and jumped. "Can't believe it, I have to go."

"That's physics—motion stops when I'm with a beautiful woman. I'll drive you back."

"Thanks."

"But remember, you owe me dinner."

"I thought it was another coffee."

"That was before I got to know you better."

"Dinner it is."

He took her back to the university. Alfonso invited her for lunch the following day.

"I'd like that," she replied as he held her hand and gave a light kiss on the cheek.

"Two o'clock, my office? We can leave from there."

"Okay, but it's my treat, remember?"

"That was dinner. This will be lunch."

Good, she thought. *I don't know how I could have paid for it*!

———

The following morning after Zumba, Mireya showered and readied herself for *A date? Sort of, I guess.*

The Lebanese restaurant they chose was busy, yet they chatted in the lobby as they waited for a table. Alfonso had to force himself not to use elevator eyes on Mireya. She wore a thin white blouse that gaped open when she leaned forward, allowing glimpses of her breasts. Her backside swayed sensuously beneath an ankle-length pleated green skirt. When they sat, he stared unabashedly. Her hair was short, dark, and purposely tousled with attitude. Eyebrows arched over large oval eyes, and her lips were pillows tinted red.

Since their first meeting, he'd felt chemicals releasing, scouting ahead for possibilities. It had been a long time since he'd had non-academic feelings for a student. He learned to set them aside, unwilling to put marriage and career in jeopardy. On occasion before the birth of his son, he'd allowed his cock to think for him. *Bad decisions were made.* Yet he had to admit, it had been exciting.

He remembered reading that mathematics was the language of nature, physics its poetry. He wondered how it would feel to test the idea intimately, to hold this young woman, feel her lips pressed to his. He and Diana had been married for fifteen years. Their son was his pride and joy. Yet, this attraction for Mireya went beyond personal responsibilities and family devotion. It skirted his conscience, which whispered, *Quit while you're ahead.*

Mireya pressed every button. She was smart, delightful to talk with, and wore sensuality like a premium perfume. She made him feel young. He harkened back to days before fatherhood, when he would've wooed her to a motel.

Before the birth of his son, he'd cheated several times, once with a colleague, twice with a graduate student, and another with an undergraduate. Each indiscretion occurred at a hotel conference. *What better place to mix business with pleasure?* His confidence had dwindled now. Coming home to a family had sheared his horns. Guilt waged a winning campaign against desire, until now. He wanted Mireya more than he could remember wanting anyone. *Nikola Tesla had a burning desire to unleash the potential of natural forces. So do I.*

"You're staring, professor."

"Sorry, was it obvious?"

———

Conversation flowed, yet never touched on the dreaded subject of availability. Mireya shared her incredible academic journey to beat the odds, not to impress him. It felt nice to tell it to an intellectual she felt comfortable with. Regardless, he was impressed and told of similar struggles—a father who beat him, and a mother who left them both.

"My escape pod was books. Science fiction was my favorite, visiting exoplanets, distant galaxies, and I even fell in love with a Mars maiden thanks to Edgar Rice Burroughs. Clarke, Bradbury, Heinlein, and Asimov took me to a better place. Because of them, I began exploring ways in which it might be possible to actually make it happen. The library ran out of physics books for me to read."

"How old were you?"

"Ten."

"About the same age, I began seeing beauty in math."

He was staring again. "Math is a mirror that reflects you."

———

After lunch, they walked in a nearby park. Alfonso boldly took her hand. Mireya gently tugged free and faced him.

"Alfonso, you're playing with fire."

"Mmm," he nodded. "Fire has its uses."

"Burning a marriage is one."

"The laws of physics are clear."

"Are they?"

"Yes, you see," taking both her hands in his, "Newton stated that whatever is in motion stays in motion, unless acted upon by an outside force."

"What's that have to do with us?"

"You're an outside force acting upon my heart."

"That's serious."

"Mmm," he nodded, lifting her hands to his lips.

"I never want to cause pain."

"You fascinate me."

"Fonso."

"Let's give it a go."

———

As the afternoon wore on, he showed a picture of his son, Alberto. She asked about his wife. At first, he was reticent.

"Diana and I met before I went to Germany to work on my PhD. She was an undergraduate in science. When I finished, we married, and she never finished. She still talks about going back."

"Happy?"

"Loaded question. Lately, I feel trapped. Yet, Alberto reminds me that my life doesn't belong just to me anymore."

"I never knew my father. You're a good man for thinking of your son."

Again, Alfonso took Mireya's hands and lifted them to his lips. "Physics can't explain why we love, and can't tell us why we fall out of love."

"It's getting late. Won't your wife worry?"

"She's not the worrying kind."

"You never know," Mireya repeated.

"You never know," he repeated.

———

On the drive to Mireya's apartment, he stopped at the side of a dirt road under renovation.

"What's wrong?" she asked.

"Nothing," he answered. Then he kissed her.

She met his lips, letting them touch a moment before extending her tongue to greet his. She placed a hand on his chest.

"This is a treacherous road," she warned.

He kissed her again.

"I'm not a homewrecker."

He kissed her again.

"It was a nice afternoon. Let's leave it at that."

"Laws of physics won't allow it."

"Hmm."

They kissed, then he drove her the rest of the way to her apartment.

Mireya didn't dare invite him in. The laws of physics wouldn't allow it. It had begun to rain, and even the blandness of her neighborhood felt renewed.

———

It was three days before she attended his morning class. She appreciated that he wasn't obsessive. In spite of herself, the desire grew. During class, he met her eyes and fumbled his presentation. Afterward, he gestured for her to stay as students filed out.

"I wanted to call," he said.

"Why didn't you?"

"I upset you last time."

"Lunch, my treat?" she tried.

"Can't today."

"Mmm."

"I called the universities. They said, we will be in touch. They weren't impressed with me, but perhaps it'll speed things along."

"Thanks for trying."

He nodded.

"I'll stop by your office tomorrow if you're not busy."

"Free as a bird around one-thirty."

"See you then."

———

The following afternoon, after teaching a morning class, Mireya visited the ladies' room to check her visage in the mirror. Her reflection seemed to ask, *What are you thinking*? She didn't use makeup or eye paint. Her only indulgence was a scarlet red lipstick that set her mouth on fire in contrast to her dazzling smile. *You know what I'm thinking.*

She wore a white sleeveless blouse and a short orange skirt that fell mid-thigh. She wasn't a classical Mexican beauty, yet men were attracted by something she had that many didn't. She didn't fully understand. Often, she'd been told she exuded an aura. *Pheromones*, she thought. Now, the glove was on the other hand. She *wanted* Alfonso, and he was playing hard to get.

Mireya entered a stall, slid off her panties, and stuffed them into her backpack. She was already moist. Confidently, she left the bathroom and walked to the physics building, climbing stairs to the third floor. His office door was open. Alfonso was wearing a pair of half-moon glasses, his head bent over a keyboard. She checked that the hallway was clear. He looked up and smiled.

"Hola Mireya."

She shut the door and locked it. He raised questioning eyebrows as she walked past him to draw the shades. Alfonso stood, and she placed herself between him and the desk. He drew her into his arms, and they kissed.

"I was just thinking of you," he whispered into her ear. "I think of you all the time."

Her breathing was labored. "Me too."

Mireya lifted her skirt above her waist and sat on the desk. Alfonso swallowed and fumbled with his pants.

"Jesus," He placed his hands beneath her knees and lifted. "Ay, Mireya…"

"Shhh." She put a finger to her mouth.

Like the tale of the Three Bears, his cock was just right. She gasped as he pushed inside, her satiny calves rubbing up and down his sides.

"Ahhh-ah-ah-ahhh." Mireya's staccato breath mixed with a deep textured moan as he stroked down and in. Their tongues danced as he pulled back and returned.

"Oyyy si," she groaned. After recent rains, it was humid in the room, and her glasses fogged. She set them on the desk. It was nearly impossible to keep their pleasure from spilling into the halls of academia.

Alfonso flexed his ass to delay ejaculation. Mireya drew a sharp breath and crested.

"Ohhh, I'm cumming, oyyy huh!" she whispered hoarsely, pulling him deep into the ripples of her orgasm.

Alfonso clenched his teeth, "O-o-o-o Jesus," he whispered harshly, then growled, "Me vengo!"

Mireya buried her face into his shirt. "Ayyy, mmm-ayyy!" It had begun to rain hard, and the patter helped filter out the sounds of simultaneous climax.

"Rawwwr! Dios mío, ahhhrrrr!"

"Huh uh-huh-uh-huh!" She panted as he saturated her with semen.

Alfonso felt her pussy grip, ease up, grip again. His powerful surge left him dizzy. He leaned forward to kiss her.

There was a knock at the door. Alfonso froze, his cock still twitching. Slowly, he slipped out, stepped back, and helped Mireya to her feet. Cobwebs of cum dripped like honey to the tile floor. The door handle jiggled.

He pulled up his pants as she straightened her skirt. Another knock followed. Alfonso put a finger to his lips. After one more try of the door, it stopped. Then there were voices outside.

"Hi Diana."

"Hola Marga. Seen Fonso?"

"No."

"Okay, thanks."

"I can open it for you if you want to wait there."

Please, god, no! Alfonso clenched his jaws.

"That's okay. Thanks."

They heard footsteps walking away, and waited in silence for a long minute.

"Napkin?" Mireya whispered.

He opened the top desk drawer and handed her the soft cloth he used for cleaning the computer screen.

"Really?" she giggled.

"Absolutely," he replied.

She fished in her backpack for the underwear and placed

the soft blue cloth over her seeping cunt.

The phone on his desk bleeped, and they both jumped. Without a word, Mireya kissed him and backed to the door. She unlocked it, checked the hallway, blew a kiss, and left.

He gazed out the door, then smiled at the globs of cum on the floor. *Christ, that was…* The phone bleeped again. He continued staring, replaying the entire scenario. His cock was hard again. The phone bleeped, and he answered. It was Diana.

"I came by."

"Bathroom break," Alfonso said.

"Lunch?

"Sure." He made a mental note to keep a box of tissues on his desk at all times.

CHAPTER 14
PETER (1995)

The fear of getting caught was exciting. He called her that afternoon.

"I'm sitting at my desk wishing you were on it," he said.

"You liked it?" she teased.

"The sexiest, scariest experience I've ever had."

"I didn't think it out too clearly. Sorry."

"Don't be. When can I see you again?"

"I have a lot of grading and homework for your class—"

"Let the homework slide. Can I come over?"

She wanted him to, yet reminded herself, *He's married. You almost got caught by his wife.*

"Now's not a good time, Fonso. Let's talk later."

He groaned, "Mmm." His hardness lifted the front of his pants.

"See you in class tomorrow."

"Mmm."

"Ay, poor Fonso. You'll live."

"Mmm."

———

The next day, things got heated again. After class, he drove them to her apartment, and they spent hours intimately connected. Alfonso was an accomplished lover. The following morning, she started her period and was reminded how lucky she was that none of his seeds found purchase. *Get on the pill, idiot*, she reprimanded.

For nearly a week, they didn't see each other. He phoned every day, and conversations revolved around saying what he wanted to do with her. She reached between her legs as he described details, climaxing over the phone.

———

She decided to have the IUD reinstalled. The process took less than five minutes. *Is it embedded in my DNA to follow in my mother's footsteps? Chela's?* It was a frightening thought. Pregnancy would stop everything she'd worked for—an excuse to end her dreams.

In a country where juicy gossip is worth its weight in gold, it was only a matter of time before the physics department secretary put one and one together. Her name was Margarita, and she was Diana's friend. She invited her for lunch one afternoon to share her suspicions.

"Diane, I think Fonso's having an affair with a student."

Diane clamped her trembling lips together. "Go on."

"She visits when it's not office hours. Twice, I knocked after she went in. He didn't answer, and the door was locked. I've seen them leaving campus in his car."

"Who is she?"

"I'll find out." Margarita reached across the table to put a hand over Diane's. "I'm sorry."

"Thanks. You're a good friend." She dabbed tears with a napkin.

———

Margarita found out her name by checking the class roster and narrowing down possibilities. There were only four women enrolled in the physics class.

"Mireya Lopez. That's all I know for now. If you like, I can find her information."

"No need. I know everything I need to know."

"What will you do?"

"Fonso has cheated before. Never caught him red-handed, but there were signs."

"Diana, I'm so sorry. Will you confront her?"

"I'm not sure what I'll do."

———

Diana cornered Alfonso in his office one morning. She considered waiting, having Margo phone her when Mireya Lopez was with her husband in his office, yet she lacked patience. *I'll deal with that bitch later. Catching him off guard is the best way. He's a terrible liar.*

Boldly, she walked through the door, closed it, and fired both barrels.

"Who's Mireya Lopez?"

Alfonso turned white. "Who?" He stalled.

"Don't play me for a fool, cabrón!"

"Diane, keep your voice down."

"I'm waiting." It was written all over his face.

"Why do you think —?"

Diane listed all the evidence. He stumbled with his defense, downplaying concerns, claiming innocence.

"She's a student, for god's sake. She comes to my office after hours, and yes, I gave her a lift because it's on the way home. Who told you this stuff?"

"Never mind, I'll ask her myself," she said.

"You've got this all wrong. Please, don't make a scene."

"You must think I'm stupid." She started to leave.

"Diane, please, I—"

She turned and left.

———

Alfonso canceled his next class and drove to Mireya's apartment. Luckily, she was there. She met him with a beaming smile, having just received word she'd be starting a Master's program in Morelia in four months. The semester at BUAP was nearly finished, and that left plenty of time to prepare. When she saw his face, she knew.

"Diane knows. I'm sure it was Margarita. They're friends."

"That's it then. I blame myself. Sorry."

"Don't put it all on you."

"I'll drop your class."

"Take the final independently."

Mireya slowly nodded. *Goddamn it.*

He tried to take her into his arms. Words crowded his mind, demanding release. They formed a crooked line—*Mireya, I love you. I know you love me too. This can't be the end! I'll file for divorce.*

Mireya kept him at bay. She was a jumble of emotions—dread, self-hatred, sadness, and finally, resolve.

"Go home, fix things with your wife. Think of your son. I'm sorry for the mess."

"Mireya, you're—"

"You need to leave, Alfonso. Please. Be a good husband and father."

Mireya effectively eviscerated the words on the tip of his tongue. Arguments died on the vine. Alfonso nodded and left, his shoulders drooping, his head hanging.

————

She walked on pins and needles the final week, expecting Alfonso's wife to be waiting in ambush.

She moved back to the ranch to save money until the Masters began. Severance was nearly complete. Now she could effectively remove him from the current memory bank and store him with hazy long-term ones.

Giselle noticed Alfonso's car parked in front of the ranch house on several occasions. She asked her daughter about it, and Mireya shared the situation.

"Ay yi-yi mi hija, a married man? Haven't you learned anything from my mistakes?"

Mireya pursed her lips. "Mmm." She nodded, and a tear trailed down to her chin.

Giselle softened. "It's good to have you here. This is your

home, and he'll soon stop badgering you."

Since her daughter's graduation, Giselle felt pride and respect for Mireya. The next time Alfonso showed up, she confronted him in his car. He rolled down the window.

"Escúchame pendejo! Go home to your wife. My daughter says she's finished with you! If I see you here again, I'll call the police!"

Heartbroken and humiliated, he drove away without a word and never returned.

———

The next week, Mireya finished her adjunct classes with the BUAP. Alfonso was trying to patch up his relationship with Diana. It would take time, months of being a perfect spouse. Even then, she'd never fully trust him.

After teaching a final class, Mireya had only to record her grades and turn them in. As an adjoin, she didn't have an office, so she walked to the library, a quiet place to enter grades. There were computers there to use. Alfonso caught up in a hallway along the way.

"Mireya."

She stopped and stared blankly at the floor tile. "What?"

"My wife…she's looking for you."

Mireya was mortified. "Where is she?"

"I don't know. She has your information and your schedule. She—"

Mireya hurried toward a flight of stairs leading out. She'd catch a bus home and hibernate—study math, exercise, paint. Alfonso followed her down.

"Mireya, hold up!"

She stopped abruptly and faced him on the stairs.

"Stay away from me, Fonso. We're through. I'm sorry about your wife, and I can't blame her." She resumed her ascent and left him standing.

"Mireya!" he called after her. "I love you!"

She opened a final door leading into the sunshine. Magnified by tears, the sun hurt her eyes.

———

On the bus journey home, she stared out the window, not even noticing that the volcano, Popocatepetl, was smoking. Her mother was waiting when she arrived.

"Mireya, the crazy wife of that professor was here. She said awful things…" Her mother's voice broke.

"Sorry you had to hear that, Madre. She's right to be angry. I was stupid."

Giselle nodded in agreement, yet her tone wasn't harsh. Her own relationships had included married men. All three of her children were from men with wives and children. In a rare show of affection, she put her arms around Mireya, who held on for dear life.

———

Alfonso's wife didn't return, yet the possibility kept Mireya in a constant state of panic. She managed to save a little money. There was a cousin, Arturo, living in Pomona, California, whom she hadn't seen since she was a child. She called to ask if she could visit.

He laughed. "Do you have to ask, prima? Our house is your house."

She procured a student visa to study English there until it was time to relocate to Morelia. Her scholarship amount increased so that she would be able to pay for books, tuition, and incidentals. She'd find work to manage rent, scraping by as she always had. She thought of Arturo and the journey he'd taken when they were teenagers.

He sneaked across the border when he was seventeen. At first, he lived in Visalia and worked in the fields. Eventually, he found construction work in Pomona and never looked back. She had fond memories of him, always smiling and laughing, taking life straight on. When he told her he was travelling a la brava to el Norte, she was disappointed.

"Why leave? You're smart, you can—"

"Listen, prima, I ain't like you. Can't stick my head in books. Gotta use these." He held out his hands. "Life don't wait, you gotta go out and grab it."

He was happy that cousin Mireya was coming to stay with his family. He insisted on sending money for bus fare from Puebla to the Northern border in Tijuana, and said he'd pick her up when she arrived. Before she left, Mireya had her IUD removed yet again.

————

"You're what?" Carmen was incredulous.

"Only for three months. I'll come back talking like a gringo."

Mireya told Carmen the whole story of her adventure with Alfonso in the comfort and safety of the ranch.

"Eres un ave rara." (You are a rare bird). "You'll go there, find a rich gabacho, get married, and eat burgers."

"What if he's black?"

"Ah, your fantasy is only twelve inches away."

"Twelve inches! Caramba!."

"You know what they say, Una vez que te vuelves negra nunca vuelves." (Once you go black, you never go back.)

"How about a friend with benefits?"

"That works?"

Mireya locked her door and thoroughly enjoyed her friendship with Carmen..

————

Mireya's English was limited. She'd taken a few classes in Mexico, yet without native speakers to practice with, it was difficult. She knew English would come in handy when she began graduate studies. Most of the textbooks she'd need for higher mathematics were in English. She thought of Alonso and the travel opportunities he had. *I'll learn.*

The bus took twenty-four hours to reach Tijuana. The trip was uneventful. A young man sat next to her for part of the journey and tried his luck. After giving it his best shot, he got off at the halfway mark in Culiacán.

When she arrived, she called Arturo from a pay phone, and five hours later, he picked her up at a Denny's in San Ysidro on the North American side.

"Prima!" Arturo called out when he saw Mireya. He gave her a hug. "What's it been, ten years?"

"Long time. How are you?"

"Surviving in Gringolandia. Nice to see you again."

Arturo was short, stocky, and easily the hairiest man Mireya had ever known. He took pride in his hairiness in the way bodybuilders show off their muscles. His eyebrows were especially impressive, thick, purposely twisted at the ends to form horns. A dark goatee finished off the look.

"Thanks for having me."

"You'll meet my wife, Maria, and my little girls. They're excited to meet their Mexican aunt. Maria made tortas for the road." He handed her a sack. "Hungry?"

"Starved. I was tempted to try Denny's."

"Shit food."

As they walked to his pickup truck, she began tearing into her sandwich.

"I hear you're gonna be a doctor, that's what your mother said. One of my little girls has the flu. Maybe you can take a look." He opened the passenger door for her.

"Not that kind of doctor," Mireya laughed. "I'm starting a Master's in mathematics, and then I'll think about a doctorate."

He entered the driver's side. "Ah, okay. I always liked

math."

"What are you doing now?"

"I work for a business that installs doors."

"Do you like it?"

He shrugged. "Pays the bills."

"Remember what you said before you left México?"

"No."

"You said that life doesn't wait for you, you have to grab it."

"Damn, I'm wiser than I thought."

"Those words inspired me."

"There wasn't nothin' for me over there. At least the gringos pay a living wage. I got a green card, Maria too. The girls have never set foot in Mex. They're gringas."

"Do they speak Spanish?"

"That's all we speak in the house."

"You're smart to do that."

"Someday we'll visit so they can see my old stomping grounds."

As they merged into the traffic, Mireya saw how organized everything was. Roads were smooth, and there were no topes (speed bumps). She began to relax for the first time in months.

"There's more tortas." He pointed to another sack sitting on the center storage console. "Help yourself."

She did, and it tasted like home.

———

Arturo and his family lived in a moderately sized house in a decent Pomona neighborhood. He'd landscaped the front and back yards, and his wife Maria kept them immaculate. Mireya was greeted with a warm welcome and shown to her room. Her arrival proved to be the calm before a storm.

Mireya's time with Arturo's family was filled with chaos. Arturo and Maria were perpetually at war. Arturo was an alcoholic and often in between jobs. When she and Maria were alone in the house, Maria complained about her husband. Evidently, he kept company with other women.

Maria liked Mireya and tried to drag her into mitigating the battles. Mireya spent time when she wasn't home attending English classes at a junior college close by. The nieces were eight and ten. Elena and Beatrice hung their heads when the fighting started, and Mireya led them into the tiny backyard of the house out of earshot.

––––

Arturo had a second-generation Chicano friend from the central San Joaquin Valley who occasionally visited. They'd worked together in the fields when Arturo first arrived. His name was Pedro, which was Americanized into Peter. He owned a car repair shop in Visalia, a moderate-sized town three hours north.

Towing a trailer behind a pickup truck, Peter came to Pomona to buy damaged cars to refurbish and sell. He was a forty-five-year-old bachelor, never married, and was smitten with Mireya. Whenever he visited, he stayed in the garage, which was Arturo's man-cave/workshop. He invited her to dinners and movies, and his visits became more frequent as his feelings for her swelled.

In the meantime, fighting between Arturo and his wife grew more frequent and violent. Mireya began weighing her options. She could return to México, or find a job here to fill in the free hours between English classes, and save American dollars.

––––

She took a job working at a small Mexican restaurant a few blocks from the house, and was still able to continue English classes. She asked Angel, the owner, to help her practice, and soon she was able to take orders and converse moderately well with English-speaking customers.

The owner, an older man named Angel, paid her in cash

and required ten hours a day. She started at seven in the morning and ended at about five. She took a bus to the college and returned by nine. It worked out fine for a month, until Angel found her alone in the kitchen one early morning and pressed up against her as she diced onions.

"Oy Mireya, seeing you looking so pretty makes me crazy. I like you."

She moved aside. "Excuse me," she said as politely as possible. "I have work to do, Angel."

"Let's take the day off." He took her by the hands. "I *really* like you."

"You've been good to me, and I appreciate it, but I'm not—"

He pulled her into his arms. "I can teach more than English." He tried to kiss her.

She pushed him away. "No!"

A terrible look formed on his face, as if someone else resided behind his eyes.

"You need to show respect and gratitude." He walked toward her.

A delivery van pulled up, and Mireya was able to dodge him to open the door for the vendor. As he came in, she walked past him and kept walking.

"Hey! Where you goin'?" Angel yelled.

She ignored him and didn't stop until she arrived home.

———

She'd managed to save her salary and tips for the month she worked in the restaurant. That was little comfort now. The arguing continued. The girls withdrew into themselves and didn't even want to be with their Mexican aunt anymore.

She called her mother every other Sunday. Giselle wanted to hear what it was like in 'gabacholandia'. Mireya could only answer based on what she knew.

"It's big. People have to take a test to get a driver's license. The food's terrible, and the air is dirty."

"Have you been to Disneyland?"

"No."

"Do you have a boyfriend?"

"Ay no." Mireya disappointed her by confessing that life in the US was boring.

"I like my English classes, though."

She didn't mention Peter. On his last visit, he asked her to return to Visalia with him. *Like it or not, it's an option.* He assured her that she could study English at the Visalia Adult School.

The night before Peter's next visit, Mireya lay in bed. Maria and Arturo were at it tooth and nail. She heard the sound of breaking glass and what sounded like a slap. The front door opened and closed with a bang. She knew she should comfort Maria, yet she didn't have the energy for it.

Out of desperation, Mireya accepted Peter's invitation. Peter wasn't young, but he was in good shape and not bad looking. He was about five inches taller, sported dark hair, gray at the temples, and a thick, well-trimmed mustachio. Tattoos ran the length of both forearms — a dragon holding a dagger, the eye of a woman with teardrops, various numbers, and the letters LA. His kindness softened her reserve. She thought of the Mexican repayment plan. *Play my cards right, and perhaps it can be avoided.*

———

Peter's eyes twinkled when he smiled. He explained that he'd quit high school in his sophomore year to work in the fields, where he met Arturo. Mireya communicated with Peter on a surface level. He expressed no opinions regarding politics or social issues. He was a simple, warm-hearted man who craved company.

With her cousin's blessing, Mireya and Peter left Pomona late one morning.

"Peter's a nice guy. You might have a future. He'll take

good care of you, help you get a green card."

"Thanks, Primo, but I've other plans."

"Well, think about it anyway."

"Okay."

Arturo gave Peter a thumbs-up as they drove away.

Along the way, Peter picked up a battered '64 Mustang, and they towed it to Visalia.

———

Peter lived with his mother in a rundown section of town. "The other side of the tracks," as he put it. The house was old, yet well-kept.

They arrived in the late afternoon. Peter's mother, Eloisa, welcomed Mireya with open arms and lots of food. She talked about life in Mexico, how her father and mother came ala brava in the days when the border was easier to cross.

"I married when I was sixteen, and not long after, I had Peter's brother Jesus. It was six years before Peter came along. Jesus had bad friends and died."

"Sorry to hear that," Mireya sympathized.

"Peter has been a great comfort."

"May I ask, what happened to your husband?"

"He died. No one knows why. I woke up one morning, and he was dead."

"Doctors couldn't give you a cause?"

"Perhaps if I'd had money to pay for one."

Ay yi-yi, she thought. *This is a very sad house.*

There was an annoying Chihuahua called Pepper. Its purpose seemed to be getting underfoot, jumping into laps, and licking its ass. She ignored its demands to be petted.

———

Late that night, while Peter spoke to a neighbor outside, Eloisa towed Mireya's suitcase into Peter's room and showed her where everything was. Mireya did the math. *This house has two bedrooms.*

She stood in the room, feeling helpless. The floors were made of wood, squeaking as she paced.

Peter came into the house, and she heard his mother say, "Mireya is settled. Buenas noches hijo."

"Buenas noches mamá."

The only bathroom was outside of Peter's bedroom. She listened to Peter brushing his teeth and using the toilet. She moved away from the door when he came, pretending to search her suitcase for something. He closed the door.

"My mother loves you already."

"She's very sweet."

He took Mireya into his arms. They'd kissed before — goodnight kisses that never lasted. These were different. His tongue sent a questioning probe into her mouth, and she felt obliged to answer. When his hands wandered, the time had come. She pulled away and looked at him.

Ground-rules. "Protection?"

Without answering, Peter reached into a nightstand for an unopened box of Trojans and took out three foil packs attached to each other. He separated one from the rest.

Without another word, she methodically removed her clothing down to her underwear and set them on a chair. Peter littered the floor with his, and faced her in his boxers.

She saw that he had more tattoos across his chest and shoulders — a pitbull, praying hands, a dagger, and a hummingbird. There were several scars too, a long white one running from shoulder to chest, and a darker circular one the size of a soda cap on his lower belly. *This man has stories to tell.*

"Dios mío, eres hermosa." His cock aggressively lifted the front of his underwear.

She offered the tip of her tongue as he found the catch to her bra. Her tits sprang forward against his chest. He kissed her shoulder, her neck, and bent to a nipple.

Mireya couldn't detach from the pleasant sensations invading her body. A moan escaped as Peter slipped the panties over her ass, and removed the boxers. His erection pulsated fiercely against her belly. She felt the warmth of the precum.

"Okay," she said breathlessly. She sat on the bed.

Peter tore the foil and hurriedly rolled a condom over his throbbing cock. Mireya set her glasses on the nightstand and laid on the queen-sized bed. Peter joined. He explored her body with his hands, cupping a breast, flicking his tongue over a nipple. Mireya felt a jolt of pleasure. She centered herself on the bed and lifted her knees.

Peter had never seen such a lovely sight. He crawled between them.

Mireya looked down at Peter's dark brown, thick, uncircumcised cock. She opened wider.

"Eres una Diosa," Peter whispered, balancing on his elbows, probing. Her pliable lips surround his dickhead. Aided by the condom's lubricant, he easily glided down and in. "Ay, Dios mío."

"Mmmahhh." She closed her eyes and arched to meet his initial lunge.

With each rhythmic thrust, guilt was absorbed by pleasure. She rested her heels on his lower back. Peter took turns on her nipples as he stroked, then kissed her. She groaned in his mouth and felt the stirrings of an orgasm.

Her breathing quickened, "Huh-huh-huh, mmm-nnn, huh, mmm-ayyy," followed by the first wave of contractions reaching shore. Mireya turned her face into the pillow to muffle her cries. "Ay si, oyyy!" Her body twisted as her pussy contracted. She knew Peter's mother could hear them. *Perhaps she's listening at the door, hoping for a grandson.*

Peter sat up to watch her soft, dark pubic hair clinging wetly to the condom. Her pussy shivered around him. The connection was complete. He wanted the condom to tear, for his seed to find an egg. *Then she'll be mine.*

"Oh baby, I'm gonna cum....ahhhh!" His prostate triggered a series of long, flowing releases into the reservoir tip. "Ah-ah-ahhh Jesus! Nnn-nnn-nnn, ahhh!"

He stayed inside, drinking kisses as aftershocks sent tremors through her body. The condom nearly slipped off after he softened. When he pulled free, she saw the tip, bulging with semen. He sneaked back inside as he kissed her.

"Ayyy," he moaned. Mireya squeezed him out again. Peter gave a frustrated sigh. *Patience. Conquer the body,* and *the heart will follow. We'll share a life, have children,* and *grow old together.*

Mireya's guilty pleasure was quickly replaced with anxiety. *What the hell have I gotten into? Twenty-one hundred miles from home, living with a man I barely know. More like my mother every day.*

———

Despite misgivings, Mireya enrolled in ESL classes at the adult school. Ms. Ramirez was a competent instructor, and Mireya was a fast learner. She planned her escape. *Poor Pete,* she thought. *Not his fault. He'll want me to stay.*

Peter thought, *She'll change her mind, learn to love me the same way she's learning English. I'll teach her.*

To his credit, he consistently gave his best, and though Mireya certainly didn't love him, she had no wish to hurt him. *There will be pain,* she knew. *In matters of the heart, there always is.* She considered the tattoos. *A violent past.* She hadn't asked, and he hadn't offered. Yet she instinctively knew that she should never make him angry.

She thought about love. *Just a word, or is there a definitive feeling when it happens?* She'd been with enough men to question whether or not it was real, or man-made myth, like characters from the Bible. *Sex has always been the defining moment in my relationships.*

———

On weekends, Pete took her on short trips to the Sierra Nevada Mountains and surrounding lakes. December 7th arrived, and she turned thirty. He'd seen her Visa card and her birth date.

"Pearl Harbor Day," he informed her.

"What's that?"

After he explained, she nodded, vaguely recalling the event from a world history class. Pete took her to an Indian casino in Lemoore, just west of the Sierra Nevadas. He gifted her with two twenty-dollar bills to gamble with. Mireya wandered around the noisy casino, studying slots before deciding which to play. Pete was busy with Blackjack.

Placing a dollar coin into a slot, she pulled the handle. The machine made a whirring sound, accompanied by a silly song, and bing-bing-bing-bing. Nothing. She moved to another one-armed bandit with the same result. She knew from statistics classes that the odds were stacked against her.

When she was down to twenty-five dollars, she stopped at the Wheel of Fortune. She inserted a dollar and pulled the handle. This time, she was rewarded with happy bells. Others glared with jealousy. The machine spit out a ticket, redeemable for five hundred dollars—enough to get home by air. Mireya quickly cashed in the ticket and stuffed the money into her pocket. Pete was absorbed at a blackjack table.

"Done already?" he asked when he'd lost all he could afford to.

She smiled and nodded. "I'm not very lucky." She handed him the unused dollars.

"It's your birthday, keep it."

They stopped at a Burger King on the way home. American fast food made her bloated, and she was gaining weight. Her pants were tighter. *I'll lose it in México.*

That night in the dimness of the bedroom, Mireya lay on her side away from Peter, planning her departure. She heard Peter turn, and closed her eyes pretending to be asleep. Undeterred, he kissed her neck and nibbled her ear. Then she heard him slipping out of his boxers.

"Mmm, I have another present to give you." His cock throbbed at the crack of her ass. He rubbed fingers over her soft tummy, gravitating to her tits. He tolled a nipple between his thumb and forefinger. He knifed and hand beneath her panties.

She lifted as he pulled them down. He rolled on top and quickly found her.

One more time, she thought. "Are you wearing—?"

Peter slipped inside without answering. "Oyyy baby, you feel good."

"Don't cum inside," she warned.

"Ayyy." He pulled back and plunged forward. "Mmm, ohhh."

Mireya's mind focused on México as Peter worked. She'd stay on the ranch until she began school. *Work, rent a room in Morelia, and go to classes. Maybe I can sell another painting—the children playing soccer barefoot in the dirt.* She'd keep one of her grandmother's wrinkled, callused hands, holding kernels of blue corn.

The feeling of his cock relentlessly working back and forth began a domino effect. The future dimmed, overwhelmed by the present. Her clit ached.

"Mmm, ay si, mmm."

He pumped faster now. Just as she was about to cum, he grunted and pushed deep. Mireya felt his cock jumping, a rush of warmth. He trapped her hips with his hands until the final spasm.

"Nnnawww sweet Jesus, your pussy's magic."

"You didn't pull out."

"Perdóname. You felt...mmm." He pushed in as he softened.

Mireya contracted to expel him, followed by a river of unwanted sperm dripping onto the bottom sheet.

Without a word, she went into the bathroom. Squatting over the toilet, she used two fingers to ream out as much as possible. Then she peed and wiped thoroughly before returning to bed.

"Mad?" Peter asked.

"No."

"I mean, if something did happen—"

"Let's hope not."

"Sorry," he said.

"Goodnight, Pete." She turned away from him.

"Love you. I think you know that."

"Should've pulled out."

"Mmm." He left it at that. *Mexican women stew before they forgive*. He was working on restoring a '64 Ford Mustang in his shop. *My wedding gift to her*.

CHAPTER 15
WYLER

The following day, Mireya skipped English class to visit a local travel agency. She purchased a one-way red-eye to México City out of San Jose, leaving in five days. Then she bought a bus shuttle ticket to the airport.

The following day, Mrs. Ramirez introduced a guest speaker—a tall, handsome gabacho who played piano and sang songs in English. He was lean, athletic, with curly brown hair that touched his collar. Students shared copies of the lyrics, and he showed how music could help them learn English. When the lesson was over, Mrs. Ramirez introduced him to Mireya.

"Wyler, this is Mireya. She's visiting from México."

The gabacho took her hand. Mireya greeted him in a thick accent, yet her English had improved considerably.

"Pleased to meet you," she smiled.

What a smile, he thought. "Pleasure's all mine."

Mireya blushed as other students looked up from their assignments to watch the exchange.

"Wyler teaches an afternoon program in conversational English," said Ms. Ramirez. "He's the director of an after-school program for teenagers."

"You're more than welcome to come," added Wyler. "It's free."

Hmm, thought Mireya, *a conversation class*.

"Wyler has a Master's in Creative Writing," Mrs. Ramirez added. "He published a book."

"Really?" She grew more interested. "What's your book about?"

"It's a short story collection. Each one is different."

"I would like to read it." She knew it would take her a long time to do so. "Is it available in Spanish?"

"Unfortunately, not. Hard to find a good translator unless you're with a big publisher."

"Oh," She didn't understand, but he was nice to look at.

"Will you come?" The gabacho asked. "I'm there by ten o'clock, and students don't arrive until after three."

"Maybe tomorrow," she replied in English. "I'll try."

Wyler smiled, wrote directions, and included personal contact information.

———

The following day, Mireya couldn't get away. Peter sensed her uneasiness. First, he took her to his shop to show her the Mustang he was refurbishing. He employed two other men, a young white man named Dixon, and a Chicano called Rafa. As he showed her around the shop, they gave each other knowing looks. When their boss disappeared into a small office with her, they whispered.

"Wow-wee," Dixon commented. "Bet the boss's hittin' that shit every chance."

"Fuck yeah," Rafa murmured. "Mexican girls take you for a ride, bro."

"Ain't never been with one."

"Don't know what you're missin'."

The shade to the office window was drawn. They strained their ears, but didn't hear anything.

"Bet he's hittin' it," Dixon predicted.

"Mmm," Rafa shook his head. "Fool not to."

———

"Not here, Peter." She reached around to pull his hands away from her ass.

"C'mon, baby, those guys won't hear anything here."

"Not here," she repeated in a sterner voice.

"Okay."

————

After their shop visit, Peter took her out to lunch and mall shopping. That evening, his mother prepared a special dinner and served a bottle of sparkling wine. There were candles and flowers centered on the table.

When they returned to the house, all was ready. Eloisa excused herself and said she had errands to run. She slipped out of the house with a funny smile on her face. *Finally, he'll settle down and give me grandchildren.*

Peter sat across from Mireya. He poured champagne and gazed at her.

"I have something for you. I've been thinking a lot lately."

Peter handed her a small box. Mireya opened it. Laying on a wad of cotton was a gold wedding band.

"I love you, Mireya. Will you be my wife?"

Blood drained from her face. She looked at this man with so much hope in his eyes. A good man. Nearly everyone she'd been with eventually wanted to make an honest woman out of her. Most were already married.

A lump formed in her throat. "Let me think about it, Pete," she replied.

He reached over, took out the ring, and placed it on her finger. Then he kissed it.

"Wear it anyway," he said, "so everyone knows you're off the market."

I sound like a product, she thought. "Give me time, Pete."

They finished eating, and each bite stuck in her throat. The sparkling wife made her hiccup. She got up from the table to do the dishes.

"Mamá will handle that." He took her into his arms. "She won't be back for hours." He kissed her, and she tried her best to return it. Then he led her to the bed and poured into her without protection.

———

When she didn't show up, Wyler visited the adult school seeking her out. She wasn't there either. Mrs. Ramirez sensed his personal interest in Mireya and remarked about how unusual it was for her to miss class. Wyler left behind a copy of his short story collection for her, along with a business card trapped inside. On the inside cover, he wrote: *For Mireya, beautiful and mysterious*.

The following day, Mireya returned to school. Mrs. Ramirez presented her with the book, and other female students teased her good-naturedly.

"If you don't want him, give him to me," said Yolanda.

"Ay no, he's mine," argued Soledad.

"You saw how he was looking at me," countered Zamantha. "He wants coochie-coochie, I'll give him coochie-coochie."

Mireya laughed. "Fight it out amongst yourselves. I'm not interested."

"Ooee-ooee-ooee, I saw your face when he was here." Yolanda wagged a finger side-to-side. "You can't fool us."

"Ay yi-yi." There was no point in continuing. "I gotta go."

"Where you going, eh?" Zamantha chided. "Tienes globos? (Do you have condoms?)

"Hasta mañana chicas."

"Qué tenga un buen viaje!"

Mireya laughed. "You guys are terrible!"

———

She walked to Wyler's business. It was in a metal industrial-looking building, which previously served as a school district warehouse. The city donated the building for Wyler's program. Teens who visited after school came from broken homes, and many were involved with gangs. The sign on the outside read, Teen City. A red Isuzu Trooper was parked there. She knocked on the steel door entrance.

Wyler was in his office working on a grant proposal to add needed dollars to the project.

"Hi Mireya!" Wyler's eyes flew open, and he beamed. She had his book in her hand.

"Sorry, I didn't make it yesterday, I wasn't feeling well," she said.

"Better now?"

"Yes," she smiled, "much better."

Feel giddy, like my first crush, thought Wyler as he pulled a chair next to his desk. His Spanish was spotty, yet he managed to combine what he knew with English into something intelligible.

"What brought you to Visalia?" he asked.

"I'm a mathematician, and most of the books are in English."

"Oh, I see. How much longer will you be in Visalia?"

"A few more days."

Wyler's heart sank. "Will you return?"

She shook her head. "Probably not."

"Students won't be drifting in for hours. Let's talk. Tell me about yourself."

"Long story."

"We have time."

The usual information was shared—she was thirty, he was forty, yes, the weather was nice lately. As the conversation dug deeper, she shared her childhood, the sadness, and her determination. She mentioned nothing about personal relationships other than to mention her best friend, Carmen. He listened attentively about her desire to use education as a conduit for success.

Wyler shared that he'd grown up on a small farm. The closest grammar school was located in a small labor-camp town called Woodland.

"Funny name for a town with hardly any trees," he

laughed. "It's where I learned about Mexican culture and grew to love it."

"Did you have Mexican girlfriends?" Mireya asked, raising an eyebrow.

He ticked off his fingers. "Luz, Adelena, Monica, Isabelle. My parents weren't too happy about it, which is why I'm not very close to them."

They shared much in common, such as a desire to travel the world. When she learned his last name was Costner, she lifted her eyebrows.

"Like the movie star?"

"Yeah, except I'm much better looking, don't you think?"

Mireya giggled. "Yes, of course." Then she asked the million-dollar question. "Married?"

"Divorced." *Almost*, he thought. *Paperwork in process.*

"Children?"

"A boy and a girl."

"Mmm."

He saw that it bothered her. "You?" He looked at her band.

She lifted the ring and took it off. "The man I'm staying with is jealous and wants me to wear it. We're not married." She slipped it back on.

"Does it have an alarm? Woo, woo, beep, beep, step away from my woman!"

Mireya laughed, "No, but it burns my finger."

"Is it burning now?"

"Yes, very painful."

"Mmm." *In a few days, she'll be history. Don't know what it is, but I feel, hell, I don't know what it is I'm feeling.* "Maybe this'll make it feel better."

He leaned forward in his chair, took her ring hand, and kissed it. Then he touched his lips to hers. Surprise muted Mireya's response. She fanned herself.

"Too soon?" Wyler pursed his lips.

"No. I mean, yes, it's just that I'm returning to México."

"Yeah, I'm sorry."

Students began arriving, and she needed to go or Pete would get suspicious.

"Come back tomorrow. I'll be here by 8:00."

"I'll try."

Something about her. Wyler's imagination took him beyond conversational English.

"Look forward to seeing you again, Mireya." He took her hand and kissed her cheek. He stared after her as she walked away.

She stopped at the door. "Thanks for the book. When I'm better at English, I'll read it."

"Good." *One unresolved kiss. Tomorrow I'll need her to answer.*

————

That night, Mireya felt cheerier. *Nearly in control of life again.* She'd seen no harm in mentioning to Peter about her visit to the conversation class. She didn't share the book he'd given her. She kept that hidden in her backpack.

"Good looking?" Peter interrogated.

Mireya shrugged, "I was there to learn." Yet she had to admit he was. *Tall, nice build, and there was chemistry.*

When she and Peter were in bed, she turned on her side away from him. He bumped his hardness against her.

"Think I'll take the day off tomorrow," he said. "A picnic in the foothills, spread a blanket, make love under the blue sky."

It was the most poetic thing she'd ever heard him say. He kissed her neck. She thought of lying, complaining of stomach pain, a headache, and cramps, yet didn't have the energy to lie. *Keep him happy a little longer.*

She wore a white T-shirt and a pair of underwear. Peter lifted the shirt and kissed her back.

"Tienes un condón?

"Don't worry."

"Said that before."

"I'll pull out." He turned on a night lamp.

He's said that before, too. "You'd better."

Mireya turned onto her back, lifted her hips to slide off the panties. Peter licked a nipple, moistened a middle finger, and slipped it inside. When she was moist, he massaged her tiny rosebud just above the opening.

"Huh!" The fleshy teardrop was super-sensitive.

Peter climbed into his favorite position (open-book missionary). He wasn't creative, but she couldn't complain about the results.

"Pull out," she reminded him.

"Ayyy Jesus," he groaned, pressing down and in. *Dear God*, he prayed, *give us a child*.

In her mind, Mireya practiced English before allowing herself a small climax. She wanted control when Peter was about to cum. Five minutes later, he growled.

"Ohhh, baby!"

Mireya twisted sharply so that he slipped out.

"Aw-aw-awww!" Peter gushed over her lower belly and pubic hair before managing to slip back in. She felt him shiver, then he kissed her deeply. Mireya dutifully answered.

As they rested on their sides, Mireya's thoughts returned to Wyler. She wanted to return his kiss. *There's a connection.* Peter interrupted her thoughts.

"What're you thinking about?" he asked dreamily, "The gabacho?" His teasing tone barely camouflaged the seriousness of the question.

"Don't be nutty," she answered and playfully slapped him. A lump formed in her throat, and she turned away. *Did he read my thoughts?*

Peter wasn't finished. He sucked a nipple into his mouth. "Mmm? Tell the truth."

"Grosero," she reprimanded. Cum coursed down her thighs. She needed a towel.

"You wanna see what a güero cock would be like."

She felt him stiffening. "Maybe you want a white woman."

"Naw, they're ugly nags."

He's not gonna let up. Just get it over with. She straddled him, lifted, and slowly impaled herself.

"Ahhh, Jesus. Promise me you won't ever fuck anybody else but me."

"Cállate y fóllame." (Be quiet and fuck me).

Mireya bridged and ground against him, becoming lost within the pearly mists of pleasure. "Mmmoh!" she squealed. "Oyyy!"

Eloisa got up to pee. She stood at her son's bedroom door listening to sounds ebbing and flowing from within, and smiled. *Dear God, give strength to my son's seed.*

"Ayyy, si!"

A grandchild, she thought, how nice that would be.

"I'm gonna cum!" Peter announced. This time, he held her so tightly that no amount of squirming would force him out. "Ah-ah-ahhh, shit...ahrrr!" He stayed buried deep so that semen wouldn't have far to travel.

Peter was sweating, gasping for breath. He kissed her slowly and put his mouth to her ear. "Marry me. I love you, Mireya. I'll make you happy."

She gave him a quick kiss, got to her feet, pulled the T-shirt down, and rushed into the bathroom with her underwear. She saw Eloisa disappearing into the darkness as she returned to her room.

"I'll take that as a yes," he called out.

Mireya used a moistened washcloth to wipe sperm. She

stood to regard the cloudy leavings that dripped into the bowl. Another surge of cum flowed and she sat again.

"Damn," she breathed. *Patience, a few more days. Wonder how much morning-after pills are here?*

When she returned to the bed, Peter was hard again. He sat with his hands behind his head, resting on a pillow, his staff pointing to the ceiling. "Look what you do to me."

"Ay Peter, I've nothing left."

"Mmm."

"Let's sleep."

"Okay, we can start the day where we left off."

She turned off the night lamp. "Go to sleep."

––––

The next morning, Mireya got up at dawn and stepped into the shower. If Peter wanted her again, she'd claim the beginnings of a yeast infection. Luckily, he was still asleep when she was dressed and went into the kitchen. Eloisa was there.

"Seems like you and my son are getting along well."

"He's been very nice to me."

"Have you considered his proposal?"

"I'm still thinking."

"Mmm," she nodded. "With matters of the heart, it's best to take your time. My son loves you very much. He was a handful when he was younger, but he's settled now.

"What about Peter's father?"

"Samuel was a hard working man. When we first came here from Michoacan, we both worked in the fields. Then he got a job as a custodian at an elementary school. He was there for thirty years. Died three weeks after he retired."

"How sad."

"Peter has a good heart, and he'll be a good father."

Mireya swallowed hard. Her throat was dry. Eloisa had touched her conscience, and now it would be harder to do what she must to regain control of her life.

Later that morning, she was ready to walk to the adult school, not far from the house.

"Off to see your güero?"

"Stop, Peter."

"Hmm. What time's class over?"

"Two o'clock," she lied. "One of the students has a birthday, and we're staying longer to celebrate." *Hate lying, but he's backed me into a corner.*

"I'll pick you up, we can get dinner, catch a flick."

Shit, she thought. "I'll walk back. I need exercise. Your mother's cooking is making me gorda."

He lifted a book from the nightstand drawer where he kept socks and the condoms that were mostly ignored. "Read about some exercises we haven't tried?" Peter lifted his eyebrows. It was a copy of the Kama Sutra.

"Ay-yi-yi. See you this afternoon." She kissed him and headed out the door with her backpack.

"Damn," he muttered as he watched her leave. *Finest ass I've ever seen.*

Mireya walked straight to Wyler's. His boxy-looking Trooper was parked in front of the building. She hadn't slept well, battling over whether or not to see him again. Her heart was whispering, and she knew if she stopped listening, it might fall silent forever. They had hours before students arrived.

When she got there, Wyler saw that she was grim.

"So happy to see you. Was worried you wouldn't make it. You alright?"

"Wyler...." She took a deep breath, still standing in the doorway. "This isn't a game for me. If you're not serious, be honest."

Wyler pulled Mireya through the doorway. "Mireya, I'm crazy about you."

This time, Mireya returned his kiss. The feel of her tongue sent electrical currents down his spine.

That first answered kiss was followed closely by others with increasing intensity. Wyler felt a surge of precum oozing. Then she rubbed his chest with her hands.

"Tomorrow I'm going back to Mexico."

"We'll make it work."

She took a deep breath. "How?"

"I'll come up with something while you're kissing me again."

Mireya obliged. Wyler's head was reeling. He felt something deeply for this mysterious woman. He pulled the door shut, and it locked automatically.

In the safety of his office, they kissed. He'd never experienced such a soft, experienced tongue. His hand migrated beneath her T-shirt, and she reached to secure it.

"Not here," she broke off breathlessly, "not yet."

The math region of her mind was calculating odds that Wyler would even phone after today. *Will he even drop a postcard*?

"We'll be together, I promise." Wyler's face was stern.

"I'll wait for a while, but not forever."

"Wait. I'll come to you, whatever it takes." He kissed her again.

She told him that she'd probably be in Morelia. She wrote all of her contact information on a piece of paper, and he gave her two business cards with additional numbers written on the back. The Internet wasn't widely available, especially in México. They agreed on snail mail, supplemented by long-distance calls.

"When we meet again, I'm going to eat you alive," Wyler said.

"What if I'm too spicy?"

"What's that Spanish saying? No picosa, no sabrosa?"

She giggled and kissed him again. Pre-cum began to soak through the front of his pants. He'd never wanted anyone so badly in his entire life.

Subsequent hours passed quickly. They talked about dreams—hers to get a doctorate in mathematics, his to write a best-selling novel. By the time students began filtering in, Mireya's mind was thoroughly clouded by the hope that Wyler was different from others she'd known.

The first student to arrive was a teenager named Joaquin. Wyler greeted him with a special handshake.

"Sup?" Joaquin said.

"How you doin', man?" Wyler answered.

Joaquin was covered in tattoos related to his gang affiliation. In Visalia, you were either Norteño or Sureño, with the corresponding numbers 13 or 14. Joaquin checked out Mireya and smiled knowingly at Wyler.

Another young Chicano came in, and the two headed to the pool table. Soon, several black girls arrived. Wyler greeted them with an enthusiastic smile, a special handshake, a series of bumps and palm slaps designed to create a connection. The one girl named Felicia smiled at Mireya and looked knowingly at Wyler.

"She's pretty, Costner."

"I know."

"Mm-hm, just *bet* you do."

They greeted the boys and went to play air hockey.

Soon, other students began pouring in—Chicanos, Mexicans, Blacks, Filipinos, all looking for an escape from the streets. Wyler made sure each was welcomed, and they showed obvious affection and respect for him.

"So impressive," Mireya commented. "They feel safe here, and they get along so well."

"Wasn't always that way. Most of them come from broken homes. They're marginalized because of circumstance."

"What is 'marginalized'?"

"Sorry. Means they aren't accepted by society. There's a lot of racism, intolerance, and ignorance in town."

"The kids seem nice."

"Most are. Given the opportunity, they do as good or better than most."

"You're spicy too." She checked her watch. "I'll have to go soon. Would you mind if I used your phone to call my mother? She doesn't know when I'm coming home."

"Be my guest. Gonna tell her about me?"

"Not yet," Mireya said.

She sat at his desk and dialed, beginning with a 001-52, followed by the number. She was glad to hear the sound of Giselle's voice.

Wyler's head was already concocting ways to stretch his limited funds and take some vacation time. *Fly to México, feed this hunger, see where it leads.*

When she finished her phone call, another shape filled the doorway into Teen City. Wyler didn't recognize the man.

He walked over and greeted him. "Hi, can I help you?"

"I'm looking for my wife, Mireya."

Wyler blanched, yet was able to hold it together.

Mireya was hidden from view in the office when she heard her name. Blood drained from her face.

"Yes, she's in my office. I'll tell her you're here." He walked into the office.

Peter stayed outside and waited, his hands flexing, squeezing, balling into fists, remembering what he'd used them for back in the day.

"Mireya, your husband's here."

Her eyes were wild with fear, yet she took a deep breath

and walked past Wyler.

"Hi Pete," she tried to sound nonchalant.

"C'mon, let's go."

"Okay, just a second. She went back into the office for her backpack. Wyler was pretending to do paperwork. "Thank you, Mr. Costner. I think some of the other students will be coming in tomorrow for their free lesson."

"You're welcome. Be sure and practice. Your husband should only speak English with you."

"I'll tell him."

She walked out to join Peter. Wyler stood at the office doorway, and Peter narrowed his eyes. Wyler saw his tattoos, letters, and numbers, and knew they represented a capacity for pain and violence.

"Have a nice afternoon, it was nice to meet you," he directed to Pedro.

"Okay," he nodded. *Don't blow up*, he thought. *That'll drive her away for sure.*

They walked out to his newly refurbished Ford F-100 pickup.

"How did you know I was here?"

"I'm good at math. I put one and one together."

"It's a conversation class."

"Yeah, okay."

———

The evening before her secret departure, Peter worked late in the repair shop. Eloisa found Mireya sitting on the front steps of the house. She sat next to her and took her by the hand.

"What's bothering you, child?" she asked.

Does she know? "I'm thinking about México."

"You miss home."

Mireya nodded.

"You'll be leaving?"

Mireya looked at Peter's mother and nodded again.

"You know how my son feels."

"Yes."

"How do you feel?"

"I'm not ready to settle."

Eloisa nodded. "Have you told Peter?"

"He knows about my plans."

"That doesn't make it easier. Can't you go to school here?"

"Not for what I need, Eloisa."

"Mmm."

"I don't want to hurt him."

"Do you love him?"

Would I even know? She shrugged. "I don't know what I feel."

Eloisa patted Mireya's shoulder and went back into the house.

————

The next morning was Wednesday. Peter was propped up on an elbow, gazing at her when she opened her eyes. She smiled, and he kissed her.

"Well?" he asked.

Mireya had put him off longer than he deserved. "Tonight," she said, "I'll give you my answer."

"Okay." He kissed her and rolled between her legs. "Swear to god, I'll make you happy."

She lifted her knees and looked over at the drawer. Peter smothered her impending condom request with a kiss and pushed to the hilt with one smooth stroke.

"Uh!" Mireya gasped.

Peter pulled back incrementally and thrusted again.

"Uh!" She repeated. "Let me turn around." *Why's he being rough?*

She got on her hands and knees to face him.

He spread her ass cheeks and lunged. "Oyyy mi cielo, te amo." *I'm gonna fill you with cum!*

"Uhnnn," her voice was deep. She rested her head on a pillow. His pendulous balls slapped with each thrust. Reaching between her legs, she found her clit as he worked. Before she could climax, Peter clutched her hips, shoved in all the way, and spewed.

———

Mireya showered and ate breakfast. After Peter left for work, Eloisa handed her a paper lunch bag.

"A little something for you to snack on. I know you don't eat enough when you're at school."

"Thank you," Mireya said.

That morning, Mireya packed as much as she could fit into her backpack, leaving everything else, including the necklace Richard had given her in Canada. The bus was departing at eleven. She thought of purchasing a morning-after pill, which had to be taken within seventy-two hours after sex, but the price was exorbitant.

Eloisa was in the small weedy garden watering roses when Mireya came to say goodbye. The old woman hugged her tightly.

"Be safe," she said.

She smiled and returned the hug. "See you after class, Eloisa."

Her eyes grew sad. "My son's expecting an answer tonight."

Guilt weighed down on her like a heavy quilt. Mireya nodded and walked away. There was nothing left to say.

———

The bus was slow getting to the airport, and Mireya had to rush to make her flight to México City. On the plane, she tried reading Wyler's book. Many words were cognates in Spanish, yet it wasn't enough to gather meaning. *Someday*, she thought, *I'll understand every word.* Her happy mood was somewhat dulled when she thought of previous experiences. *Prepare for disappointment on the front lines of love.*

From México City, she took a bus to Puebla, finishing her journey in a combi (minivan) to Xoxtla. She walked the remaining distance to her home, passing the big oak tree, where she'd made Enrique cum simply by kissing him.

Her mother was happy. Gisselle delighted in bragging to neighbors that her daughter was studying in the US. She peppered her with questions about food, school, her cousins, and work at the restaurant. She was clueless about Peter and the whole Visalia debacle. *Keep it that way.*

Mireya's immediate plan was to forget Wyler. She was determined to focus on education. *He's probably already forgotten me*, she thought. *Güeros live in a different priority zone.* Pete was Chicano, but she'd learned that in politics, most Chicanos voted for policies that hurt immigrants. *I don't understand*, she reflected. *Why would you vote against your own people?* Pete had a house, cars, spending money, and shopped in department stores. She remembered leaving the engagement ring inside the nightstand, next to an unused box of condoms. Pete would be forgotten too, and prayed he hadn't left a permanent reminder in her womb.

Late that night, Arturo called, and her mother handed her the phone.

"He's upset."

"It's okay."

Her mother gave her privacy.

"Hola, Arturo."

"Hey, cuz, what happened with you and Pedro? He called, all desperate and crazy—said you left without a word. What's up with that?"

"Primo, try to understand. I'm going to finish my education. Pete knew—"

"You didn't tell him you were leaving." Arturo interrupted. "That's not the way to treat people who care about you. He wants to go there. Said he wants to marry you."

"Wasn't sure he'd let me leave."

"You weren't a goddamn prisoner! He said you shared a bed!"

"I take full blame." Her voice trembled. "Just want to finish school."

"He's all fucked up. Talk to him."

"Sorry."

"Yeah, well, poor Pete. He got mad."

"I feel terrible."

"Don't leave him hanging."

"Okay, primo."

"Alright, I'll let you go. Glad you got back safe. You're welcome here anytime."

"Thanks. Please say hi to Maria and the kids."

"Yeah, sure." Arturo hung up. It was ironic that her cousin, who treated his marriage with such disdain, should advise her on matters of love. *I'll never go there again.*

———

That night, Mireya was worried. Her period was due in a few weeks. Pete managed to pump her full of semen repeatedly. She thought of throwing up a small prayer, but stopped.

Science can explain the universe without the need for a creator. God, the Easter Bunny, and the tooth fairy are on the same team. She didn't call Pete.

CHAPTER 16
CARMEN REVISITED

A week after her return, Carmen stopped by. They hadn't spent much time together the past few years, so they caught up on the latest gossip. Mireya confessed about her time in the US—Peter, Wyler, the entire mess.

"Damn! You stay busy, don't you?"

"Wyler's forty, but has a young heart," Mireya explained.

"Hell with that, how's he in the sack?"

Mireya shrugged, "We haven't."

"Better find out. What if the shoe doesn't fit? I've heard gabacho's lack rhythm."

They burst into laughter. Mireya thought back to her grandmother, who advised that the way to a man's heart isn't through his stomach.

Carmen brought tequila. They reminisce about a certain hotel room in Tetéla where they deepened their friendship. Mireya drew the blinds, locked the door, and returned to the worn couch.

"Jorge and I are finished," Carmen said.

"He was messed up."

"I wanna forget him.

"Let me help."

Mireya brushed a lock of hair from Carmen's eyes and kissed her. With tequila on their tongues and fire in their loins, they were soon out of their clothes. Carmen stayed sitting, and Mireya kneeled on the cement floor before her and lifted her legs.

When Carmen felt the tip of Mireya's tongue on her clitoris, she shivered and gasped. Mireya worked her tongue fast and slow, until Carmen was writhing. Then she curled two fingers inside to find the G-spot.

Carmen's voice changed. "Oy si, mmm right there, ay qué rico! Huh-huh-huh, Ayyy!" Her pussy drew inward and relaxed repeatedly until she was satiated. Then she traded places.

Afterward, they kissed tenderly.

"We taste like coño," said Carmen.

"Mmm," Mireya moaned. "I missed you."

Mireya invited Carmen to stay the night, but she was on her way to the neighboring state of Hidalgo to visit her parents.

"Stop on the way back," Mireya suggested.

"I'll try."

———

Carmen's alcoholic boyfriend persuaded her to come back to him. A week later, Mireya started her period, and Wyler called the same day.

"Your friend came by looking for you the other day."

"What did he say?"

"Said he thought you might be in my class. I told him I hadn't seen you since the day he came in."

Do you think he knows something?"

"I don't think so."

"Good."

"Remember Joaquin?" Wyler asked.

"The one with all of the tattoos."

"Yeah. No one would hire him because of that. He was frustrated, so I had an idea. On the back of the phone book, there's an advertisement for a laser specialist named Michal Johnson. I called to see if it was possible to remove tattoos using the laser. He said he'd never tried. I asked if he'd like to experiment on Joaquin."

"What did he say?"

"Joaquin's already had the first session. Laser fades the

ink so you can barely tell. Hurts like hell. I held his hand, can you believe it?"

Mireya giggled. "That's exciting. Because of you, his life will change. I'm proud of you."

"The best part is, Dr. Johnson isn't charging a dime. I contacted the local newspaper, and they covered the whole story. His photo was on the front page yesterday!"

"Fantastic!"

"When the tattoos are faded, he has a job waiting for him. Now I just have to protect him from norteño gang members. They wanna hurt him."

"Why?"

"Once you've jumped in, it's for life. To quit, you're supposed to get jumped out."

"What does that mean, jumped in?"

"Sorry. To get into a gang, you have to let them beat you up. Getting jumped out, they beat you up worse. You could possibly die."

"That's awful! Poor Joaquin."

"He's staying with me until I find a safe place, especially now that he's a celebrity. Let's change the subject. I'm making plans to visit you."

"When?"

"Not sure yet, but soon I hope. I'm going through withdrawal for your kisses."

"I'll save them all for you."

"Mmm."

———

Wyler wrote to Mireya every day, and called on Sundays. The language of desire allowed them to communicate without having a firm grasp of their respective languages. They exchanged photos. Mireya thought of sending the erotic photo Marco, the photographer, had taken years earlier, yet worried Wyler wasn't ready to be privy to her wild past. The photo she sent was taken by Carmen at a dance club—Mireya, smiling, hands above her head, a look that bespoke of her passion for life. He wrote her after receiving it:

My beautiful, exotic Mireya,
How I ache for you! Here's a puzzle to practice your English. Remove the words, to and see from the following sentence:
I want to see you so badly.
I'm working hard, saving for my ticket. Please wait for me! No doubt there are others lined up to try their luck!

Two months, thirty letters, and eight phone conversations later, Mireya wrote a proposal:

Handsome Wyler,
It would be much cheaper to meet me in Tijuana for a weekend, no? I can take a bus and wait for you at the border crossing. Please call at 7:00 your time on March 5th for an answer.

Wyler had been scrimping since she left. On the 5th of March, he called with a reply.

"The weekend of May 27th is Easter holiday. I'll use some personal vacation time to extend it! It's a six-hour drive. If I leave by 6:00, I can be there by noon. Does May 25th through the 28th work for you?"

"Yes! I'll buy my bus ticket today."

"How long's the ride?"

"From Puebla, it's about seventeen hours."

Wyler was flabbergasted. "Jesus!" Then a thought came to his head. "I'll send money for a plane ticket."

"Too expensive. Don't worry, I've taken buses all my life."

"Remember, I was saving for a round-trip to México City. I

have the money. Please, let me do this. Then you'll be well rested when you arrive."

She closed her eyes for a moment. *He isn't Richard,* she reminded herself. *I want to be with him.* "Okay," she said, "but I'll pay you back. I don't know when, but I will."

"Find the ticket and I'll wire the money. We'll be together in twenty days!"

"Ay, my handsome gringo."

"I have your picture on my truck's visor."

"Keep your eyes on the road. I need you in one piece."

"Where should we stay?"

"Let me take care of that." Her voice was coquettish. "There's a restaurant right across the border called Sanborns. I'll wait there for you."

"Red or white wine?"

"I'm not pretentious," she replied.

"Both, and a bottle of champagne."

They talked a while longer, and the entire time, he was as hard as dry salami.

———

Two days before the trip, he called.

"Still spicy?"

"Muy picante."

"Mmm."

"You should bring protection."

Her words gave him an instant hard-on. Then he eased her mind.

"Know what a vasectomy is?"

"Like when a man has his tubes tied?"

"Exactly. I had one after my divorce. You'll never have to worry."

"Wow, you're full of surprises."

"Mmm-hm."

"We'll take a taxi to the hotel as soon as you're here."

"You can't imagine how much I'm looking forward to this." Pre-cum oozed.

"Drive safely."

"See you soon, gorgeous."

"Hasta luego guapo."

He has kids. That complicates things, she thought. *I remember how it felt to be on the other end of a parent relationship. Calm down, relax. Don't get too serious.*

―――

After the call, he went to the Trooper and flipped down the visor to stare at her photo — perfect ass, short powerful legs, soft tongue. *TNT.*

Immediately, he posted a notice that Teen City would be closed for five days beginning on May twenty-fifth and informed the board members, who approved it immediately.

Mireya's four-hour flight would arrive in Tijuana early Friday morning. She'd find a hotel and meet him at Sanborn's. The rest would unfold by itself.

―――

Wyler drove his gas-guzzling Trooper six hours to the border and parked in San Ysidro on the North American side. He pushed through a turnstile without being searched or questioned by Mexican border guards. Sanborn's was close by, and he hurried across a busy street. It was noon, and Mireya wasn't there. He sat in the lobby and found a discarded Mexican newspaper filled with gory pictures of car accidents and murders. He put it down.

Ten minutes later, Wyler saw Mireya exiting a taxi and walking toward the restaurant. He thought his heart would rupture. She wore a short blue form-fitting flower-print dress, sandals, and bright red dangling earrings. He met her outside the front entrance and pulled her into his arms. Her welcoming kiss nearly made him spurt.

She hailed a taxi to the hotel. On the way, Wyler kissed her cherry-red lipstick off. They hardly spoke a word, choosing to communicate in a language as old as time. The driver peeked at them in the rearview mirror and sped to the Hotel Azteca.

Mireya had already paid for the first night. Wyler paid for two more. The next three days and nights were spent almost entirely in room 302.

In the elevator, Mireya kissed his neck, trapping skin between her teeth to leave a blue mark. He lifted her dress to cup her ass, and she tugged it down as the bell sounded, and pulled a shoulder strap back up. They rushed to 302. Wyler slid the door card into a security slot. Mireya opened, pushed past him, playfully ran to the bed, and threw herself on it.

Wyler laughed, toe'd off his shoes, and flopped down next to her. Her kisses filled his head with helium, his cock with so much blood it lifted the font of his pants with every heartbeat. His fingers played over the smooth brown skin of her back. Precum trickled steadily from his cock. He pulled down the straps of the dress and unlatched her bra, unleashing firm mounds topped with tall, light chocolate nipples. He took one into his mouth. Her hand tangled in his hair.

"Ayyy, si."

"Jesus, Mireya, I want you so much."

"I solved the puzzle you sent. Now you can have me."

In their haste, she kept her dress, sandals, and glasses on, only pulling off her underwear. Wyler tugged down his pants, kicked them away, and crept between her satiny legs. Mireya had seen his cock, swollen tight, throbbing. She was pleased.

Splaying his legs beneath hers, he cupped his hands beneath her knees and lifted them.

"What do you want?" she whispered, running fingers through the hair on his chest.

"You know." He inched forward.

She twisted away. "Tell me."

This is torture! "I want this." He pushed against the soft outer petals of her cunt until they surrounded his broad helmet.

"Mmm, I want that too." Her hips wiggled.

Wyler slipped his arms beneath her shoulders and pushed down and in. "Oh my gawwwd."

Mireya's pussy slowly surrendered to the full measure of his cock.

Suddenly, he stiffened to give warning. "Don't move, baby."

"Ahhh, I want to move."

"Don't." His voice was desperate.

With great effort, she kept still, her mouth slightly open, showing her front teeth.

Wyler closed his eyes to concentrate, allowing a steady stream of cum to escape without breaking his hardness.

"Mmm, I feel something warm."

Not answering, he kept his eyes shut until the urge was vanquished. Then he drew back and returned.

"Ayyy que rico, ayyy si." She lifted her knees until they were even with his shoulders and swiveled around him.

The sounds Mireya made were exotic. Utterances—ay's, oy's, sah's that sizzled in his ears and made him super-sensitive. He focused on the flowers decorating the faded quilt, a reprint of a windmill on the wall. Buried within the velvety walls of her pussy, he tapped the door to her antichamber. Mireya rubbed calves over his ass. He avoided her lips, knowing they'd lead his 'short-cumming'. He clutched her hips to keep her still again.

"Don't move," Wyler repeated through clenched teeth.

Mireya wanted him to let go. There'd be other chances for her. After a few tense moments, he pulled back slowly and plunged.

Mireya arched her back to counter-thrust. "Uh-huh, oyyy

si baby. uh-huh." Her almond eyes glazed over as Wyler pumped.

Now recovered, he sat up to watch. The black hair surrounding her cuntlips clung to his shaft, her clitoris swayback and forth across the top of his cock. Her tits jiggled with each forward thrust. She tightened her hands on his shoulders, and her voice grew husky.

"Huhnnn," Mireya took a deep, jagged breath. "I'm cumming....Oooayyy, Ay-ay-ayyy!" Her voice rose higher and higher. A second orgasm followed close behind. Her whole body trembled as she lifted and twisted, inner walls collapsing, squeezing him.

"Oh shit!" Wyler bellowed. "I'm gonna cum....rawww! Oh dollface, awww, aw, aw, awww!"

"Oy sí mi amor, ayyy sí !"

Jets of semen were pulled up from his balls. "God*damn*," he growled. It poured as if his balls were bellows heating a flame.

"I'm cumming again....uhnnn, oyyy!" Her head snapped back and twisted side-to-side.

Wyler nearly swooned with pleasure. Mireya felt warm cum glaze her lining, oozing from her pussy, gathering at the delicate scalloped edges of her lips, creeping thickly down the crack of her ass.

Wyler kept moving even when it was ticklish.

"Spicy enough?" she breathed.

"Ay yi-yi," he said.

She giggled, lazily rubbing her heels over his ass. "You called me dollface. What is that?"

Wyler kissed her. "It means you have a lovely, beautiful face."

"Mmm, okay. I'll be your dollface."

Mireya liked his's cock—broad-tipped, moderate length, thick enough. Wyler stayed inside, and slowly, as they kissed, she felt him swelling.

"Are you going to make me cum again, Mr. Costner?" Mireya whispered into his ear.

"Do you mind?"

"Let me think about it while I take off the rest of my clothes."

"Good idea."

When they were naked, she straddled him, placing her hands flat against his chest. Her head tilted back and her mouth opened as she rocked.

"Oyyy baby." Her hips undulated.

He watched his cock disappear beneath the mocha lips, and reemerge. His previous leavings were matted in her pubic hair. She licked her fingers, found her clit and moved faster, forward and back, up and down, stirring him. Wyler reached up to twist her nipples, and she responded with a deep groan, followed by a hawkish cry.

"Eeeayyy, ayyy, uh-ayyy!" She circled until the strength of her orgasms made her dizzy. Then she rested against his chest. "Huh-huh-huh," she panted. "Ohhh, uhnnn."

He thrusted upward as her tits dragged over his chest.

"Ohhh!" He kept his eyes open, watching her face, deep in rapture. Erotic noises filled room 303. "Nnnawww!" He nutted so hard that he lost consciousness for a moment.

———

Mireya rested on top, casually leaving blue marks on his chest. He smelled her hair and rubbed his hands over her shoulders and back. *Smells like cinnamon, nutmeg, night-blooming jasmine, rare flowers in an exotic jungle.* He realized then that he was already writing about her.

"Guess we still like each other," Mireya managed.

"In English, that's called an understatement."

"I don't understand."

"Means I'm very serious, Dollface."

Mireya smiled. "Good." She lifted, and his cock slipped out. Cum dripped like egg whites onto his upper thighs.

"You called me 'amor'.

She nodded. "Mmm-hm."

"I love you, too."

They barely left their bed for the next few days. With Wyler, she felt at ease with her sexuality. He welcomed experimentation. She sipped red wine and dribbled it over her body for him to lick, and jacked him off in the downstairs Jacuzzi. Wyler licked until her clit pulsed and kicked. She suggested anal sex, yet they didn't have lubricant. That would have to wait.

They fucked until frothy bubbles of cum issued from her swollen cunt lips, punctuated by the escape of trapped air. They fucked until she was too sensitive to continue — until she smelled like the sea. Then she gave him head, swallowing his cum. She left monkey bites all over his body. She threw everything she had into making sure, when asked who was the best fuck of his life, the name Mireya Lopez would effortlessly float from his lips.

When the weekend was finished, promises were made — the kind born on wings of dopamine. Wyler watched Mireya board a bus that would eventually arrive in Puebla. He lost count of how many times they balled.

"You nearly fucked me to death," she complained just before leaving.

"What a way to die."

"Mmm."

He hugged her tightly. "I love you, Mireya."

"This isn't a game. Better mean it."

"A thousand percent."

"Interesting calculation. Te amo, Wyler Costner." *I said it.*

———

Wyler floated across the border, feeling better than ever. When he arrived at his parking spot, he saw that someone had vomited on the hood of his Trooper. He didn't care. Mireya filled his thoughts as he paid at the tollbooth and drove further and further North, away from her.

Wyler hadn't mentioned that his divorce wasn't final, and saw no need for it. He was certain he loved Mireya more than he'd ever loved a woman. Distance and time were enemies to love. He needed a better job, something closer—San Diego or Los Angeles. Perhaps she could return to the US, and they could begin a life together. His mind whirled with thoughts of Mireya in his bed forever.

Recently, he applied for a teaching job at the California Youth Authority in Paso Robles, a small central coast town. The interview had gone well. Paso Robles was only twenty-five minutes from the cold Pacific. He'd always wanted to live near the sea.

As fate decreed, Wyler was offered the job. Mireya was excited for him when he called with the news. His first week on the job, he stayed in a cheap hotel before finding a tiny cabin in the nearby mountains. Housing was tight, and it was the only place available.

Every week, he called Mireya with tales regarding the one-bedroom cabin. It was dilapidated, and the strange landlord who lived next door wasn't inspired to make repairs.

"You can see bare ground through the wooden floor-slats," he said. "One night, I came in from work, and a gopher snake was curled up in a corner of the living room. Frogs live in the shower behind the hot and cold valves."

"Why do you stay?"

"Nothing else for rent. Last week, during a rainstorm, a big tree fell and wiped out a living room wall."

Mireya loved hearing the stories. He promised to fly to Puebla during Thanksgiving break. In the meantime, Mireya received a letter from Morelia. The university was asking her to put off her Master's for another semester, citing over-enrollment. It didn't seem possible that there were too many math enthusiasts in Mexico.

From Paso Robles, Tijuana was six hours away, yet Wyler made the trip at the first opportunity and paid for her flight. He had five days off, including the weekend.

They met at the Sanborns. Mireya wore an Indian skirt and a Mexican blouse. It'd been two months. Overcome with passion, he sank to his knees.

"Mireya Lopez, will you marry me?"

Everything changed from that moment on. Mireya looked at him, and tears formed in her eyes. At first, she couldn't form the words, then she did.

"Yes," she said, "yes, I'll marry you."

———

They returned to the Azteca Hotel, and this time Wyler remembered lubricant.

The first night, they made love twice before resting. After dinner in the hotel, they returned to the room. Wyler waved Astroglide in her face.

"Ready for something different?"

"Go slow." Her experience was limited, yet she remembered that much.

Wyler was already stiff as they quit their clothes and took to the bed. Mireya lay flat on her stomach. He straddled her, kissed her neck and shoulders, teasing the length of his cock between her ass cheeks.

Mireya got to her knees, and she heard him flip the plastic lid open, the squishy sound as he slathered jelly over his hardness. Incrementally he slipped a jellied finger up her ass.

"Slow baby, sssahhh."

He moved the finger as deep as it would go, regressed and entered again, over and over until he felt the walls relax. Then he placed a dollop of lubricant on his cockhead, and pushed against the wrinkled brown ring of her sphincter until it disappeared. She bore down, allowing him to progress.

"Mmm si, mmm." She reached between her legs to find her clit.

Halfway, Wyler pulled back an inch and pressed forward until he was fully buried.

"Uh-huh, mmm, that feels good."

As he stroked back and forth, Mireya massaged her tiny bud. Inserting fingers into her cunt, she felt Wyler's cock through the thin separating membrane, and felt an intense climax on the skyline.

"Ohhh, that feels tight." He never mentioned that it was his first time entering the back door. "Cum, baby."

"Oy si, I'm cumming....Oof! Ohhh!" Her voice was deep and guttural. She gulped a lungful of air. Her asshole and cunt spasmed synchronously, and her clit jittered with an all-encompassing climax. "Ooo-ooo-ooo-sss," followed by a cacophony of gasps, screams, groans, and prayers. "Oh god, ohhh my god! Ayyyy!"

Wyler watched her anus wink around him, and he plunged deep inside her bowels to empty his nut sack. "Oh Jeez, awww, awww!" He grasped her hips, reached to cup her tits in his palms, and twisted her nipples.

She shuddered with smaller follow-ups before stretching out on her stomach. Wyler exited slowly, and as he popped free, a queef of bubbly semen followed.

"God*damn*," was all he could think to say.

"Mmm."

"I'll get a hand-towel."

When he returned, Mireya held it to her ass and shuffled to the bathroom. The toilet magnified the sound of trapped air and semen.

Wyler joined when he heard a flush. Skin-to-skin, they kissed, then stepped into the shower to lather each other.

Yeah, she thought, *I'll marry this man.*

———

"Are you crazy?" Her mother argued when Mireya returned. "You hardly know him!"

"I love him."

Giselle couldn't argue with that. She'd had many men, and though she loved a few, none led to a proposal. *How can I advise against something I've wanted all my life?*

"Ay hija, I hope you know what you're doing. Be careful with the 'L' word. What do you love about him? That he's kind, gentle, makes you laugh, or do you only love the way he stirs the pot?"

"Mother!"

"When do I meet him?"

"Soon, I hope. He's coming for Christmas."

Mireya's mother pulled Mireya into her arms for a rare hug. It felt so good that she held on for as long as possible. Then Giselle pushed her to arm's length.

"Are you being careful?"

She tried to explain the concept of a vasectomy, but it got lost in translation.

"El arma todavía funciona sin las balas?" she asked, causing Mireya to fall into a fit of giggles.

"Yes, Mami, the gun still works without bullets."

———

In December, when Wyler flew into Mexico City, he was enraptured by the whole experience. They took a bus to Puebla, another bus to Xoxtla, and a combi to the ranch. Wyler had a carry-on luggage and a backpack. As they approached the ranch, it was like traveling back in time two hundred years. People were walking along dirt roads, riding horses, and bicycles. He saw an ancient Renault creating a dust cloud, rusted bumpers held together with baling wire. Bony burros pulled wooden carts filled with corn, grass, and alfalfa.

They passed a small church with an open field next to it. Barefooted children played soccer, pieces of concrete representing the goals. There were several intimidating factories hulking up in the distance. Mireya pointed to one.

"That place makes semi-truck bodies, and over there, they dye fabrics. All the waste gets poured into the river." She shook her head. "I used to swim in that river when I was little, before the factories."

"Why doesn't anyone stop them?"

She lifted a hand and rubbed two fingers together, making it clear. "Corruption."

"It's the same in the US. Corruption's like gum stuck beneath a desk. You can't see it, but you know it's there. Power makes monsters."

Mireya squeezed his hand and leaned into him as the combi approached their destination. High in the sky, several red-tailed hawks circled. Street dogs lay along the side of the road or moved slowly, sniffing at the ground. Cement dwellings dotted the area, each sporting rebar horns at the corners of the roofline. Families left them there with the hope that one day they'd add another story to their dreams.

"Por favor, nos baja después del tope." (Please let us off after the speedbump), she requested the driver.

The house loomed on the right. They thanked the driver, and he drove away slowly to avoid kicking up too much dust. Wyler gazed at the property.

"This is it, Mr. Costner. Home sweet home."

The house was a two-story cement affair fenced in by beautiful, deadly looking maguey cactuses. She led them through a steel front door and into a dirt courtyard. Mireya studied his face and was pleased to see it full of wonder.

"This is amazing," he said.

She giggled and called out, "Madre!"

Mireya's mother stepped out of her house and into the bright sun.

"Hija."

She spoke to her mother in Spanish and translated back and forth.

"This is Wyler."

He took her hand, "Mucho gusto, Señora."

"Mucho gusto," she replied with a smile just like her daughter's. "Bienvenido a Mexico." She gestured them inside.

They sat on a grouping of worn furniture, and she offered them a glass of water from a burbling five-gallon plastic jug. Four crates wired together made up a coffee table. She sat across from them on a white plastic chair with a beer logo on the backrest.

"How was your trip?" Gisselle asked Wyler. Mireya translated.

"Very smooth. They served tequila, and that made it even smoother."

Gisselle laughed. "Is this your first time in Mexico?"

"I've spent some time in Tijuana." He looked at Mireya, and she gave him a knowing smile.

"How long will you stay?"

"Five days." Then he turned to Mireya and took her hands. "I want you to tell your mom something."

"Okay." She scrunched her forehead with curiosity.

"Tell her that I'm here to ask her for your hand in marriage."

Mireya blushed and fanned herself. "You don't waste any time, do you?"

"Nope."

Gisselle leaned forward and waited.

"Okay. Mamá, dice Wyler, me gustaría pedir la mano de

su hija en matrimonio."

Gisselle shook her head emphatically. "No." She paused for effect. "No solo la mano, la enchilada entera," she replied.

Mireya laughed so hard that she had to get up and hold her stomach.

"What did she say?" Wyler wore a confused smile.

Mireya caught her breath and sat. "Mom says, no, you can't have just the hand, you have to take the whole enchilada." And then they all laughed.

"I take that as a yes?"

Mireya nodded, and Wyler thanked Giselle.

Giselle welcomed him into the family with a real hug.

Then came tough questions. Giselle wanted to know the plan. Mireya was surprised at how linear and logical her mother's queries were. *She could have been a mathematician.* She shot them rapidly in Spanish, all at once.

"Where will you live, how will you marry, you don't have papers, what do you really know about each other, what about your education?"

Her questions pushed buttons that Mireya's heart hadn't allowed access to. They caused her to draw back, to think clearly about what she was doing. *True, I'm jumping into the unknown.*

Wyler assuaged some of her anxiety by promising that she would reach her educational goals in the US. Yet, doubt bred by logic plagued her thoughts.

That evening upstairs, when they were making love as quietly as possible, she felt better. *Life is short*, she philosophized. *It's taking me somewhere I never dreamed of going. Fear and ignorance are enemies.*

Facing each other, he stroked her face with his thumb. "I love you, Mireya. I'm going to make you very happy."

"Too late, you already have," she answered.

———

"Pinche gabacho," Pete fumed. He had learned from one of the Teen City board members that was his car worked on, that the güero had taken a new job in Paso Robles, teaching at a prison.

"I met him once. He seemed like a nice guy. He was teaching a class."

"Yeah, a conversational English class, I believe it was," said the board member.

"Yeah. I want to keep in contact with him. Did he leave a number, a forwarding address?"Pete probed.

"He may have. I'll check. If I find anything, I'll bring it when I pick up the car."

"Too bad he left, he was good at reaching some of those knuckleheads."

I got something to go on now. Arturo had talked to Mireya's mother, who said she met a nice güero in California, and they were serious. *I'll show that cabrón what it means to be serious.* He surveyed the artwork on his arms and recalled his reasons for the dagger getting inked lengthways down his left forearm. *Armando.*

He and his brother, Armando, were teenagers looking for a bit of spending money. They were members of the South Side Loc's (Loco's), and wanted to prove their worth. After casing a particular neighborhood, they decided on a house owned by a grandmother living alone with half a dozen cats. *Didn't have no car, so we walked.*

"Catlady keeps money layin' around, what I heard," Mando said.

Went wrong from the beginning. Got in through a window, found the kitchen, and the old lady was there, petting a goddamn cat and sipping tea. Mando showed her his knife, and she collapsed.

"Fuck!" he said, after recognizing her as his eighth grade English teacher. "That's Mrs. Davenport."

We didn't stick around to see if she was dead. I found her purse, took out the wallet, and we split up to go home. Things got worse when a cop stopped Mando on a sidewalk to question him. It was three in the morning by then. The old lady had woken up and called the cops. They put one and one together, took him in for questioning.

Mrs. Davenport recognized him. "As I recall, he didn't care much for school."

Mando took the fall and spent a couple of years at the Wasco State Prison.

Mando. Where are you now, cabrón? Pete refocused on the task at hand. *Find the motherfucker, throw a scare into him so I can get Mireya back.*

———

The next few days were filled with activity. They visited beautiful downtown Tlaxcala, made a trip to the zócalo in Puebla, and walked in the open markets of small towns. Occasionally, they invited Gisselle, yet she was always busy. Mireya's brothers made an appearance one evening. Hugo and Edgar took turns grilling Wyler and threatening him if he did anything to make their sister unhappy.

She tried to react good-naturedly, yet it came out stronger than she intended. "Cállate. Neither of you took an interest in my life."

They pretended to be saddened by the remark. Then Hugo slapped Edgar's shoulder.

"You know what this means, eh?"

Edgar nodded and went along. "That's right. Tell him."

"Wyler has to pay a dowry to us. I want a car, and Hugo, what do you want?"

"I think a car would be nice."

"Pinches cabrónes. You'll get a six-pack of Corona and a bottle of Jose Cuervo Especial."

They pulled disgusted faces, and Edgar shrugged. "Better than nothing."

Hugo nodded. "Pay up."

———

On a trip to Cholula, a quaint little town in Puebla, they encountered three ex-lovers. The first was Antonio at an open-air artisan market. She hadn't seen him since the days of juggling a sex triangle with him and his best friend.

"Mireya!" He waved and walked over.

"Hi, Antonio." She was embarrassed, yet happy to see him. She flashed on the memory of them upstairs in his bedroom, Billie Holiday singing All of Me as they fucked on the floor.

They hugged, and he kissed her cheek. "It's been a long time. You dropped off the face of the Earth."

"Antonio, this is my fiancé, Wyler."

She was sure she saw disappointment in his face. They shook hands.

"Nice to meet you. Wow, getting married. How did you meet?"

"I was studying English in the US."

Wyler saw it written on his face. *Something serious happened between them*, he thought.

"Well, congratulations. You're a very lucky man."

"I know."

"Well, I have to go, but it was really good seeing you again." He lifted a card from his wallet and handed it to Mireya. "I teach at Madera University close by. Please call when you get a chance so we can catch up."

He shook Wyler's hand again and hugged Mireya.

"Call me," he whispered.

———

A half hour later, Mireya spotted Javier in a bookstore with his new wife, a pretty woman her age. This time, she wasn't embarrassed at all. Javier had been her good friend. She had coaxed him out of depression with mind and body, after his wife's lover impregnated her.

Wyler was more comfortable with Javier, yet sensed Mireya had been more than close friends with him.

"Still teaching at BUAP?" She asked.

"Yes, no one else would hire me." She giggled, and he smiled at her. *Always loved the way she laughs.* "You know where to find me."

"I will."

His wife kept a neutral face, yet began showing an impatient smile.

"Wyler, it was good to meet you. Congratulations on your marriage plans. Please make sure she doesn't stop at a Master's. She has an amazing mind."

"I'll support whatever she wants to do."

They said their farewells and sat for lunch at a small bistro. Wyler was full of curiosity, yet didn't want to come off as a jealous asshole. He tried a subtle approach.

"Antonio seems like a nice guy."

"He is. His best friend did community service with me in Tetela."

"Just friends?"

"Well, a little more, I suppose." *This is a good test*, she thought.

"Thought so."

"Jealous?"

"Dollface, I know I'm not your first, but I hope to be the last. What about Javier?"

"Friends with benefits."

"Oh, I see. Was he very beneficial?"

"Mutually."

Wyler's heart was pounding, and he felt dizzy with a sudden need to get her into a bed. They finished their meal and walked to Cholula's famous pyramid, Tlachihualtepetl. It was one of the few you could enter, climbing up to reach a plateau at the surface. There were human burial remains under glass, green lizards darting around, and a place where you could clap your hands and have it repeated back in an echo. On the outside steps leading down, they bumped into Marco (the poet) as he was climbing up. They stopped at the same time.

"Hello, Mireya."

"Hi." She was stuck for words. A rush of mellowed anger filled her for a moment. *The gambler who lost.* He looked sad and embarrassed.

"Never thought I'd see you again."

Her eyes narrowed, and the next words had the same effect as when she'd pushed him off of her and ordered him to leave.

"Marco, this is Wyler, my fiancé."

Moonlight and Ravens, he thought. *What could have been, yet never shall.* In that instant he relived the feeling of his cock slipping into paradise. Then getting denied. *All because of a stupid bet.*

He reached for Wyler's hand and received a warning grip.

"You're marrying the most beautiful flower in México."

"Sooner the better," Wyler replied. *Before someone else picks her.*

"Good to see you again, Mireya. "Are you still writing poetry?"

"When I get the time. Well, it was nice seeing you again. Congratulations."

She put her arm around Wyler's waist and leaned into him.

Marco slowly trudged up the steps.

At the bottom, an old woman was selling chapulines (fried grasshoppers).

"Ever tried?" She asked..

"No. What are those?"

"You call them grasshoppers, I think."

"Mmm."

The lady gave them a handful to try. Mireya had tasted them many times. Wyler popped one into his mouth and smiled with satisfaction. At that moment, she loved him more than ever. She buried herself in his arms and told him so. When they drew apart, he smiled.

"Did Marco enjoy the benefits?"

"Not really. He bet with one of his friends who would bed me first."

"Who won?"

"They both lost." She didn't say more, and he didn't ask, though he wanted to. *Someday she'll inspire a novel.*

―――

On his final day at the ranch, vendors were announcing themselves through loudspeakers attached to vans and pickups. Some played songs. The man selling gas played the theme song for The Good, the Bad, and the Ugly. The garbage man was heralded by a boy on a bicycle riding ahead with a bell rung by hand. The pastry truck was accompanied by El Panadero, sung by the famous Mexican comedian Tin Tan.

Three hours before Wyler was scheduled to leave by bus to the airport in Mexico City, Mireya led him upstairs. After the first lovemaking, he stayed hard and was able to cum again. Then, just as he was finished packing his small carry-on, she kneeled to take him into her mouth.

They rode to the bus stop in Puebla for a tearful farewell. She'd never cried for a man, even for Domingo after he cheated. Yet, when boarding was announced, she did.

"I love you, Wyler." And she knew it was true.

"Love you, Mireya." He also knew.

―――

"Why are you going to Paso Robles? Eloisa asked her son.

"Picking up a car this evening. Should be back sometime tomorrow."

"Drive carefully."

"I will, Mama."

She moved her fingers over his heart in benediction, and he kissed them.

He took the F-100 pickup. *Still need paint, but it runs good.* He went over the plan in his head. He knew that teachers worked from 2:00-10:00 p.m. *Strange hours*, he thought. *Wait for the cabrón in the prison parking lot, follow him, find the right moment to make him an offer he can't refuse. Can't blame Mireya. He confused her. She'll come around.*

Peter stopped for gas before heading over to the Paso de Robles Youth Authority. Males between the ages of twelve and twenty-five were housed there. The parking lot was unguarded, large enough so that no one noticed him sitting there, close to a red Isuzu Trooper. *Remember it being at the Teen Center. Got a head for remembering cars.* He checked his watch. *Nine forty-five.* He'd brought his .45 automatic. *Throw a scare into him. That's all.*

At five minutes after ten, the workforce exited. Peter saw him coming with a briefcase. He was tall and looked the same as before. A Trooper, he thought. *Gutless gas-guzzlers*, he thought.

It was a moonless night. Peter followed Wyler, leaving plenty of room behind them. He took the 101 freeway for eight miles. Just past the small town of Atascadero, he exited on a lonely gravel mountain road. Peter slowed, took the exit, pulled over, and shut off his lights. Then he followed Wyler's tail-lights. A mile up, the Trooper parked in front of a tiny cabin. Peter pulled off to the side, turned around so that he was faced for a quick escape if needed. He shut off the engine, close enough to see the tall gabacho disappear into the shack.

Sit tight. Let him settle in. He saw another house close by with lights on, and could see a shape moving in there.

He thought of Mireya, their time in his bed. *Spoiled me for any other.* He remembered how she felt inside, and a lump formed in his throat. *Can't give that up. Go over the plan. Knock. Talk your way in. Soon as he opens, show him the gun, sit him down, have a nice little chat. Hit the freeway, head home. Give it a week. Get her number from Arturo. Patch it up.*

Pete stood by his car. He left the keys in it and slipped the .45 down the back of his pants. Leisurely, he began toward the cabin. *All goes well, I'll soon have the chance to make Mireya forget all about the pinche —*

The door to the cabin opened, and Wyler walked toward the Trooper.

"Shit!" He whispered harshly. He hurried back to his truck, got in, and laid flat across the seat.

————

Wyler saw the Ford F-100. *Wasn't there when I came in.* His headlights didn't show anyone in there. He crept past, raising as little dust as possible on the gravel road. Breakdown? *Friend of the landlord, Wally?* He kept driving. If he's still there when I get back from the grocery store, I'll tell Wally.

When he was down the road far enough, Peter got out and walked quickly to the cabin. It was a simple job to shoulder the old wooden door open. A light was left on in the kitchen. He stepped inside and listened. A few steps took him everywhere in the shack. On the ancient refrigerator, a magnet held a picture of Mireya, dancing, smiling, her arms held high.

Wait for him to return? He looked at the door. A few broken pieces of wood on the floor. *He'll know someone broke in. Damn it!* He took the photo and slid it into his back pocket. He rifled through a few drawers and found a phone book with his phone information. He wrote it down. A new plan emerged.

He left a .45 round on the plastic kitchen table. *Call from a payphone in Paso Robles. Warn him about Mireya.*

He set her photo on the passenger seat with the .45 on top. He used his lights on the way out and found the freeway. His anger pushed his speed twenty miles over the limit. The sudden flash of bright lights followed by winky-blinky's caused all the blood to drain from his face. His brain went numb. He pulled over to the right shoulder and waited, his heart thumping in his chest.

The officer approached from the passenger side and shined a flashlight. Immediately, he saw the .45, which Pete had forgotten in his panic. Drawing his weapon, he commanded Peter to keep his hands on the steering wheel. Each command was barked, ending in "Do it now!"

Soon, Pete was face down on the pavement. Other CHPs responded. *Star of the show,* he mused. *All for the love of a woman.* The cuffs were too tight. They helped him to his feet and put him in the back of a cruiser. Pete looked at the wire barrier in front of him.

––––

Wyler reported the breakin, what was missing, and what was left behind. Wally was curious and hung around until the responding officer asked him to go away.

Wally murmured, "I'm the landlord, it's my business to know what happened."

"Yes, sir," the kind officer responded. "I'll take your statement when I'm finished with Mr. Costner."

When the investigation was done, it coincided with what the perpetrator confessed.

"We'll be in touch if we need anything more." He gave Wyler a card.

"Do I need to worry that he'll return?" Wyler asked.

"He's looking at some serious time. Two to five years, possession of a stolen firearm, breaking and entering with the intent to cause bodily harm. Don't think you'll need to worry. By the way, we'll need the photo for evidence."

"Okay."

"Seems like you two shared a love interest, am I correct?"

"Mireya's my fiancée. He's just some guy she met."

"Where is she?"

"Mexico, until she gets her fiancée visa."

"Well, I wish you luck."

———

That evening, Wyler called Mireya to tell her the story. She sobbed, repeating how sorry she was. He reassured her that everything was fine.

"You're not to blame."

"Thank you for loving me."

"Easiest job I ever had."

"Are you looking for a new place?"

"Nothing yet, but when we're married, we'll look together." He didn't mention the child support payments that were biting into his budget. Luckily, the union negotiated a hefty pay raise a few weeks later.

———

Wyler rented a cheap apartment for Mireya in Playas, close to Tijuana at the border. Every other weekend, he drove to the border town of San Ysidro to meet her at Sanborn's. She was waiting for a fiancée visa appointment at the American embassy in Ciudad Juarez. They were told it could take up to six months for an appointment, and she would only be given a two to three-day notice. Moving closer to Juarez made sense.

Mireya began searching for work around Playas. She took a math-tutoring position at the Autonomous University of Baja California to pay for food. In the evenings, she studied math.

The apartment was walking distance to an unkempt beach littered with plastic bottles and trash. Her first day there, helicopters hovered close by, and the landlady told Mireya that police were closing in on a drug lord. The loud pop of firearms was heard, and that evening, they watched news teams gather. Three drug dealers and one officer were killed. The drug lord escaped.

The unmarried landlady's name was Micaela, Miki for short. She was short and stout with a booming personality and bawdy humor. They took an instant liking to each other, and Mireya spent many hours accompanying her on business errands, shopping, beachcombing, and attending Zumba. She drove a Nissan Tsuru, which she nicknamed 'Deathtrap,' because it lacked any safety features, including seatbelts.

Miki hated exercise and kept up a steady stream of curses during class. She stopped often to catch her breath. Sometimes the things she said made Mireya breathless with laughter. Instructors admonished Miki, but enjoyed her humor too.

"Move your arms and shake your booty!" They encouraged the class.

Miki shouted back, "Who do you think I am, a backup dancer for Shakira? I'm sweating so much, my leotard is sticking to my skin like Saran Wrap on leftovers."

"Cállate, Miki!" The instructor reprimanded with a smile.

After class, Miki suggested that they share a caguama (forty-two ounce bottle of beer). They found a family store close by with chairs outside. At this point, she hadn't met Wyler. Money for the apartment was wired. He was due to arrive for his first visit on a three-day weekend in February.

Miki raised her glass. "One beer, two beers, three beers, four. Then I hit the fucking floor. Salud!"

They tipped glasses. Miki gulped down half, burped through her nose, and pinched her nostrils. "Ouch." Then she smiled mischievously at Mireya. "Your güero's coming."

"Yes."

"Que la Chinga. He must *really* like something about you."

"Ay, Miki."

"Wonder what it is. You're gonna wake up the whole apartment complex."

"We'll try to be quiet."

"Where's the fun in that? Make all the noise you want. Does he have a brother?"

"They don't get along."

"Too bad. I had some güero's. They get the job done. How's yours?"

"Can't complain."

"Tiene una gran polla?"

Mireya giggled. "Just right."

"What you gonna do besides fuck?"

"What do you suggest?"

"There's a strip club close by."

"Hmm."

Miki shook her shoulders, "Boom-boom chicky-boom!"

"You should be a stripper," Mireya suggested.

"Ay no, Zumba's enough. Let me lose twenty more pounds. I can't even do table dancing. I'd break it."

Mireya giggled. "Miki, thank you for being so nice to me."

The sentiment caught her by surprise. She smiled and put a hand over Mireya's and patted it. Then she took a long swallow of beer.

"My cabrón husband is living with his puta on the other side of town. We were married for eight years, and he shot blanks, so I didn't even get a baby from him. But he owned apartments, and I got a good lawyer. If he divorces me, he'll pay. Anyway, having you here…" She choked up. "I needed a friend like you."

Mireya pursed her trembling lips.

"Share the güero. I'll Zumba all over him."

"I'll ask him."

Wyler arrived at 6:30 on a Saturday morning. He was exhausted, but lust overrode the need for sleep. Miki saw them arrive and went out to meet them. After a short introduction, Miki let them go with a caveat.

"Go on now. Your güero's starving."

"Ay, Miki. See you later."

"Call me if you need help."

Her Spanish was so rapid that Wyler only grasped part. Mireya led Wyler to her small apartment. It was furnished tastefully with basics, including cookware. The bedroom housed a queen-sized bed with a firm mattress.

Although she preferred vaginal sex, lubricant was close at hand. On the second night, Mireya doubled up a pillow beneath her stomach and presented herself.

"Slow, baby," she cautioned.

Wyler applied jelly to his cock, circled the rim of her anus, and slipped in.

"Ayyy, huh." *Bear down*, she reminded herself. Her voice deepened, and she grunted. "Oh, oh, ohhh.." She reached between her legs and circled her clit with two fingers.

When she flinched, Wyler paused before pushing deeper. He gripped her hips, pulled back slowly, and thrusted more aggressively, faster and faster until his balls slapped against her ass.

"Uhn-uhn-uhn," she groaned until he spurted.

Semen rushed warmly into her bowels. She'd never really enjoyed anal sex with others, yet it was different with Wyler. They purchased a copy of the *Gourmet Guide to Lovemaking* and systematically tried everything. Many were variations of traditional positions.

"You're a goddess," Wyler said as he pulled out.

A flatulent fountain of frothy semen flowed down and

over her cunt lips.

That evening, they went to a strip club, and a beautiful woman wearing a cowboy hat and a set of pistols straddled Wyler. Later, he paid for a lap dance. He and Mireya sucked her nipples and took turns kissing her.

As they left the club, he took his future wife in his arms. "You're a *wild* woman, you know that?"

"I'm *your* wild woman."

———

Four months later, she received a postcard for the fiancée visa appointment, three days hence.

"Ay chingada," Micaela murmured when she heard the news. "Ciudad Juárez, What a shit hole."

"We're only going for as long as it takes to get the visa."

Juárez was the murder capital. Women disappeared on a daily basis. In fact, Mireya had read that there were 8.5 homicides per day, often as many as twenty. North Americans had built maquiladoras (factories) there, paying twenty dollars a week to workers. *NAFTA works out well for gringos*, she thought. *They bribe authorities, use México like a puppet. They pollute the air, foul rivers, and disregard worker safety.*

"Be careful. Promise you'll visit."

"I will. Maybe you can get a visa to see us."

"Good idea."

———

Mireya had second thoughts about marrying, living in a place where Mexicans were treated like dirty laundry. Yet, something inside said it was the right thing. She felt safe with Wyler. *We'll make it work.*

Wyler arranged to have her university transcripts analyzed stateside, so that her bachelor's degree would be recognized in the US. Her dream was deferred, yet still alive. Wyler was helping her to finish what she'd set out to do many years ago. Her English improved dramatically with Wyler, and she was confident she'd master it with time.

———

When they arrived in Ciudad Juarez, it was worse than they imagined. The city seemed to have given up hope. Trash lined the streets, graffiti covered walls, and the American Embassy was a drab and prison-like—not a place where dreams were issued.

Wyler wasn't allowed to accompany Mireya for her final interview. He sat outside on the hard outskirts of a broken fountain for two hours. Finally, she emerged, looking older than her thirty-one years, wearier than he'd ever seen her. She carried a folder in one hand and a chest X-ray in the other.

He took her into his arms, and she broke into sobs. "They treated me like a criminal. It was so humiliating," she said through tears.

"It's all over, we're together now."

They crossed the border into El Paso, Texas, to complete the process. Compared to Juarez, it was a cakewalk. A border guard at the final turnstile entry into the United States examined Mireya's visa one last time.

"You know," he chided, raising an appreciative eyebrow, "it doesn't say anywhere here that you gotta marry *this* guy. I'm available."

They shared a laugh, yet Wyler realized, in a single glance, he'd identified Mireya's sexual potential.

Bet she fucks like a tightly packed explosive, the officer was thinking.

———

They caught a puddle-jumper (small jet) to Las Vegas. Without leaving the airport, a final flight took them to San Diego. While waiting for the plane, Wyler played a few slots and actually won over two hundred dollars.

"What a great way to start our life!"

After the flight, a cab took them to Wyler's dusty Isuzu Trooper, parked at a pay-lot in San Ysidro. Someone had pissed on his front windshield. Once they'd eased out of heavy traffic, Mireya rested her head in his lap. She was exhausted. He stroked her short, dark hair.

"Mrs. Costner," Wyler said. "Has a nice ring to it."

"Mmm," she replied.

"Have I told you how much I love you?"

"A few times," she said, "but I don't mind hearing it again." She felt his cock throbbing against her head.

"What's happening, Mr. Costner?"

"An involuntary response."

"Mmm." Mireya unzipped him. "Concentrate on the road."

"I'll keep to the slow lane."

Mireya played her tongue on the sensitive tip until he was oozing precum. The musky man-smell faded once she wet his length.

"Jesus...ohhh shit." The sounds of licking and slurping filled his head with cotton. Wyler spurted on the I-5, twenty-five miles north of the border, and Mireya swallowed.

I must really love this man, she thought. She found a pack of gum in the glove compartment and put two sticks in her mouth, offering one to him. They stopped to refuel, use the bathroom, and she rinsed her mouth out in the sink.

At one-thirty the next morning, they arrived at the cabin. The rental sat off a lonely mountain road above the town of Atascadero, the Spanish word for deep mud.

Mireya's first impression was that it looked like an abandoned shack. The landlord was a strange, eccentric man, slow to respond when repair skills were needed. The windows were uncovered except for the bedroom, where Wyler taped a bedsheet. The refrigerator in the tiny kitchen sounded as if it were powered by crickets, and there was no heating. The bedroom had a tall freestanding closet that took up a third of the space. A queen-size air mattress lay on the floor with an alarm next to it.

They were exhausted. Mireya looked around her new home.

"Poor Wyler, you've been alone in this place for six months?"

"We'll find a better place."

"As long as I'm with you, we could live in a circus tent."

"Wanna see an elephant with an afro?" he asked.

"Sure."

Wyler unbuttoned his pants, pulled out his cock, and trumpeted."

Mireya giggled, grasped it, and tugged him into the bedroom.

———

They kissed beneath a single dangling light bulb, and Wyler removed her clothing one piece at a time, leaving her glasses on.

"God, I love your body."

She batted her eyes, "Thank you, sir."

"Crazy about you."

Wyler's cockhead looked like polished ivory. He sucked on a nipple.

"Mmmahhh," she moaned.

He kissed and licked his way down to her fragrant meadow and parted the soft, dark hair surrounding her lips. He flicked his tongue over the hood of her pearl.

The taste, the smell, and the texture of her snatch, he loved everything about it. *Magical*, he thought. *Velvety snugness, the way she cums*. She welcomed his cock like a happy birthday, an unexpected check, or student loan forgiveness. Fucking Mireya was always the best day of his life.

"Get inside," she demanded.

The air mattress squeaked. He sat up and lifted her knees, fascinated by how the outer lips surrounded his cockhead, the way her face softened as he pushed. A large black beetle was making its way up the bedroom wall, and he focused on it to keep from nutting.

Mireya moved her hips, and his concentration shattered. He buried himself to the hilt and cried out. "Ohhh shit, awww!" Beneath the dim bulb, his leavings emerged, glowing thickly. He surprised her by pulling out and bringing her off with his tongue and fingers. He tasted cum, marvelling that she'd swallowed it.

After working his tongue for five minutes, she lifted and twisted her head side-to-side. "Ay sí mi amor, ayyy!"

Wyler apologized for his early exit and volunteered to get toilet paper. Mireya pulled him back down.

"It's okay," she said, "don't leave."

They fell asleep in each other's arms. She draped one satiny leg over his hips and was soon breathing softly.

When they awoke, late-morning sun was streaming through the bedroom window. They made love beneath the natural light, and Wyler lasted until Mireya was exhausted and satisfied.

"Your turn," she panted.

Wyler looked into her face as he stormed back and forth, unloading violently.

They shared a shower with the frogs. Then they dressed and went into the tiny kitchen. A small gopher snake was curled up in front of the ancient, unusable stove.

Mireya gave a short scream.

"He's harmless." Wyler captured it and set it free outside.

"Sí, amor, we'll find another place."

There was a knock at the door. The landlord, Wally Brewster, said he needed to check a gas line leading to the stove.

It was an excuse to get a long look at Mireya. He suddenly acted friendlier than Wyler had ever known him to be. Wally's eyes stole glances at her as he pulled the stove away from the wall, pretending to inspect the connections.

So, this is the woman who caused such a stir. I can see why. The previous night, Wally Brewster leaned against the outer bedroom wall of the cabin to listen to their lovemaking. Cock in hand, he came when she did. *Long time since I had a woman. Boy, is she purdy.*

When Wally finished his fake inspection, he took Mireya's hand. "Welcome to the US. Anything you need, just ask. I'm usually around."

"Thank you, Mister—"

"Wally, just Wally."

"Thank you, Wally."

"Pleasure's all mine."

After he left, they returned to bed to catch up on sleep.

———

Wyler drove Mireya into Atascadero for lunch. It was a quaint inland coastal town. Buildings had a dress code, required by a city ordinance to be white, beige, or light blue. Streets were spacious, roads were smooth, and there were no speed bumps. Mireya asked why.

"Well, Dollface, in the US, everyone's tested before they're allowed to drive—a written test, eye exam, and a driving test, where an examiner gets in your car with you and grades how well you drive."

"México needs something like that. We pay for a license— one, three, or five years, and no tests."

"A recipe for disaster."

"I will need my license here."

"I'll teach you."

She held him. "So glad nothing happened to you when

Pedro came looking for you."

"Me too. He was completely obsessed. Can't blame him for that. He has a lot of time to think about it."

"I called Arturo to tell him."

"What did he say?"

"He blamed me."

"Is he a macho?"

"Yes, very much so."

"Me too."

"Machomenos," she joked.

"What's that?"

"Never mind."

"Oh yeah?" He tickled her until she told him.

"Okay, okay, stop! It means you're gay but still macho."

CHAPTER 17
WALLY

After breakfast, they cruised the streets, and Mireya's eyes were wide, like a child's. She was impressed by how organized everything was—no litter on the streets, double-parked cars taking up an entire lane, or facing the wrong way. There were clearly marked crosswalks, no street vendors, jugglers, fire-breathers, or beggars at stoplights.

"You have corruption?" She asked.

Wyler furrowed his brows as they crept along. "Like gum stuck under a table, hard to see, but it's there."

"México's the fifth most corrupt nation in the world."

"Why?"

"Education."

"Makes sense. Kids I teach at the Youth Authority are gang members, never really went to school."

"I was raised by my mother. We didn't have much, but I never considered being a criminal."

"Americans celebrate ignorance like a badge of honor." He pointed to a gym. "That's where I work out. They have aerobics, dancersize, and martial arts."

"I took Zumba in México."

"We'll get you signed up."

They passed an adult store. "Wanna check it out?"

"What is it?"

"An adult toy store."

"I've never been."

Wyler turned around, and they parked in back of the store. They went in holding hands. Immediately, a smiling young woman greeted them. She wore a nose ring, and her medium-length hair had a pink stripe.

"Anything I can help with, let me know."

"Thanks," Wyler said.

"*Toy* store?" Mireya narrowed her eyes.

"Yeah."

As they browsed the aisles, Mireya asked what certain items were for. She pointed to odd-shaped vibrators, two-way dildos, butt plugs, and various restraints. Wyler explained as best he could.

"Tried any of these?" she asked.

"Not really."

Mireya nudged him. "Liar."

Wyler smiled sheepishly. He pointed to a thick black dildo. "Ever had a lover like that?"

Mireya picked up the box. "Realistic, ten inches, two inches thick—exact replica of pornstar, Maxwell Steele. She looked at Wyler. "Too big, isn't it?"

"Wanna find out?"

"I'm a tiny woman."

"Curious?"

At this point in their relationship, Mireya wanted to please. Going to see the strippers had been her suggestion. New positions they tried from *The Gourmet Guide* were her idea. The black dildo reminded her that she was once black-curious. In México, black people were rare, mostly Cubans. In Pomona, there had been many, but limited English made her shy.

Once, on a walk to the grocery store, a handsome young black man kept pace. He spilled words so quickly she didn't understand, yet from his body language, it was clear what he wanted.

"You going to buy it?"

"Maybe." He picked out a small curved vibrator and a

blackout blindfold.

When they stood at the counter to pay, the girl said, "You'll want a good lubricant." She reached beneath the counter for a small tube. "Here's a free sample, works really well. Oh, and you'll need a triple-A for the vibrator."

"Thanks." Wyler bought batteries as well.

When they returned to the truck, Mireya noted, "She wasn't embarrassed."

"Gabachos can be pretty open-minded."

"In México, intellectuals are more likely to try new things."

"Let's head home and...?" He patted the bag, "Be intellectual."

"Grocery store first if you want to be fed tonight."

"Okay."

————

They shopped for fish taco ingredients. Along the way home, Mireya asked to stop at a second-hand store. She found a small lampstand with a drawer for the bedroom. When they returned, Wally was pruning the roses that grew in their front yard. He waved enthusiastically as they parked.

"Settling in?" he asked Mireya.

"Yes, thank you."

"Just a sec." He removed the thorns from the long stem of a yellow rose and handed it to her. "Yellow ones smell the best."

"That's sweet. I'll put it in water right now."

When they entered the house, Mireya looked around. "Curtains," she said. "Do you have any newspapers?"

Wyler showed her a stack he'd thought to use in the fireplace before Wally told him not to.

"Tape?"

Wyler found duct tape in a toolbox he kept in the bedroom closet. Mireya placed squares of newsprint over the living room windows. She doubled the sheet covering the bedroom window.

"This'll do for now."

"We won't be here much longer." Wyler waved the bag from the adult store. "Wanna try it on for size?"

"What if I really like it?"

"You'll want the real thing." He grew hard as he said it.

"How would you feel about that?" she teased.

"Pretty small."

"You're just right."

He opened the box, lifted the impressive black silicon shaft, and handed it to her. Her fingers wouldn't fit around it. She tested the tip with her tongue. "Yech!"

He read the box. "Says to wash in warm, soapy water before use."

Mireya removed the vibrator from the molded plastic container. It unscrewed from the back. She inserted a AAA battery and screwed it back on. The cap also controlled the intensity of the vibration. She turned it on and touched the tip.

"Really works."

"Never used one?"

She shook her head. "I'm sexually organic."

Wyler laughed. "Your English is getting so much better."

"Thanks. Wash that thing, and I'll get ready." Mireya unbuttoned her Levis, and slowly tugged them down.

Wyler hurried into the bathroom with the dildo. When he returned, Luca was naked on the air mattress. On the newspaper window covering above, the Yankees defeated the Red Sox six to three. She lifted her knees and spread. Wyler set the toys on the bed, removed his clothes in a rush, and lay on his side facing her. The first kiss connected them to a sexual power outlet..

Wyler kissed and licked his way down to her soft, beautiful nest. He separated her labia with his thumbs and lapped. "Mmm, you're so wet."

Mireya arched and groaned. "Ay si, right there baby."

Wyler knew that pleasure zones were located at or near the surface of the vagina, where most nerve endings can be found. He loved eating her pussy, the way it tasted, the way she smelled. He loved the texture of her lips, the feel of her clit on his tongue.

He grasped the vibrator, set it on low, and applied the curved tip to her clit.

"Huh! Ohhh, mmm."

When her hips began lifting, Wyler flipped the cap on the jelly tube to squeeze a good amount on the tip of the dildo and worked it over the length. He speeded up the vibrator and placed the cockhead, rubbing it up and down. She twisted with pleasure.

"Oyyy sí."

Wyler watched the inner labia surround the bulbous tip. He pushed.

"Huh!" Mireya gasped, her head lolling side-to-side. Lubricant gathered at the edges.

Slowly, down and in he pushed, lubricant making a crinkle sound as he progressed.

"Ooommm, huh-huh-huh, oyyy sí." She'd never felt so occupied. Deeper and deeper he pushed, the passage of the shaft making the sound of pasta stirred with a wooden spoon. "Huh!" He reached her terminus. "Ayyy."

Wyler was astonished that she'd accommodated nearly the entire length of Maxwell Steele's legendary cock. "Feel good, Dollface?"

"Mmm, ayyy sí." She was lost within the misty world that lies between reality and fantasy.

They'd played fantasy games when she lived in Playas, yet this was more intense. Wyler slowly pulled back and returned. "Wanna try the real thing, baby?" He kept the vibrator on her clit even though her hips were gyrating.

"Ayyy sí."

Wyler was lightheaded. The lips of her pussy yawned around the cock. He worked it steadily back and forth. Mireya circled her hips. The combination of Maxwell Steele's cock and the vibrator proved overwhelmingly delightful.

"Ohhh, baby." Mireya's voice deepened. She began trembling. "Ohhh baby, I'm gonna cum." She drew a deep breath. "Ohhh, guh!" Her ass lifted off the mattress, and she began thrashing. "Ay-ay-ay-ayyy!"

Several times, he lost his place with the vibrator. Mireya was delirious. She took control of the dildo, thrusting it all the way in — tap, tap, tapping, pulling back, and returning. Wyler sat back and watched.

She was a screeching hawk, a crooning seagull, falling into a contralto groan as her anus winked, her clit jumped, and her cunt lips spasmed around the thick shaft.

"Ahhh, I'm cumming again! Huh-huh-huh, ayyy!" Milky liquid emerged from around the dildo, soaking the mattress. "Uhnnn, huh-huh, uhnnn!" The tiny bedroom was filled with primitive, desperate sounds. She pulled the cock almost to the brink, and snaked it in, cumming again. Then she pulled the cock out, and sprayed Wyler.

He knew about women who occasionally squirted. He replaced the dildo with his cock. Mireya was stretched out so that he hardly felt her, yet he imagined a black man plying her, and spurted immediately.

She felt Wyler twitching and wrapped her legs around him.

"Yes baby, cum." She lifted to kiss his chest, inspiring another outpouring.

———

They lay exhausted in each other's arms. Her racing heart took time to normalize, and her breathing to soften. She was embarrassed by the squirting. It didn't happen regularly.

"Wowzers," Wyler managed to say.

"Sorry for the mess."

"That's the most erotic thing I've ever seen."

"Yeah?"

"To the world, you're one person, but to me, you're the world."

She kissed him. Never in her wildest dreams did she imagine finding such a man. He allowed self-discovery, celebrated her intellect, and inspired her to dream. She kissed him again.

"I love you," a kiss, "I love you," another kiss, "I love you," she moved the next kiss to his chest. Subsequent kisses migrated downward. She lapped his cock, jacked him, and used the vibrator on his frenulum until he shot a high arching spurt that found her face and tits.

———

When Wyler left for work the following day, Mireya studied math and wrote a list of chores to keep her busy. She covered the kitchen windows with newspaper and cooked enough to last three days. Then she cleaned the cabin and searched the phone book for universities where she could begin her studies, once her transcripts were approved, and she received a green card.

Wyler's shift kept him at the youth prison from two in the afternoon until ten. She eagerly awaited his return and had a late dinner waiting. Invariably, Wyler wanted her for dessert. There was a can of whipped cream in the refrigerator. That night, she planned to squirt it on her body and have him lick her clean. Then she'd use it on him.

———

At eight, the landlord came to the door. He was dressed nicely, freshly shaved, and wore cologne. He was trim, had muscular arms, and sported a greying goatee. He was pleasant enough, yet something was missing from his eyes — unfocused and distant at times.

"Hey, Mireya."

"Hi, Mr. Brewster."

"Just Wally. Brought these." He handed her a bouquet of fresh-cut roses. "I was trimming this afternoon, and thought, why waste these? "

"Very nice, thank you."

"Listen, if there's ever anything you need," He nodded vigorously. "Just ask."

"Thanks, but I can't think of anything right now." The hair on Mireya's neck began to rise, and a chill ran down her spine. *Creepy the way he looks at me.*

"Know you're just startin' out and all. Could lower the rent a bit if you wanna clean my house a couple times a week."

"We're trying to find something in town but—"

"You're leavin'?"

"Just looking."

"I can build on a couple more rooms."

"That's kind but—"

"I've really enjoyed havin' you around, you and Wyler. Those flowers aren't half as purdy as you are."

Blood drained from her face. She knew she had to turn the conversation.

"I...that's nice of you to say." She checked her watch. "Wyler's on his way home, I'd better check on dinner."

"Doesn't he get off at about ten?" Wally's eyes clouded for a moment.

"Said he'd be earlier tonight."

"Alright then, just came to give you those."

"Thanks, Wally."

"Have a good evenin'." He turned to leave, then stopped. "Creative, those curtains you put up. Pick some out in town, I'll pay for 'em."

"Okay."

As soon as he was gone, Mireya locked the door. When Wyler arrived, she told him everything.

"Damn. He's not playin' with a full deck. You shouldn't be here alone anymore."

———

The following day was Friday, and Wyler considered taking a personal day off to hunt for apartments.

"It can wait until the weekend," she advised.

"Then I'll drop you at the city library or something so you won't be alone here."

"I'll spend the afternoon looking for apartments."

"Good. But where will you wait until ten?"

"The gym is open until eleven. You can pick me up there."

"Genius." He kissed her. "Be there by ten-fifteen."

Wyler dropped her off at the library, and she searched the papers for rentals. There was nothing available. As planned, he picked her up from the gym. After her dance-aerobics class, she used the stationary bike, then wandered around experimenting with various exercise machines to kill time.

Two men eagerly volunteered to show her how they worked, subtly interviewing her at the same time. She politely answered their queries and followed the advice.

"Like your accent," one said. "Never been to Mexico, but it must be beautiful," said another.

"Ever been to the new microbrewery?" asked the boldest. "They have good food too. My treat if you'd like to go after your workout."

She kindly fended off each approach, yet she had to admit she liked the attention. Since she'd lived in the US, she'd been isolated.

When Wyler arrived, she hugged him, and the others slinked away.

———

On Saturday, Mireya was in the kitchen finishing up a casserole. Wally had recently installed a new oven. She needed a few other ingredients, and Wyler offered to get them.

"Come with me," he said.

"There are things in the oven."

"Got something for your oven."

"Later, Mister Costner."

"Be right back." He kissed her and backed the Trooper out until he could turn on the gravel road leading down to the main highway.

———

Wally peeked from a mini-blind as Wyler drove away. He splashed his face with cologne, swallowed hard, and went to look again. Mireya took a bag to the outside trash can and returned to the cabin. She wore a knee-length Mexican skirt and an Indian blouse, and he thought she looked exotic.

———

While Wyler was shopping, he ran into Andy, a guard from work. They stood in front of a wine display and chatted. He asked how Mireya was adjusting to life in the US.

"She's doing fine. We're waiting for the green card and work permit."

"Still livin' in the boonies?"

Wyler smiled and nodded. "Trying to find a new place. Cabin we're in is ready to collapse, and the landlord's weird."

"Yeah?"

"Fuckin' Wally. He went to see Mireya yesterday when I wasn't there, and creeped her out."

"Last name Brewster?"

"Yeah."

"Listen, Wyler, if it's who I think it is, you oughta get outta there. He did five years at the Atascadero State Hospital, and he's a registered sex offender. There's a website where you can find out where pervs live. I've got two kids, so I looked it up. Wally's mom died a few years back and left him that mountain property."

"Christ." He turned to leave. "Thanks, Andy."

"Need help movin' outta there, give me a holler. I gotta truck." He took out a pen from his shirt pocket and wrote his number on a receipt. "Here you go."

"Appreciate it, Andy." Wyler tore a piece of the same paper and wrote his information.

———

Mireya stepped into the shower after Wyler left. Immediately, two frogs escaped from around the nozzle and clung to the wall. She had to make it fast because the water heater was only good for ten minutes. There were so many holes in the cabin, and some she hadn't noticed, like the shoulder-level gap in the wood above the steel shower stall.

Wally had a full view of Mireya. He watched her rinse before soaping, then she lathered her tits, her dark thatch, the crack of her ass. When she shampooed her hair, her breasts lifted. His cock was in his hand, and he sweated as he tugged at it. *Not yet*, he thought. He zipped up, went to the front door, and used his key. Silently, he crept into the bedroom.

They fuck like rabbits, he thought. He looked at the inflatable mattress, her clothes laying there. He picked up the underwear and raised it to his nose. The shower stopped, and he heard the plastic curtain pulled aside. *Shit*! There was no time to escape through the front door, and the cabin didn't have a back one. *Damn, she takes short showers. The closet*, he thought.

Mireya dried off and hung the towel over the curtain rod. She padded into the bedroom, drying her hair, and paused at the full-length mirror nailed to the closet door.

"Mireya!" Wyler's voice filled the cabin.

"Bedroom!" She called.

Wally began trembling. *Sonofabitch!* He felt dizzy and

began sweating profusely.

Wyler hurried in. "Get dressed. We're out'a here."

"What's wrong?"

"Bumped into Andy from work. Told me Wally's a nut-case."

"What?"

"Later. Leave everything. Get dressed, Dollface. We'll stay in a hotel until we find another place. Andy says he'll help us move. He's got a truck."

Mireya quickly stepped into her panties and finished dressing."

"Fuckin' asshole," Wyler murmured.

They left the bedroom together. Wally was frustrated and furious. If he'd remembered his big folding knife, he would've made short work of Wyler and taken his time with Mireya.

He was stock-still until the Trooper pulled away. Then he crept from the closet to explore. When he drew back a drawer in the nightstand, he found the vibrator, dildo, and a tube of jelly beneath pairs of socks. He drew down his pants, applied the vibrator to his cock, and recalled how fine Mireya looked in the shower. After a minute, he grunted and spurt into the palm of his hand. He shivered, used the comforter on the air mattress to wipe with, and took the dildo back to his house with him.

Wally found a notebook and wrote a rental advertisement: FOR RENT, CHARMING MOUNTAIN COTTAGE, QUIET, CLOSE TO TOWN, $400 PLUS FIRST AND LAST.

Find someone like her, he thought.

———

Mireya was in luck. After checking into a Motel 6, Wyler dropped her downtown before he left for work. She read about an apartment for rent in a free EZ-AD, called, and was able to view it. The landlady was in her late seventies, and she greeted Mireya with grandmotherly charm. The apartment was perfect —

one bedroom, a living room, a small kitchen, and a tiny outdoor patio.

The following morning, Wyler put down a deposit and paid first and last month's rent. As planned, he picked up his stuff with Andy's help. Wally shuffled over as Wyler loaded the Trooper. There wasn't much, and with both vehicles, it would require one trip.

"Sorry to see you go. Where you headed?"

"San Luis Obispo," he lied, teeth clenched in anger.

"Should stay until the end of the month," he said, alluding to the rent.

"That's okay."

"Need to do an inspection before returnin' your deposit. Give me your address, and I'll send a check."

"Keep it."

"San Luis Obispo. Nice town." Wally scratched his beard. "Expensive as hell."

Andy stood quietly with his arms folded. They were loaded, ready to go.

"Alright then." Wally turned to go and stopped. "You left some stuff behind. If you want, I'll load it in my pickup and drive it over for you."

"Keep it."

"Alright then."

Wyler turned away and got into the Trooper..

"Vamanos," Andy said with finality.

As they pulled out of the driveway, Wally stood watching until they distanced themselves down the road.

CHAPTER 18
FAVION

When Wyler returned home from work that night, Mireya was sitting with the landlady, sharing a bottle of white wine. Her name was Ethel. She was a widow, and they soon knew her as Grandma Ethel. Ethel and Mireya were laughing when Wyler came in. He joined them for a glass. Obviously, Ethel had a deep affection for Mireya. It was good to see Mireya safe, relaxed, and happy.

The following day was Saturday, and they spent the day unpacking, shopping for furniture, and hooking their new television up to cable. Wyler also purchased a desktop computer, floppy disks, and connected to the internet. He was amused by the strange sound it made when it activated—Shhhhhh, bigong bigong! He'd been writing on a Sears SR1000 electric typewriter for years. He found a desk and a decent office chair at a secondhand store.

Ironically, when they turned on the television, the evening news with Dan Rather was on. He was talking about a Canadian man from Quebec arrested for drug dealing:

"Canadian Mounties arrested Byron Smythe early this morning at his mountain estate, where he is reported to have headed the largest drug-dealing, sex trafficking operation in Canada."

Mireya's mouth flew open. "I know that guy!"

The TV showed police escorting a handcuffed, dour-faced Byron to a police cruiser.

"What? How in the world?"

"I was in Canada with a friend. We met in Quebec."

They watched in silence as the news report continued.

"Here's what we know so far," said the reporter, his breath fogging as he stood at the gates of the castle. Police are keeping the area locked down until the investigative team arrives, but sources say at least six greenhouses have been discovered, located on the forest property behind this imposing palace." He swept his hand theatrically. Then he provided a brief history of the castle before giving updated information.

"Just in, police found twenty-six women living in a large guest house behind this property, believed to be victims of human trafficking."

A split screen showed the anchorman shaking his head in disgust. "We'll share more as this breaking story develops."

Wyler turned off the television and spent the next hour listening to Mireya's experience. She left Richard out, as well as the black-out night in the castle.

"I stayed to myself while Lourdes was with him."

"This is the makings of a novel." He went to the desk to retrieve a notepad.

"Don't be silly."

"I'm not. Tell me more, I'll turn it into a book."

"No, I want to forget about it. I hope he rots in jail."

Wyler made a note to himself to read all the news feeds he could find about Byron Smythe. "You've lived a remarkable life. I'd like to write about it. What's your earliest memory?"

"Alone, scared in an apartment in Mexico City. My mother worked cleaning houses, and couldn't afford daycare."

"Jesus. How old were you?"

"Three."

They sat on a worn couch facing each other with their legs entwined, sipping tequila. Mireya felt more comfortable talking about herself after a few shots. Sharing her story helped sort out who she was and which direction she was headed. It was a rollercoaster chronicle, and she happily recognized that because of Wyler, it was more ups than downs.

She recalled the revolving door of boyfriends her mother entertained, the teacher in sixth grade who tried to kiss her, the award she'd received as the top student in ninth grade, Valedictorian her senior year in high school, working in a jacket factory with her cousin Chela, who was always pregnant. Mireya was impressed with her life as she told it, clarifying certain aspects. She remembered the university, having her first real boyfriend when she was twenty-one.

"What about your first sexual experience?"

"Enrique. We were together for nearly a year."

"Why'd you split?"

"He wanted an ordinary life — marriage, kids, to give up my dreams."

"How old were you?"

"Twenty-two."

"Pretty old to be a virgin."

"Had my reasons."

"Where did it happen?"

"An empty classroom at the university late one night."

"Academic fuck. I would expect nothing less."

She giggled. "We were doing Algebra."

He made some notes. "After Enrique?"

The mathematical part of her brain was able to provide a precise chronology of events — battles with her mother, the long-distance program, and René. Other lovers, including Carmen, Antonio, Sebastián, and Peter in Visalia.

"How did you end up with that guy?"

"He was nice, but possessive."

"Yeah? Tell me about it."

"Mmm."

"Was he good in bed?"

"I don't want to think about it."

"Okay. Can't wait to meet your friend, Carmen."

"I'll bet you can't."

So many lovers, about two a year. Wyler wanted details, yet even with tequila, she was reticent. Toward the end, his questions evolved into a game.

"Who was your favorite lover?"

"Hmm."

"Hard to decide, eh? Ever been with a black man?"

"Not yet."

"Is that a warning or a request?"

"Do I need permission?" she teased.

"The dildo got lost in the move somehow. But you want the real deal."

"Mmm, it might be fun."

"Gotta friend at work named Vern—tall, good looking, green eyes. Think he's originally from Jamaica."

"Want me to meet him?"

A lump formed in Wyler's throat. It was exciting to think about, a mixture of jealousy and trepidation. *A safe fantasy*, he thought.

"Nice guy, works as a teacher's aide."

"What if he wants me?"

His heart was pounding. "No question, he will. I'll watch you with him."

"I'd be nervous with you there."

"I'll listen in the next room."

"Too close."

"From the outside window."

"We'll find a motel, and you can wait at home."

"You'd be filled with his cum." He set down his pad and pen to kiss her. Precum was soaking through his pants.

"Mmm."

"Vern would fuck you with his big cock over and over."

"Ay sí, ahhh."

Their clothes were soon strewn, and their love-making became a desperate frenzy.

———

A few weeks later, Wyler and Mireya were married in a simple, civil ceremony at the courthouse in Paso Robles, with Grandma Ethel as their witness. He slipped an emerald stone ring over her wedding finger, and they shared a long kiss.

"It's beautiful," she gazed at the ring.

"Has a built-in alarm that beeps when another man gets too close."

"So, I won't wear it when I see Vern."

"It'll beep if you take it off."

"Where are you going for your honeymoon?" Ethel asked.

"To our island apartment," Wyler said. " I need to build up more vacation time for a real one."

"I won't come knocking," She grinned.

———

A king-size mattress was delivered just as they returned to the apartment. They placed a fitted bottom sheet and fumbled out of their clothes.

They lay on their sides, Mireya's leg hooked over him, his cock pulsing at her entrance.

"First time as man and wife," Wyler said.

"Mmm, think it will feel different?"

"I'll have to give up my other girlfriends."

"Very funny, Costner. Want to spend your first night on the couch?"

He scooted so that his cockhead was hidden beneath the outer tuffs of her cunt hair. Wyler didn't mention that his divorce was only finalized the day before.

Mireya kissed her husband. It didn't feel different, yet

something had changed. *My husband. Faithful in sickness and in health.* For a moment, she was apprehensive, then her body relaxed as Wyler pushed inside.

They fucked on and off until mid-morning, getting up for potty-breaks. They fucked until they were exhausted. Wyler had the next day off. After breakfast they fucked again. Her inner labia was visible by then.

"You almost fucked me to death. I smell like an aquarium."

"Shower time."

In the shower, Wyler soaped her tits, lathered her pussy, and scrubbed her back with a soft washcloth. Mireya cleaned him too, then squatted to take his cock into her mouth.

Yeah, thought Wyler, *Married life.*

Married life—Wyler worked, Mireya waited, and weekends were spent exploring the coastline, hiking local mountains, and fucking—lots of fucking. They fucked in the Trooper at a lookout point in Big Sur, beneath a blanket hidden by a beach dune—they fucked off-trail in national parks. They fucked so much that Mireya developed honeymoon cystitis, and her cunt swelled inside out. The medication took a week to bring things back to normal.

In between fucking, Mireya spent time being exercising, being a housewife and hanging out with Grandma Ethel. She was waiting for a work permit, which would eventually be followed by a green card. Then she'd get on with her life. She was feeling antsy.

Ethel told Mireya stories about her strange, secretive husband who died five years earlier. He'd worked for thirty years as a building inspector.

"Max mostly kept to himself. He was kind of a strange man. We were married for almost forty years, and I feel as if I never really knew him. Our daughter lives in Santa Rosa. She rarely visits. Kids—they grow up and leave the nest," Ethel explained.

"She doesn't call?"

"Once in a while."

"How sad," Mireya said. Slow tears emerged from Ethel's eyes. "Sorry, Grandma." She hugged her and felt the old woman's body trembling.

Ethel pulled away, "It's okay, that's just life. Want some wine?"

Mireya was disturbed by the callousness of life in the US. She saw that North Americans were missing something. Their lives were full on the surface, empty inside.

———

A month into marriage, her university transcripts were returned with reciprocity, which meant her BA in Mathematics was valid in the US. She received a work permit and applied to a Master's at Cal Poly in San Luis Obispo. While she waited to hear from them, she looked for a job. Bill Clinton was the new President, and the economy was humming because of the tech industry in Silicon Valley. It was a hopeful time.

Wyler and Mireya frequented the gym. He'd always stayed fit and had attended university on a baseball scholarship. The past ten years, he trained and competed in a dozen triathlons and four marathons. Lately, he was content to lift weights three days a week. Serious training took a lot of time, and he no longer had a competitive need. He was forty-one, married to a beautiful Mexican woman ten years younger. Mireya took dancercise classes, and rode a stationary bike as Wyler sweated out an hour and a half with weights, situps, and a rowing machine.

She rarely asked Wyler to do anything in the house unless there was a minor repair. Yet, one morning, she asked him to cut and clean papaya for a fruit salad. She walked to a small grocery nearby with a bag to buy other fruits she'd need. When she returned an hour and a half later, the papaya was untouched, and Wyler was on the internet looking at sports news. She held onto her anger, yet it seethed.

Later, she asked him to get dry clothes from the community laundry room.

"Okay, in a minute." He kept pursuing the internet. When the fruit salad was ready, she went out to the laundry to retrieve the clothes. Then she dumped the basket on the bed and folded them. Anger bubbled closer to the surface.

After lunch, he got up to shower before work without putting his dishes in the sink or waiting for her to finish eating.

"Where are you going?"

"To get a shower."

"You don't want to sit with your wife until she's finished?"

"Sorry." He sat down.

"No, it's okay, go get your shower, I'm almost done."

"You okay?"

"I'll be fine." She got up and began collecting dishes to wash.

"Did I do something?"

She whirled around. "You did nothing. I asked you to do a few simple things: clean the papaya, get the dry laundry. That's fine, I'm not working."

"Mireya, I'm sorry."

Is this just the beginning? She went for a walk. When she returned, he'd already left for work. There was an apology note on the kitchen table:

DollFace,
Sorry. I was selfish. Please forgive me. I love you. See you tonight.
XOXO

The apology made her angry, too.

———

Three months later, Mireya had a morning appointment for a physical. After getting a work permit, she applied for a teacher's aide position at Atascadero High School, something to keep her busy until she was accepted into a Master's program. The job required a recent physical. Grandma Ethel recommended Dr. Reyes because she'd heard good things about him.

A middle-aged receptionist named Rita greeted Mireya at 11:30 that morning. "Dr. Reyes will be right with you."

As if on cue, the door opened.

"Mireya?"

"Yes," she stood, and the doctor greeted her with a handshake.

"I'm Dr. Reyes. Please come in."

His name was Favion Reyes, and he was a handsome Cuban immigrant. Smiling broadly, he led her into an exam room. His hair was cropped short, and his face was dark brown, with well-defined cheekbones and nicely shaped lips. He was trim, fit-looking.

She immediately felt comfortable because he spoke Spanish. They chatted for a few minutes, and it felt good to speak her language.

Dr. Reyes handed her a green paper gown. "Please change into this, and I'll be back shortly."

Five minutes later, Reyes arrived with her chart. As he examined Mireya, he asked about life in México and her motivation for coming to California.

She explained. Dr. Reyes listened intently as he examined her heart, blood pressure, then shared his path — a homemade raft with forty others to Florida when he was a boy. After hearing this, Mireya was more determined than ever to study mathematics and eventually earn a doctorate.

Dr. Favion Reyes explained that most of his Latin patients

worked in vineyards or cleaned houses. He was impressed with Mireya's plans. She was passionate, gesturing with her hands, moving her body when she talked. He liked how she pursed her lips as she pondered a response. *Expressions speak volumes*, he thought.

"How do you like it here so far?" He asked, taking the gown down over her shoulders to feel for lumps in her breasts."

"Anxious to start school again."

"Where will you be going?"

"I applied for a Master's at Cal-Poly."

"Ah, a very nice school. You'll study math?"

"Yes."

"Impressive." He pushed his fingers in circles around her breasts.

Favion couldn't help admiring Mireya's tall, brown nipples. He listened to her lungs through a stethoscope, noticing an increase in heart rate when he leaned close.

"Do you exercise?" he asked.

She nodded, "Dancercise, the stationary bike."

"Good. Your lungs are clear, heart rate, and blood pressure. Normal. You appear to be in tip-top shape." *Indeed.*

She smiled.

He asked her a few rhetorical questions from the chart to double-check, then he set it down.

"We'll do a pelvic exam now to check for abnormal growths or irregularities." He pulled the gown back over her shoulders.

"Okay."

"Lie back and relax." He guided her feet into metal stirrups.

She lifted to allow him to pull the green gown higher. He'd seen thousands of vaginas, all different, like fingerprints. Mireya's was beautiful. He pushed on her lower stomach.

"Any pain or discomfort?"

"Nope."

"Good." He slipped on a latex glove and applied lubricant to his first and second fingers.

"This will feel cold at first." He slipped them slowly into Mireya's pussy. As he curled the fingers upward, she took a sudden breath. "Are you and your husband planning a family?"

"He had a vasectomy before we met."

"Oh, I see. How long have you been married?" His fingers explored the inner lining, then probed deeper.

"Huh! Less than five months."

"Miss México?"

"Very much." Mireya looked away and shivered as his thumb rested on the hood of her clitoris. Then he slowly slipped his fingers out.

Dr. Reyes removed his glove and jotted information on her chart, feeling an unprofessional knot in his throat. He conducted a pap smear, and the exam was concluded. *Keep your mind on work*, he scolded himself.

"Have you been back to Cuba?"

"No, the US embargo makes it complicated. I'm hoping this new President will lift it."

"It's not a problem for Mexicans." Mireya said, "North Americans leave from there all the time. When they arrive, they ask immigration not to stamp their passports."

"I didn't know that."

"Immigration just puts a blank piece of paper over the passport entry page, then stamps it."

Favion laughed. "So in essence, they're helping Americans travel there."

Mireya nodded and smiled, "There's always a way around the system."

He laughed again. "Okay, Mireya, get dressed, and I'll take these samples to the lab. Be back in a few."

As Mireya slipped into her underwear, her pussy tingled.

It hadn't escaped her attention that Favion's interest was more than professional. The thought made her shiver, and a pleasant warmth ensued.

As she slipped on her shoes, Dr. Reyes returned.

"Everything looks great. Lab results will be ready by tomorrow after three."

"Thank you. Should I call before I pick them up?"

"I have your number." He gestured to her patient chart. "I'll call *you*."

"Okay."

"This is off-topic, but do you know anything about computers?"

"A little bit. My husband has one I've been playing around with."

"Do you have a printer?"

"Yes."

"My printer won't connect with the computer. Could you maybe take a look?"

She pursed her lips and nodded. "Sure."

"When you come for your results."

"Alright. Where is it?"

"My house, less than ten minutes away."

"Okay. I'll see you after three."

"Perfect."

After making a copayment at the reception desk, Mireya walked home, still tingling. When she arrived, Wyler was ready for work. He wasn't allowed to bring anything inside the youth prison but lunch in a paper bag.

"Wards make weapons out of anything," he explained. "There's a story about a kid rolling up a newspaper tight, and peeing on it. After it dried, he sharpened one end on the concrete floor to make a spear."

"I don't like you working there," Mireya said.

"Don't worry, Dollface. We carry little beepers on our belts with pins. It sends a distress signal to guards, and they come with pepper spray and wooden clubs."

"That's not very comforting."

Wyler kissed her, "How was your appointment with the doctor, what was his name?"

"Reyes. He's Cuban and speaks Spanish. Lab results will be ready tomorrow, but he thinks I'm healthy. He asked me to help him connect his computer to a new printer."

"Aren't there techs for that?"

"I guess not."

"Mmmm."

"What?"

"Is he married?"

"He didn't say."

"Where's the printer?"

"His house."

"Look, Dollface, you're beautiful, exotic, and you share the language. I'm sure he wants you to connect *something*, but I doubt it has anything to do with a printer."

"Give me your beeper if it'll make you feel better."

Wyler laughed, then turned serious. "Remember what I said. When's your printer date?"

"It's not a date, Costner. Tomorrow afternoon."

"See you tonight, love you." He kissed her and walked out the front door.

Mireya smiled after him. *Is he right?* She thought of the papaya incident and grew angry again.

———

After Wyler left for work the next afternoon, Mireya had a few hours before her meeting. She cleaned the house, did laundry, cooked the evening meal, and showered..

Her life had been a constant struggle to stay in school.

Obsessive men tried to quash her dreams. She loved Wyler. Any misgivings would eventually be resolved once she was where she wanted to be.

Mireya dressed in a form-fitting pair of Pepe jeans, paired with an indigenous blouse from Oaxaca. She wore red lipstick to match red-seed earrings and a pair of red sandals. Checking herself in the mirror, she felt presentable. She dabbed Coco Chanel behind her ears and walked to the clinic.

When she arrived, the receptionist handed her test results. "Doctor's finishing up with a patient. He'll be right out to discuss your results."

Mireya sat in the lobby and picked up a copy of *Parents Magazine*. Thumbing through, she saw mothers and fathers smiling with beautiful children. There were times when she thought that having a child would be nice. Wyler's children visited every other weekend, and they arranged bedding in the living room for them. Visalia was a two-hour drive, and they stayed in a cheap hotel when visiting the kids there. She always breathed a sigh of relief when they were safely back in Atascadero.

Wyler's children were sweet. Lydia was six, and Owen was nine. They loved going to the beach in Pismo and seashell shopping in Morro Bay. The water was so cold that Wyler purchased surf-suits. Although she knew how to swim, Mireya didn't enjoy the frigid ocean or the feeling that there were living things she couldn't see swimming all around.

Sometimes they drove to Coalinga, halfway to Visalia, to pick up the children or drop them off with Wyler's ex. Her name was Karen, and she didn't give the time of day to Mireya. Sometimes she arrived with her new boyfriend in tow, a Wal-Mart manager in Visalia. Mireya rarely asked questions about Wyler's previous marriage. Karen's attitude explained a lot. Her lips were tight, eyes narrowed. Yet, Mireya knew there were always two sides to a story. *If he wants to tell me, I'll listen, but I won't ask.*

Favion came into the reception area, interrupting Mireya's thoughts.

"Hi Mireya." He took her hand. "Let's have a look at your lab results."

Mireya handed him the folder, and he sat close to her, perusing the values for blood and urine. Then he smiled and handed them back.

"Estás muy saludable," he reported. "When do you start your job?"

"Next week," she replied.

"Teacher's aide?"

"Yes."

"Overqualified, aren't you?"

"I don't have a teaching credential. Education is a business here."

"That's true. But once you finish the Master's, you can teach at a college."

"Mmm," she nodded.

"You'll get there, I'm sure of it. Let's be off, shall we?" He gestured toward the exit. "Hasta mañana, Rita," he said to the receptionist.

"Have a good evening, doctor." She stared after them, secretly wishing she were the one walking toward his red BMW.

Favion took out his key fob and opened the passenger door for Mireya. As she entered, he admired the perfect curve of her ass. Then he settled into the driver's seat and swiveled his head.

"You look lovely," he said as she settled into the leather seat. "Where's your top from?"

"Oaxaca."

"I have patients from there."

Mireya stared out the windshield, trying to drown Wyler's

warnings.

They drove up a hill and turned down a private street lined with impressive homes. Dr. Reyes' house was at the end of a cul-de-sac, a two-story Mediterranean with a fountain in front.

"You live here alone?" Her question would make things much clearer.

"Yes."

"Never married?"

"Finished med school less than five years ago. There's been little time for romance. But work is starting to ease up now."

"It's a huge house."

"Bought it when interest rates were low." He parked in the driveway and hurried to open her door. "An investment."

Other questions came into her head, yet never made it past her lips. He used a keypad next to the front door to disarm the security system and ushered her into a spacious, well-appointed family room. The floors were Mexican tile. Beyond was a large kitchen filled with light from the bay windows, and hallways that led to other rooms.

"Glass of wine, Tequila?" He gestured to a wooden corner bar.

"No thanks."

"Printer's upstairs," he gestured.

He put a hand on her back as they walked up. They passed three bedrooms before arriving at the office. A desktop computer was centered on a large mahogany desk facing another bay window, with a panoramic view of an oak grove below. The office was furnished with a tan leather sofa, a matching loveseat, end tables, and built-in bookshelves lining an entire wall.

Favion turned the computer on. Then he peered over her shoulder as she worked from a high-backed office chair.

"Sorry, forgot to log in." He reached over her to tap on the keyboard.

Mireya was glad he no longer had a stethoscope pressed to her heart. His cologne and his proximity made her pulse quicken.

She easily found a window that allowed the addition of a printer. All that was required was the name and style of the printer. Clickity, clackity, clack, very simple. *Hard to believe he couldn't figure this out.*

"Do you have an Email account?" he asked.

"Haven't set that up yet."

"I use Hotmail. I'll give you my user address and we can write. It's free."

"Okay."

Favion leaned into her as she worked. His closeness gave her dizzying notions. After a few minutes, she printed a test page. He began kneading her shoulders. *Where's this going?* Logic asked. *Papaya,* libido answered. She wondered why logic surrendered control to desire so easily. *Wyler warned me.*

"There," she announced, as the printer buzzed and spit out the page.

"You made it look easy," he continued, massaging her shoulders. "Thank you so much."

Mireya stood and pushed the chair in. When she turned, he was inches away. He lifted a hand to her shoulder and squeezed. His other hand went to her face, and his eyes softened.

"I've a confession."

Mireya's traitorous body was already guessing what it was. *Papaya,* she thought.

"You're intoxicating."

"I'm married." Trying unsuccessfully to make it sound like a rebuke.

"Yeah." He smiled, took her by the hands, and kissed them one at a time.

"What're you thinking?" Mireya asked in a quavering voice.

"About how natural it is for two Pisano's to enjoy an afternoon together.

"Quieres follar. (You want to fuck.)"

Favion's eyes flew open. Then he slowly nodded and pulled Mireya into his arms. The first kiss was short, speculative, begging for definition. Mireya pulled away and put her hands flat against his chest. Rules had to be in place before caution was blown away in the winds of passion.

"Let's be clear, " she said breathlessly. He kissed her, and their tongues slipped together. Her body relaxed into his. "Two Pisanos." He kissed her again. "Enjoying an afternoon."

"Mmm."

He led her to his bedroom. Drapes were open, and light spilled over a king-size bed covered with an emerald green comforter. A giant oak stood witness. He found the catch to her bra and lifted her blouse.

"Qué hermosa," he whispered into her ear before bending to suck.

Mireya ran a hand over his hair and sighed. *Papaya.* Favion's tongue circled. *My wild nature.* Trying to change it was proving impossible. She toed off her sandals and unbuttoned her Pepe jeans. He pulled the blouse over her head and dove hands beneath the waistband of her panties, pulling them down along with her jeans. Mireya stepped and kicked them away.

"So beautiful," he whispered.

Mireya helped him out of his clothes, and they stepped back to admire each other. Her eyes rested on his cock, and her mouth opened with astonishment. Favion's staff was long, dark, thick, throbbing with life. *Maxwell Steele*, she thought.

Mireya kissed his chest, trapping a nipple with her front teeth. A shiver ran down his spine. She pushed him to sit on the bed and kneeled before him, grasping a pole of muscle that pulsed with every beat of his heart. She licked the broad tip, and a cobweb of pre-emergent stretched between her tongue and his beautiful staff. She painted down and up, pausing at the sensitive frenulum.

"Ssssahhh, oh yeah, mmm." Favion watched as she licked. "Oh baby, mmm."

After a few minutes, he pulled her onto the bed and guided her onto her back. Kneeling between her uplifted knees, he kissed the soft skin of her tummy, then dragged his tongue down.

"Huh-huh-huh!" Mireya was panting.

He found her clit with his tongue and flicked there, slipping two fingers inside her humid cunt.

"Oyyy si, eso se siente bien!"

He darted over her tiny almond sliver until she was ready to burst. Then he sat up and scooted forward. His cock lay heavily over her slit, and he rubbed its length back and forth over it.

"Huh-huh-huh! Ohhh god," Now he was sucking her tits again, trapping a nipple between his front teeth. She dug her heels into his ass, trying to pull him inside.

"Get in there," she pleaded."

"Bella diosa," he said, shifting so that his helmet was between her pink inner labia. Mireya gasped as he pushed, stretching her pussy on its journey down, down, in, in. Her pleasure was cataclysmic, and she climaxed immediately.

"Ayyy sí, ayyy!" She arched and lifted to meet him. Her cuntlips closed together with each titanic contraction.

"Oy mi vida," he whispered hoarsely. "Do you like this?"

"Huh," Mireya gasped when he withdrew, groaning appreciatively when he returned. "Ahhhmmm, oy si, me gusta." Another climax was approaching.

He stopped abruptly. "Wait...don't...move." He shut his eyes tightly. "Nnnn, no-no-no, wait...." A slow, steady stream of semen flowed. Favion clenched his ass to avoid a full ejaculation.

Mireya wanted to churn, lunge, and pepper him with

kisses, yet she waited. She recalled several lovers who spurted by kissing her. *Want him to fuck me into oblivion.* Briefly, she thought of protection. *Russian Roulette with this incredible cock.*

After his recovery, Favion pulled back slowly and returned deeply. Air was forced out, accompanied by thick globules of spunk clinging to his shaft.

Mireya's head lolled to the side. "Ayyy huh, oyyy sí!"

He cupped his hands beneath her knees and lifted to watch his gleaming staff slide in and out of her snugness. The top brushed back and forth against her clitoris. Semen swirled in the thick hair surrounding her brown outer fronds. He loved the way she moved, the sound of her voice—deep groans when he tapped her cervix door, high staccato notes as he pumped back and forth. She smelled of perfume and sex.

"Oh!" her warning cry. "Ohhh!" deeper, more desperate, "Huh! I'm cumming!" followed by a long, ragged gulp of air.

When she started bucking, Favion didn't move at all. She sent him in and out of her with lifted hips. Her voice was crenulated with passion, lost in time.

"Ohmmm, huh-huh-huh, Ohhh god, ohhh god….ayyy! Mireya's cunt rippled with a strong continuous series of spasms. "Ay-ay-ay, ayyy!" Her whole body shuddered as her pussy contracted, and her head thrashed side-to-side.

Her orgasms gripped so firmly that Favion had difficulty pushing through. *Never felt a woman cum like this.* A delicious feeling rose deep inside his bowels, flowing into his nut sack. It was time to join her.

"Oh baby…Ohhh, baby!" He pumped furiously. "Ooos!" He plunged to the hilt, growling and releasing. "Aw-aw awww, Jesus!" His balls twitched, lifted, and compressed. "Uhnnn, awww!"

Sperm lacquered her insides, escaping from the tight seal. It marched down the channel of her ass to gather at her anus, before trickling in long, viscous strands to the comforter. And still, he was jumping inside, adding fresh spurts.

She added her own mysterious juices into the mix. When she thought he'd finished, he shivered again.

Exhausted, he collapsed and gasped, as if he'd run a hundred-meter dash. After catching his breath, he kissed her slowly, deeply, as if life depended on it. She caressed his shoulders, kissed his shoulder, and neck.

His mouth rested against her ear. "Let's stay like this forever."

"Mmm," she responded.

"Never want this feeling to leave."

"Mmm," she was unable to form words. He was still inside.

"Mmm, is that all you have to say?"

"Mmm." She felt him slipping out, and clamped her legs tightly. "Don't go yet."

———

Favion stayed. Size gave him the option. Her tongue went to work in his mouth, teasing, sucking.

"I love your cock," she whispered in his ear.

"It's found home."

She kissed him again, teasing with her tongue, nipping his bottom lip, rubbing smooth calves over his thighs and lower back. A few minutes later, their tongues triggered a surge of fresh chemicals, and she felt him swelling.

"Turn around," he said.

"Okay."

He pulled out, accompanied by the sound of breaking suction, a moist queef, and a river of pent up semen. She doubled a pillow beneath her stomach. Favion opened her cheeks. Cum coursed from her cunt, still agape from being stretched by his conquering black serpent. He clutched her hips, placed himself, and shoved in all the way.

The suddenness of his occupation nearly drove Mireya into oblivion. Each climax that followed gave voice to natural forces controlling her body. Air escaped wetly as his balls slapped against her. She ejaculated, and her wet, rhythmical queefs synchronized with his thrusts.

"Gawwwd, I'm gonna cum!" he announced. And she joined him.

When the aftershocks had run their course, they lay in each other's arms, legs akimbo, sperm seeping from her yawning entrance.

"How married *are* you?" He managed.

"Mmmm." She uttered, unable to answer. At this moment, she was all his.

Five minutes later, he asked, "Shower?"

"Need to get home, pull myself together. I'll shower there."

"Okay."

Slowly, she rolled out of bed and got to her feet. He watched her collect clothing and walk into the bathroom. He lay with his hands clasped behind his head, staring at the ceiling fan. The sound of peeing and queefing reached his ears. Absently, he reached for his cock—still moist. He lifted fingers to his nose to sniff the essence of their fusion.

"Lord," he said into the emptiness of the large bedroom. *She's the one*, he thought. He could foresee no end to his desire for her. *With a woman like this, I'd be king of the world.*

In the bathroom, Mireya managed to stem the flow, yet even as she pulled up her underwear, more soaked through. Favion was still in bed when she returned. She could tell he wasn't ready to call it an afternoon. He captured her hands, pulled her on top of him, and kissed her slowly.

"I need a ride back." She gently pushed him away. Favion stood on wobbly legs and pulled her into his arms.

"Seriously," she said weakly, hands flat against his chest. "When can we meet again?"

She heaved a great sigh. "Favion, it might not seem like it, but I love my husband. You made me forget for a few hours."

"Mmm." *Be patient. Wait for her to diagnose her feelings.* "Okay." His cock jutted like a length of driftwood.

Favion dressed, and they drove back to the clinic. On the way, he pulled off the road.

"One more kiss before reality sets in."

She obliged. With difficulty, she broke away. "Ay Favi."

Arriving at his office, they sat for a moment.

"That was a nice afternoon."

"No one will ever know," he said. "We'll plan carefully."

"I can't separate the two worlds."

"Let's talk later, Mireya. Everything is fresh right now. Tomorrow the path will be clearer. All I know is, nothing is impossible but the word itself."

"It has to be clear right now. You have so much to offer a woman." She smiled at her pun and shook her head. "Not just that." She glanced at his crotch.

He lifted his eyebrows, shook his head. "I want to feel you skin-to-skin, until we forget where one ends and the other begins."

"Thank you." She got out of the car.

He rolled down her window as she walked away. "Hey!" Mireya stopped. "Key's under the front door mat. I'm changing the alarm code to M-I-R-E-Y-A. Mi casa es su casa."

She smiled and nodded without answering, and kept walking.

———

When she arrived, she threw her clothes in a community washer and stepped into the shower. Before turning on the water, she inhaled their combined musk. She reached down to feel her opening. *If he sees, he'll know.*

That night, Wyler asked about her visit with Reyes. Mireya generalized and handed him the results of her tests, hoping it would distract him. It didn't. As a writer, he was already concocting a story to use in bed.

"Handsome?"

She shrugged.

"Did you have lunch together?"

She shook her head. "I fixed the printer, and he drove me back. He had appointments."

"Yeah?" Wyler raised a mischievous eyebrow.

"Stop writing, Costner. I need help filling out paperwork for my job."

"After you tell me everything, right down to the last detail."

"Ay-yi-yi."

————

As she served his late dinner, her pussy tingled. She battled her conscience as he ate steamed vegetables and baked fish. Already her body begged for any excuse to visit Favi—punch in M-I-R-E-Y-A, spread herself on his bed. Yet, the part of her brain that reminded her that her wild nature was subversive and dangerous. *Am I using Wyler? Papaya or not, he's a wonderful man.*

After dinner, she kept Wyler up late helping her with paperwork. Afterward, she fended him off by complaining of a stomach ache. *Heartache.*

He went into the kitchen and brought Pepto-Bismol and a spoon.

————

Chorro, the Spanish name for diarrhea. She fended off his early morning erection by lying that she had it. The following morning, the phone rang just before eleven. When Wyler answered, there was a pause before the caller hung up.

"Your lover," Wyler teased.

"Not a chance, Mr. Costner. I tell them never to call when you're home."

"Mmm."

After Wyler left for work, Favion called again.

"Can I see you this afternoon?"

"Favion, didn't you hear what I said?"

"If you can break free—"

"No." Her cunt warred with her brain.

"Just say when."

His flexibility created bells and whistles, inferring it would only get worse. His obsession would grow, obliterating everything in its path. *Then what*?

"I don't know."

"Sorry, I sound pushy. Give me a buzz anytime."

"Okay."

"Can't stop thinking about you."

"I have to go."

"We'll talk later," he said.

"Bye."

"Hasta luego, guapa."

———

Grandma Ethel came over and noticed something funny about Mireya's behavior.

"What's eatin' yuh sweetheart?"

"Nothing.

"You and Wyler okay?"

"Yeah."

"I used to get into some real catfights with Max."

"It's nothing like that."

"You miss Mexico?"

"That must be it."

———

A slew of weekly invitations from Favion weakened her. He invited her for lunch, art galleries, local wineries, music concerts, all out of town and carefully orchestrated to coincide with Wyler's work schedule. Mireya steadfastly refused, even as her head swarmed with the memory of his thick dark cock, and her shattering climaxes. When desire got the upper hand, she masturbated in the shower with the vibrator or let it build until Wyler returned. Her enthusiasm made him forget his suspicions regarding Dr. Reyes. One morning in the shower, she began cramping and smiled.

That afternoon, Favicon called again. Mireya resorted to a stronger voice, aided by the crankiness caused by her period..

"Favion, I was foolish and self-indulgent. There's a saying, 'Can't have your cake and eat it too.' Stop calling me."

"I get it. You know I'm here if you change your mind." *Be patient. So much can happen in a few months.*

"Thanks, bye."

———

Weeks after the afternoon with Favion, Wyler moved them to a larger apartment in the neighboring town of Paso Robles. Mireya breathed a sigh of relief — less opportunity for chance meetings, subsequent temptation. Wyler dropped her off at work in Atascadero in the mornings, and a public bus returned her close to home in the late afternoon.

She found time to set up a Hotmail account. A day later, she received one of her first inbox messages. It was from Favion:

Mireya, what we experienced was magical. I know you feel the same. Let's make magic again!

She answered, How did you get this address?

Response: I typed your name in the finder box.

That's all there is to it? Already, she was feeling wary of the new technology. *Don't open his messages, problem solved.* But she did, one more time. A simple message was there:

M-I-R-E-Y-A.

———

She began work at the Atascadero High School, thinking she'd put the issue behind her. A few weeks later, as she walked to the bus stop, Reyes surprised her.

"What are you doing here, Favion?"

"I want to cook dinner for you."

She remembered a quote she'd heard as an undergraduate: 'Sex is like math—add the bed, subtract the clothes, divide the legs, and hope you don't multiply.'

"We've been through this."

Favion's patience was thinning. "Mireya, we can't change what happened. It was supernatural."

Mireya walked past him toward the bus stop. For once, her body agreed with her brain, and there was no turning back when he called out.

"Want a lift?"

"No."

"Think about it!"

"God*damnit*," she breathed. The bus was five minutes late.

———

With time, she rededicated herself to Wyler, and the memory of Favion slowly faded. He stopped trying, and she stopped wanting him to try.

She only saw him once more, while she and Wyler were shopping the aisles of the Albertsons supermarket in Paso Robles. They bumped into him at the meat section. She introduced Favion to Wyler, visibly blushing.

Wyler shook his hand and felt a tentative pressure. *You can tell a lot about a man by his handshake.*

"Nice to see you, Mireya. How's the new job?"

"Good. Still waiting to get into CalPoly."

"You will."

"Ojalá."

"Nice to meet you, Wyler." Then he took both of Mireya's hands. "Adios."

He left without waiting for a reply.

————

While making love that evening, Wyler concocted a fantasy fuck.

"Dr. Reyes wants to give you another pelvic exam."

She kissed him. "Think so?"

"Satisfy your black curiosity."

"Mmmm, yeah baby." Her hips moved. *An open marriage. The ultimate solution.*

"You'll tell me?" He moved back and plunged forward.

"Huh, ayyy....you'd divorce me."

"Mmm, god*damn* you feel good." He moved faster. "He'll flood you with jizz."

She took a deep breath. "Oy si baby, I'm gonna cum.... huh-huh-huh! Ayyy, ayyy!"

It was one of the strongest orgasms she'd experienced with Wyler, inspired by Dr. Reyes.

CHAPTER 19
SETTLING IN

Mireya sorely missed México, where she'd felt needed and respected as a professional by students. Mexican students were eager to learn and treated her as if she were important. In California, her bachelor's degree only qualified her as a teacher's aide.

Her Atascadero High School experience proved disappointing. Teachers had low expectations for limited English speakers, and her job was more babysitting than instruction.

She tried explaining to a few colleagues that newcomers to the US were highly intelligent and enjoyed challenges. They listened politely. The male teachers were more interested in viewing her than her viewpoint.

The instructor she helped was Mrs. Killian, and she ran the class as if students were Kindergarteners. Mexican students were anxious to learn, yet Mrs. Killian effectively dumbed down the curriculum so that the look on their faces was one of complete, utter boredom. She didn't even speak Spanish. Students loved Mireya, often whispering in Spanish that she should teach the class.

Mireya missed the life-sustaining energy of everyday chaos, living the moment in Mexico. She longed for the feeling of aliveness—laughing, dancing on weekends, deep conversations, freedom to be herself.

In California, Mireya was just another Mexican, albeit an exotic one. Her self-esteem was dissolving, replaced by apathy—terror that her life would run on automatic for the rest of her days. There were periods when she went through the motions and gave thought to hopping a bus to the border, yet logic came to the rescue. *Running never solves anything.* She'd run from Enrique, Alfonso, her cousins, Peter, and Fabion. *Pendeja*! her conscience screamed. *Remember who you are, where you came from*! *You're smart*! *Quit acting like an idiot*!

———

Almost a year to the day of her arrival, her green card came in the mail. In essence, the card was a license to enter a university with the same rights and privileges enjoyed by all North Americans.

Mireya was accepted into a Master's program at Caltech San Luis Obispo, based on her outstanding academic record in México, and because the school had a (race) quota to meet. She fit the profile to a 'T'. Minorities were encouraged to apply, and Mireya had all the prerequisites —female, Mexican, studying a STEM (science, technology, engineering, math) subject.

The news instantly revived her excitement for life. She was determined to study hard, not stopping until she was Dr. Mireya Lopez-Costner. Her renewed enthusiasm translated well for her marriage. She steered clear of temptation and kept Wyler content. He taught her to drive, and she passed her exams on the first try. One morning, he surprised her with a low-mileage used cherry-red Volkswagen Jetta.

Costner, this is…" Tears rolled down her cheeks.

"Red, like my passion for you, Dollface."

She held him as if letting go would shatter the dream. Now she would drive herself, no more buses, relying on Wyler to take her everywhere. The red Jetta was freedom.

———

Easily, Mireya became the best student in her classes. A Master's in mathematics took an average of two years. Mireya earned it in one. The program allowed for the exploration of a variety of mathematics—Chaos Theory, Differential Equations, Combinatorics, and Algebraic Topology. She was thirty-two, and the world was her oyster.

Meanwhile, Wyler grew weary of his job at the California Youth Authority. He was getting lazy. His passion for teaching waned. The recidivism rate for incarcerated wards of the state was a whopping 91%.. He began searching for another job.

On weekends, he woke up at five to work on writing, hoping for a break that would allow him to pursue it as a second career. He wrote apocalyptic fiction, literary fiction, mysteries, horror stories, and erotica. The erotica was Mireya inspired. Female leads were Latina, and his steamy descriptions were steeped in his reality.

Wyler's stories usually took place in small California towns. *Write about what you know*, his Master's thesis advisor told him years ago. *Show it, don't tell it*. He'd been working for years on a novel entitled *Desperate Living*. Each time he thought it was done, he read it through and found it wasn't.

Wyler's job search landed them both job interviews in the small immigrant community of Greenfield, an hour north of Paso Robles. They drove there one morning for a meeting with the principal.

Carlos was a late fifty-something Chicano who affected a ruggedly handsome Gene Hackman look. His obvious interest in Mireya made Wyler uncomfortable, yet he was getting used to it by now. They were asked a lot of questions regarding experience, and Carlos challenged them with hypotheticals.

"Wyler, what would you do if students started fighting in your classroom?"

Wyler took out his wallet, flipped it open, and said, "Beam me up, Scotty."

Carlos laughed, and Wyler followed with a real answer that seemed to satisfy him.

"Mireya, you're gonna have a lot of kids who hate math. How will you change that?"

"By showing that they already use it every day for almost everything, and making it fun for them." She gave several examples of ways to entertain using math concepts.

"Great. I think the students are gonna love you. I taught math before I became a principal."

"Math is beautiful," she remarked.

"Mmm," he smiled. "Well, jobs are yours if you want them."

They smiled and nodded. Carlos stood to congratulate them.

"Go see Lydia in human resources. I'll call, let her know you're on your way. She'll get you all set up."

"Thank you." Wyler shook his hand.

"This is a nice Mexican community," Mireya said.

Carlos took her hand. "Pleasure to have you as a part of it. Lydia will give you a calendar with start dates and in-services. Found a place to live?"

"We're gonna buy a newspaper and look around today."

"I've seen several houses for rent recently. In any case, Soledad's only ten minutes away if you don't find anything here."

————

The rental house they found was perfect. It had two bedrooms, situated on a quiet street between Elmer, the landlord, and Rudolfo, the town mayor. Elmer was a widower, and Rudy was married with two young children. Friendly morning hellos accompanied Wyler and Mireya every morning.

Mireya taught basic math and algebra with an emergency credential, valid for a year. She'd need to enroll in a credential program to continue the following year. Wyler taught six English classes per day, which required an enormous amount of planning.

After a day's work, they returned home and talked about the day. Mireya noted the lack of respect students had for teachers. Wyler informed her that the teenage pregnancy rate in

Greenfield was among the highest in the state.

"Nothing for kids to do here except join a gang or fuck."

"True," Mireya said. "But I also have some really great kids."

One late afternoon on the short drive home, Mireya burst into tears.

"You know what a student said to me today?"

Wyler held her hand and shook his head.

"Tony. He never does anything in class."

"I have him too — lazy, belligerent."

"I walked to his desk to help him. He said, 'Fuck off, bitch' in front of the entire class."

"Jesus Christ! What did Carlos do?"

"Suspended him, but can you believe it?"

"Can only imagine what his parents are like. "

"I'm having a conference with them tomorrow."

"That should be interesting."

"What a difference between Mexicans and Chicanos," Mireya remarked. "Chicanos are ashamed of their heritage. My best students are the Mexicans, or Chicanos, who cling to their culture."

"Replacing tacos with pizza and hot dogs. Assimilation."

Mireya was jolted into remembering a vow she'd made to herself. That weekend, she began searching for a doctorate program.

———

The next day, Tony's mother came in. She was a timid woman who appeared much older than her years. She spoke only Spanish and was pleasantly surprised by Mireya's kindness. When she asked about Tony's behavior at home, the mother burst into tears.

"I don't know what to do. His father isn't around, and he won't listen to me — just wants to be with his gangster friends. I don't know what to do," she repeated. "He's been arrested four times since sixth grade."

"Ay, señora." She stood and hugged her. Then she looked into the defeated eyes of the woman. "There's a program in Paso Robles called The Grizzly Academy. It's a military style school that emphasizes discipline. I've read that the program has a pretty high success rate."

"How do I get him in?"

"I'll look into it for you. They provide food, housing, everything he'll need, including uniforms. The program takes a year and a half."

"Please, help me. He yells and throws things. I'm afraid of him."

"The father?"

"He doesn't have anything to do with us."

"Brothers or sisters?"

"No."

"What is Tony doing during his suspension?"

"Out with his malos amigos."

"Ay yi-yi."

———

Three weeks later, Tony was admitted into the Grizzly Academy. In the kitchen that evening, his mother gave an ultimatum.

"You either go to the academy or the streets."

"Fuck you bitch. It's my house, you can't kick me out!"

Two beefy men in uniforms were ready in another room. They entered. Another waited outside.

"That's enough," said one.

Tony darted for the door, blocked by another large man. They forced him to the ground and hogtied him with plastic ties.

"Motherfuckers! I got rights! You can't do this shit!"

Without a word, they lifted and carried him out to a white, unmarked van.

"Mama, call the cops! This ain't fuckin' right! Mama!"

His mother stood in the doorway and quietly sobbed.

"I wanna fuckin' lawyer!" was the last thing she heard him say.

The van sped away. Tony's mother went inside and closed the door.

———

Carlos tried his luck with Mireya toward the end of the school year. One afternoon, he asked her to drop by his office. He asked her to join him for a three-day California Math Standards conference in San Jose. She respectfully declined, instinctively perceiving ulterior motives.

"I've a lot of work to do, and my students will fall behind."

He folded his hands in his lap and gazed at her from across his desk. Then he smiled.

"Mireya, you know how I feel about you. You've earned everyone's respect. The scores on the State test went up considerably in your classes. Hope you'll reconsider. All expenses paid. I'll take you dancing."

"Carlos, that would be awkward, don't you think?"

He smiled. "I'm pretty good."

"Carlos…?"

"Okay, no dancing."

This kind of bravado didn't faze her. She liked Carlos. He was fair, funny, and at least he was honest.

"You remind me of a physics professor I once knew."

Carlos smiled mischievously. "I love physics almost as much as math."

"My marriage is important." She felt like a hypocrite, recalling the sultry afternoon with Favion Reyes.

He shrugged. "Been married thirty years. There's a saying, 'Just because I bought something doesn't mean I can't shop around'."

"You'll need to shop elsewhere," she countered.

"Only one store has what I want."

Mireya smiled. "They're out of stock."

"Damn you're smart." Carlos stood and walked her to his office door. "Think about it."

"Okay, I will."

"Have you applied for a credential program yet?"

"Not yet."

"I can help with that."

"Okay." *A last resort if I don't find a doctorate program*, she reflected.

He kissed her on the cheek. "Please don't mention our talk to Wyler. He's a lot bigger than me."

She shook her head. "Don't worry."

"Oh, by the way, Tony seems to be doing pretty well at the Grizzly Academy."

"Happy to hear that. His mother deserves some peace and happiness."

"We all do," Carlos added.

End of Book One

Sneak Preview of,
Mireya in the Wild

Nigel insisted on paying the tab, and they walked to his apartment building. It was mid-December, and the air was cold. Soon, snow would pile up and get shoved aside by snow plows. It was after one in the morning when they arrived.

Nigel lived on the first floor of a well-kempt apartment building. He opened the door for Mireya and flipped on a light. His space was larger than hers. On the walls hung pictures of family and friends, as well as a few African masks. He led her into the living area, and she saw a portrait of him.

"What're you wearing, Nigil?" Mireya pointed. "It's so beautiful."

"It is called a Kanzu, traditional dress for men, made from silk and cotton. We wear them for ceremonies. The women wear a gomesi, and they're equally beautiful." Nigel had an ancient record player, and he set the needle to an album of African instrumentals.

"Will you be a politician like your father when you return to Uganda?"

"Little choice."

"Ever dream of something else?"

"I wanted to be a professional soccer player. Yet, those are the dreams of youth. What about you?"

"I wanted to change the world, but it's too big and messy." She cocked her head toward the music. "I like this."

"It's called Kadongo Kamu."

"A lot of bass."

"You have an excellent ear. Bass is the main instrument in Kadongo. Do you play an instrument?"

"I sing."

"Sing for me."

She cleared her throat and began:

"Bésame, bésame mucho como si fuera esta noche la última vez, bésame, bésame mucho, que tengo miedo a perderte, perderte después."

"You sing like an angel."

"Thank you. It's been a long time."

"What does the song say?"

It says, 'kiss me, kiss me a lot, as if tonight were the last time, kiss me a lot, for I'm scared to lose you, lose you again'."

"I love it! Tell me about México.

"You should visit. Then you can know it for yourself."

"Now that we've met, I know it must be a magical place."

Mireya blushed, and Nigel took her into his arms, swaying to African rhythms filling the room. When another song began, he leaned to kiss her, and without thinking, she returned it. He looked into her eyes, and they kissed again. Each dance movement journeyed them toward his bedroom. She didn't think about stopping to set the rules. Tonight, she was ready to break them.

Another dance started, unrelated to what was spinning on the turntable. Without a word, they stood at the edge of the bed and undressed each other, kissing exposed flesh as it was revealed. She cupped his cock in the palm of her hand, and it was thick and heavy. Accompanied by African music, they laid on the bed to begin an ancient ritual.

"You're such a beauty, Mireya." Nigel kissed her and followed a downward path with his tongue, arriving at her mound. She gasped as he lashed there. "Mmm, delicious," he whispered.

Considerations crowded into an obscure corner of her mind. At the forefront was his tongue.

"Oyyy Nigel, sí, oyyy." She arched and lifted. Her clit was a rigid teardrop. She wanted him inside. Gently, she lifted his head away and guided him over her.

In the Bantu language, he said, "Nkwagala, Mireya."

Nigel pulled back on his dark shaft to streamline the broad mushroom tip. He rubbed it between her moist, chamois-soft lips and pushed until his crown penetrated.

"Ahhh, Mireya." He took a nipple into his mouth as his shaft was slowly welcomed by her satiny walls. Down, down, stretching, filling, immersing nearly all of him.

"Uhnnn," Mireya grunted deeply and panted, "huh-huh-huh." She rested her heels on his ass. "Oh my god, oh my…. nnnahh!" He filled every space within. "Ohhh, I love this!"

Hang on, he warned himself. He reached her tissue barrier with several inches to spare. Mireya's head tilted and lolled to one side. Her textured groans filled his apartment with a universal language. Nigil pulled back and returned.

"Oooosss, ahhh," He tapped her border.

She took a deep breath and let out a slow hiss. "Ssssayyy!"

"Nkwagala," he repeated.

———

African music played as they fucked. Mireya lifted, circled, dug heels into his ass. Her first climax was monumental, her pussy pulsing like an elephant's heartbeat, moans deep and primitive. He greeted each orgasm with a kiss and waited for them to subside before resuming long, powerful strokes.

"Huh! Ohhhayyy!" her voice swung up an octave. "I'm cumming again!"

She had sobbing, ground-shaking orgasms. He felt a warm liquid surround his cock. Nigel arched his back and pushed as far as possible. A dizzying rush clouded his head.

"Ohhh Mireya." For a moment his whole body became rigid. Then he erupted. "Uh!" His spurt was astonishing, as if a kinked garden hose were suddenly straightened. Mireya bucked, twisted beneath him as he grunted, growled, and emptied.

Ty Spencer Vossler, MFA, is the Xman (ex-farmer, ex-truck driver, ex-powerlifter, ex-cop, expatriate). He currently lives in Tlaxcala, Mexico, with his BMW (beautiful Mexican wife) and daughter. He has taught English and creative writing for twenty-eight years and is currently a professor at the Colegio ADA in Puebla, Mexico. His rich life experience has shaped his writings into a reflection of contemporary society. Vossler's published short stories, essays, and poetry have won worldwide acclaim. He attributes his original and creative work to the fact that he shot his television over two decades ago. To learn more about Vossler, visit: www.tyvossler.com.

www.ingramcontent.com/pod-product-compliance
Lightning Source LLC
Chambersburg PA
CBHW021504240626
47154CB00002B/495